The Mango Murders

Also available by Lucy Burdette

The Key West Food Critic Mysteries

A Poisonous Palate
Lucy Burdette's Kitchen
A Clue in the Crumbs
A Dish to Die For
A Scone of Contention
The Key Lime Crime
A Deadly Feast
Death on the Menu
Killer Takeout
Fatal Reservations
Death With All the Trimmings
Murder With Ganache
Topped Chef
Death in Four Courses
An Appetite for Murder

Other Novels

The Ingredients of Happiness
Unsafe Haven

The Mango Murders

A KEY WEST FOOD CRITIC MYSTERY

Lucy Burdette

NEW YORK

Books should be disposed of and recycled according to local requirements. All paper materials used are FSC compliant.

This is a work of fiction. All of the names, characters, organizations, places and events portrayed in this novel are either products of the author's imagination or are used fictitiously. Any resemblance to real or actual events, locales, or persons, living or dead, is entirely coincidental.

PUBLISHER'S NOTE: The recipes contained in this book are to be followed exactly as written. The publisher is not responsible for your specific health or allergy needs that may require medical supervision. The publisher is not responsible for any adverse reaction to the recipes contained in this book.

Copyright © 2025 by Roberta Isleib

All rights reserved.

Published in the United States by Crooked Lane Books, an imprint of The Quick Brown Fox & Company LLC.

Crooked Lane Books and its logo are trademarks of The Quick Brown Fox & Company LLC.

Library of Congress Catalog-in-Publication data available upon request.

ISBN (hardcover): 979-8-89242-165-2
ISBN (ebook): 979-8-89242-166-9

Cover design by Griesbach/Martucci

Printed in the United States.

www.crookedlanebooks.com

Crooked Lane Books
34 West 27th St., 10th Floor
New York, NY 10001

First Edition: August 2025

The authorized representative in the EU for product safety and compliance is eucomply OÜ Pärnu mnt 139b-14, 11317 Tallinn, Estonia, hello@eucompliancepartner.com, +33757690241

10 9 8 7 6 5 4 3 2 1

For Dorothea, Henry, and Callum:
I can't wait to see the people
you become!

Chapter One

Tea, biscuits, a good gossip? Yes, we will provide you with those. Money, heroin, diamonds? No.
   —Richard Osman, *The Last Devil to Die.*

Key West's Sunset Celebration on Mallory Square has been a magnet for visitors to our island since the 1960s. An hour or two before sunset, the square on the waterfront begins to bustle with food and drink carts, performers and buskers of many kinds, a sprinkling of homeless folks, and purveyors of Key West–themed trinkets and tchotchkes. Everyone loves it—except the police tasked with keeping people safe, including my hubby, Nathan Bransford. I tease that for him, from his police officer's perspective, that deliciously fun event is all about what could go wrong.

As the sun drops closer to its nighttime resting place in the Gulf of Mexico, the square grows more crowded with chattering tourists, the air ringing with performers' calls to action (Give donations to the artists! Come watch my act!) and scented with buttered popcorn and sweet minty mojitos. The water off the square hums with the sounds of happy revelers on sunset cruises.

I'd visited the scene hundreds of times since I moved to the southernmost point in the Florida Keys, sometimes with out-of-town guests, sometimes to check in with my dear friend and tarot card reader Lorenzo, and sometimes on my way to dinner at a nearby restaurant or a musical or dramatic performance. Tonight, for the first time, I would be experiencing it from the water, sailing on a cocktail cruise cosponsored by my mother's catering company and my employer, *Key Zest*—the e-zine that aspired to be the go-to source of information on all things Key West for tourists and locals alike. (Everyone knew this truth—if you wanted the real dirt on our island, you went to the locals' Facebook group.)

All three of us *Key Zest* employees—our boss, Palamina; Danielle, my newly married, newly promoted reporter friend specializing in style and real estate; and me, Hayley Snow, food critic and aspiring author of deeper opinion pieces, had been roped into hosting. Our cruising vessel would be the stunning *Pilar Too*, docked in front of the Schooner Wharf at the bight aka the harbor. The website had billed this boat as fashioned in the manner of a hand-crafted wooden Hemingway yacht lookalike—only it was much bigger and a sailboat/catamaran instead of a motorboat. Sheesh. The owner wouldn't have been the first Key Wester to have a Hemingway obsession.

We were to be joined by a raft of Key West luminaries ranging from businesspeople to artists to government types and most important to me, foodies. We'd each had the chance to contribute to the guest list, and my people included chefs, restaurant owners, and a few folks who wrote about those topics for local magazines.

Our route would take us around the point containing the Pier House, past chichi Sunset Key and abandoned Wisteria

The Mango Murders

Island, and out into the open Northern Channel. We'd be able to see the magic of Mallory Square, but we wouldn't be immersed in the gritty, chaotic details. As we sailed with our fairy lights twinkling, we'd schmooze and ply our special guests with libations and amazing hors d'oeuvres prepared by my mother and stepfather's catering business. By the end of the voyage, with sun set and bellies full, we hoped to have developed a bigger footprint in Key West, outshining the other magazines, e-zines, and blogs in town. We'd become the go-to place for both finding content and spending advertising dollars.

Danielle and I were stationed on the dock next to the sign that read: *Pilar Too, Captain Amos Roche*. Our jobs were welcoming our guests to the boat, while Palamina circulated on the deck, escorting our dignitaries to the bar stationed at the bow, manned by my stepfather, Sam. Weather permitting, we'd assumed that most people would prefer to be outside, even though the main cabin space was stunning.

The salon was twice the size (at least) of my houseboat's living area, with an open kitchen including a full-size Sub-Zero refrigerator, dining and lounging spaces done up in antique wood and old-fashioned rattan furniture with deep green cushions to die for, and perfectly comfortable modern berths with private baths down below. There was an auxiliary kitchen space north of the bathrooms, where private chefs could store supplies and do prep work. With the installed dumbwaiter, food and other items could be easily transported from the upstairs to the down. Any number of nooks and crannies and small cupboards had been designed to store gear so that nothing would be unsafe in foul weather, or for that matter, messy. An office with a normal desk, computer and printer, and file cabinets was also located downstairs. This boat made my home seem a little cramped and crowded in comparison. I tried not to steam with envy.

My octogenarian houseboat row neighbor Miss Gloria had desperately wanted to work the event with us, but the siren call of her best friend's birthday trumped our business outing. The ladies were birthday twins, as Miss Gloria described them, Mrs. Dubisson's 85th birthday this week and Miss Gloria's same big day next week. She couldn't miss the opening notes of their celebrations at a dinner for her pal, but she hated to be left out of anything.

I'd spent many hours assuring her that the excitement she'd experienced with the Scottish scone sisters on a tiki boat tour would always top corporate cruising, as I'd taken to calling this event. Which Palamina would hate. She preferred to think of it as a jolly cocktail party among friends. Good friends. Who happened to have a lot to offer a slightly flailing magazine.

For the next fifteen minutes, we experienced a rush of guests that Danielle and I could hardly keep track of. I hoped we'd welcomed everyone properly, but there was also a steady stream of tourists passing by on the docks at the same time as our embarkation so it felt chaotic.

"VIP's incoming!" said Danielle. She looked frazzled and worried, same as I felt. We'd all wanted to invite as many people as possible who might support our e-zine and the catering company. Probably we'd been overambitious, and there was a good chance we'd also overestimated the regrets. A sunset cruise on a gorgeous night with a great caterer and free booze was hard to refuse.

"Welcome to the *Pilar Too*," I chirped to our new mayor and one of the city commissioners, the one who most often voted with him. The mayor was a few months into his first hot-headed term, and I really missed the calm perspective of our previous leader. I grinned and shook each hand vigorously. "We are thrilled to have you here."

Close on their heels, two of the most controversial businesspeople in town along with the marketing director of the Tourist Development Agency approached. I slowed them down a bit by blocking the gangplank and chattering mindlessly about the history of the yacht and our e-zine. I remembered they'd clashed horrendously with the new mayor at the last city commission meeting. There was shouting—something about clowns running the circus. Or was it "not my monkeys, not my circus?" Though I wasn't certain who were the clowns and who were the monkeys and what was the circus. At any rate, no one was literally ejected from the meeting, but it was not a shining Arthurian round table moment for the government of the city of Key West.

"This particular craft is a sailing vessel, note the enormous mast and sails," I told them. "Hemingway's *Pilar* was in fact a motorboat, but this boat is actually more in the *decorative* style of the *Pilar* than anything else. I suspect the owner wanted to ride on Hemingway's coattails by constructing it of wood, and who wouldn't? Actually, this craft does have a motor in addition to the sails, but they mostly use it to launch and dock, or more broadly of course, in cases of low wind. Not to worry, we have plenty of fuel." Like I said, babbling.

Their eyes were glazing over but since these men and our mayor had not yet been on the same side of an issue, I wanted to keep them separated, at least at the beginning. I hated to spoil our launch with an instant fight. Though Key West appeared to most visitors to be an island paradise without worry or care, underneath the surface there were always conflicts. How much development was too much? Should larger cruise ships be allowed to dock, sucking up the air and water around the square and sullying our precious environment? How many new housing sites should be reserved for low-income people? The town was getting more and more expensive, even as the workers that kept it humming were being priced out of the rental market. If we did build more units, would they really be reserved for low-income residents or sold to the highest bidder? If the city crammed in more people, could they evacuate safely in case of a big storm? Good gravy, Joni Mitchell with her paving of paradise song had been positively prescient.

Last December, Miss Gloria and I had joined the throngs of tourists and locals jostling to watch the hometown holiday parade make its noisy, celebratory way across Duval Street. We'd spotted our former mayor ride by, perched on the back seat of a yellow convertible, waving at the crowd. She was smiling so broadly and looked so happy, and we screamed our greetings like lovesick teenagers.

A woman standing near me, who wore reindeer ears on her head and a string of colored Christmas lights flashing on her chest, carried a plastic cup of beer in one hand and her iPhone in the other. "That's the job I want once we move down here," she announced to her friend, pointing to the mayor.

No, you don't, I thought to myself. *You have no idea how hard she works—how many intractable problems she juggles and how many buffoons she's required to manage.*

One of the crew on the *Pilar Too* trotted down the gangway to let me know we would be launching shortly. I waved in the businesspeople, directing them to Danielle with her clipboard, followed by two local artists, John Martini and Peter Vey. They were trailed by a tall, blonde woman I didn't recognize.

The Mango Murders

"All aboard the *Pilar Too*!" another crew member called.

I glanced around to be sure we weren't cutting off any important dignitaries, noticing that several crew members of the boat next to the *Pilar Too* were watching our event with super sour expressions. Three women dressed in short khaki shorts plus a man who had to be the captain stood next to their own sign, *Carpe Diem, Captain Buddy LaRue*. I didn't have time to worry about their possible envious feelings—they needed to carpe some of their own diem. I waved cheerfully, then boarded the ship myself.

My mother was circulating among the passengers with a tray of champagne flutes in one hand, and a plate of her special spicy cheese wafers in the other.

"Anchors away!" shouted the captain as a crew member pulled up the gangplank in preparation for moving away from the wharf. Captain Roche smoothed his rough black beard as he welcomed the passengers through the sound system inside the boat. He explained the location of life jackets, lifesaving rings, and two zodiacs for use in the unlikely case of emergency, made a few obligatory jokes, and then wished everyone a good voyage.

"If you need to visit the head down below, remember to go down the ladder backwards—toes grip and heels slip!"

We glided out of the harbor, passing yachts and sailboats and catamarans and a few chugging tikis, and then crossed into the open water, around the unkempt greenery of Wisteria Island and the manicured island of Sunset Key. Wisteria had been fashioned out of the spoils of dredging by the US Navy in the early 1900s. Sometimes called Christmas Tree Island, the twenty two-acre undeveloped land had been claimed by both a private corporation and the federal government and was now home to a smattering of otherwise homeless Key Westers. This was yet one more hot button issue for some of our passengers—they would have very different opinions about what the island's future should be.

As we emerged from the back side of much fancier and more exclusive Sunset Key, the crowds on Mallory Square came into view. A performer on a ladder towered over his audience, juggling what appeared to be bowling pins. Flames in acts had been forbidden on the square ever since a juggler had accidentally set an audience member on fire. (See note above regarding things that could go wrong.) He'd panicked and thrown her into the sea to douse the flames. Predictably, the city was sued.

Carrying bottles of champagne in both hands, I joined a small group of revelers and began to chat about our plans for expanding *Key Zest*. "Of course, I'll continue to do restaurant reviews," I said, nodding at one of the owners of Seven Fish, who was standing with my pal Chef Martha Hubbard. I also waved at Chef Edel Waugh, who had taken a break from the zaniness of our island, but then returned and was about to reopen her upscale restaurant near the Key West Bight. "But I've started working on bigger pieces too. This time of year, because it's the season, I'm writing one article focusing on mangoes. Don't miss the bartender's take on a mango daiquiri tonight, or the caterer's mango shrimp fritters."

"Since when are mangoes a big story?" I heard one of the guests mutter.

I flushed hot and pink, madder than I probably should have been at her careless remark. She obviously had no idea how hard it was to churn out fresh topics and new spins on old ones. In truth, maybe I was a little over sensitive on this subject, as I had yet to pitch an opinion piece to Palamina that she'd deemed worthy of pursuing. Sometimes I worried I'd be stuck with recipes and local foodie gossip for the rest of my career. Don't get me wrong, I adored food and foodie people, but still, I felt pressure to write something bigger with more impact, too. As I mentally scrambled for a polite retort, my mother approached from the other side with a tray of shrimp fritters and mango mozzarella skewers interspersed with fresh basil leaves.

"We are so lucky with tonight's weather," she said, her smile glittering. "My husband is the bartender and very prone to seasickness, so we weren't sure how this would go. It wouldn't do for him to disappear into the head for two hours!" She laughed gaily. "Luckily, the water's like glass, and you better believe that I loaded him up with Dramamine for good measure." She nodded at Sam, who was mixing frozen drinks in a blender at the bar. He grinned back at her, looking a little loopy from the Dramamine I thought.

"These fritters are made with Key West pink shrimp, a bit of chopped mango for sweetness, eggs, a sprinkle of flour, and a splash of dark beer, in case anyone is concerned about allergies," she added. "I also added a whisper of heat with a hot pepper to balance the sweetness of the mangoes."

I was about to explain how she cleverly deep-fried the fritters in her professional kitchen but warmed them up in the boat's small kitchen in the toaster oven, when we heard a panicked voice.

"Fire! Fire!"

My heart pounding, I spun around to see what could possibly be on fire and figure out where to get help. Maybe there was a fire extinguisher nearby, and I could handle this myself? Maybe the captain already had it under control? Around me the worried guests were milling and sputtering in various degrees of concern to panic.

"Mom!" I called. "Is someone taking care of this?"

She shrugged, her hands still full of hors d'oeuvres, her expression dismayed.

Then one of the crew members—a lanky, youngish woman wearing white short shorts, a striped shirt, and a coppery ponytail bouncing out of her ball cap—pushed forward to stand on the prow. "Abandon ship!" she shouted through cupped hands. I couldn't help thinking that she would be in so much trouble if this was a prank. I prayed it was a prank.

A large bang startled all of us and the boat's deck heaved. As I grabbed for the railing, I lost my grip on one of the bottles I was carrying, and it shattered against the railing into a million pieces. The first noise was followed by a louder explosion that seemed to come from below the cabin. Before I realized what was happening, I was thrown off the deck and sent cartwheeling into the air.

There were flames and the smell of fuel, and screaming—was that my voice? I hit the water hard.

Chapter Two

The fruit thudded to the ground, splitting and scattering everywhere, its pink fleshy pulp looking like blood.
—Harini Nagendra, *A Nest of Vipers*

My first thought was that I couldn't breathe. I was going to drown right here in the murky sea off Mallory Square. *Don't panic, Hayley! Fight!*

I pushed the water away with both hands and kicked hard until I finally burst through the surface and gulped down some air. I could hear yelling, both from the people splashing in the water near me, and from those watching the disaster unfold from the shore. What had just happened? The boat appeared to have erupted into flames and then exploded, flinging its passengers and cargo and all our carefully planned libations and nibbles into the drink. Now flames licked around the edges of the remains like ravenous dogs.

My second thought: Where was my mother?

Once I got over the first shock, I didn't appear to be hurt. I saw no blood in the water around me and felt no sharp pains.

I began a slow breaststroke around the area, keeping my head above the surface to search for all the people I cared so much about—my mother and Sam. Danielle and Palamina. And the mayor.

"Mom?" I yelled out.

"Hayley!" The answering call came. "I'm right over here, we're fine."

I nearly burst into relieved tears, except I needed to save my wits and strength to stay afloat and help others who might be struggling.

The remains of the boat floated about thirty yards away, flames flickering around the part of the deck and cabin that was not underwater. A patch of something was spreading over the water's surface, leaving an oily slick. Now was not the time to wonder what caused the explosion. We all needed to move further away from the wreckage in case the fire spread and there was another blast.

In the distance, I heard the whoop, whoop of sirens, both from onshore and from the Coast Guard and pleasure boats that were speeding into the harbor. I spotted a gray and red zodiac from the Key West Fire Department, heading right toward us. More sirens, louder this time, probably fire engines. Nearby, I recognized a woman who co-owned an ice cream shop on Duval Street—she had a panicked look on her face.

"I can't swim," she yelped. She was slapping the surface with her palms, dog paddling madly, which would only use up precious air and energy.

"I'm coming over," I called to her. Her name miraculously popped into my head. "Amanda, don't hit me. I'm going to help

The Mango Murders

you." I remembered this from my Red Cross training as a teenager: People who think they are drowning become filled with an adrenalin-fueled panic and can take their rescuers down. An orange life preserver floated by. I grabbed it and swam over to the distressed woman.

"Take hold of this," I said, pushing the life preserver to her. "Take a deep breath." I breathed along with her. "And another. Roll on to your back and float. You'll be fine." I gestured at the fleet of boats that had sped into the harbor. "The Coast Guard and the fire department are here, and they'll pluck us all out and we'll be right as rain. Hang on and try not to kick so hard."

The small boat that ferried passengers to and from Sunset Key pulled up alongside the woman.

"Take my hand, and grab the bottom rung of the ladder," said a woman in a khaki uniform. She leaned over the side of the boat and hauled Amanda aboard.

I waved my thanks and continued my slow breaststroke to look for other people who might need assistance. One man was floating calmly on his back, as if enjoying the pool on a cruise ship, only a gash in his head oozed red blood into the sea. A memory of taking a tour on a shark boat that attracted those fish by throwing bloody chum overboard rushed into my mind.

"Are you OK?" I asked. "Can you stay afloat until the rescue boat comes around? They're on the way."

"I'm OK," he croaked. "Help the others."

Flotsam and jetsam had begun to surface around the bobbing heads of the passengers. A faux silver tray floated by. Somebody's pink linen sweater. Two striped floats that had been tied to the boat's railings. I grabbed one of those and scissor-kicked back to the bleeding man. "Hold onto this so you don't get tired." Even though he looked calm, I thought he must be exhausted and scared. I felt both, as the initial wave of adrenalin had begun to recede.

On the shore, a phalanx of blue-uniformed police had appeared, and were pushing back the sunset celebration crowd. The juggler had been waved down off his ladder, and three ambulances edged through the crowd and arrived at the dock's curb, where cruise ships sometimes parked. One cop had a megaphone, and he was shouting to the crowd.

"You must clear the area immediately so we can help victims of the disaster who need assistance."

Victims. Disaster. That way of describing it made it sound worse than I had hoped it was.

The Coast Guard ship and the Key West fire department boat were motoring closer and had begun to pull people from the water and toss flotation rings out to others.

"This man is bleeding and needs assistance," I yelled.

I was close enough to the pier that I thought it would be faster to swim to shore and climb out of the water onto land than to wait for a boat. I wasn't cold—this was May, and we'd already had months of above-average temperatures. But I couldn't wait to be dry and safe, far away from the smoking remnants of the *Pilar Too*. Motioning to my mother and Sam, who had bobbed up beside us, I breaststroked toward the square. Once we reached the dock, two officers knelt to the cement to help me climb the rusty ladder, followed by my parents, and two local chefs who had followed our lead. I was glad not to have lost my sandals in the melee as I did not want to get tetanus on top of everything else.

That was such a ridiculous thought that I wondered if I was in shock.

Chapter Three

Investigations are launched, fingers are pointed, potentially dangerous liaisons unfold, and I was turning those pages like there was cake at the finish line.
—Moira Macdonald, Seattle Times Must Read
Books for Summer 2022

Fifteen minutes later, as we huddled on a bench under some palm trees, wrapped in Mylar blankets, Nathan's SUV cruiser roared up. He sprang from the vehicle and jogged over to us. He pulled me into a fierce hug, and then hugged my mother and Sam.

"I'm so glad to see you, so glad you're all OK. I've arranged a ride to take you home," he said, his voice brisk, "right after the paramedics check you out."

"We're fine, just wet and a little stunned," my mother said, "no medical assistance needed for us." Sam was shaking his head in agreement beside her.

"I'm not going anywhere," I added, my shoulders stiffening under the foil wrap. "I might have noticed things that others didn't. I can help. I want to help the other people. It was our party, and I feel responsible." I could feel tears threatening but I refused to cry.

Nathan's eyes flashed with irritation, then softened as he absorbed my struggle. He stroked my arm, which was covered with the emergency blanket I was clutching. "Let's be reasonable. You're in no shape to be useful," he said in a stern but loving voice. "You'll be in the way. Right now, the medical professionals need to assist the people who might be hurt, and later we can figure out what happened. I know you'll be helpful with that," he added, more gently. "Either you go with Officer Ryan, or I'm going to take you." Handsome, dark-haired Officer Ryan stepped up next to Nathan to show he was ready to shuttle us home.

Part of me realized he was right, and I did not want to pull him away from his important job right here. He would not be happy about sending me home alone, but he needed to interview people who might have witnessed something important from their perspective on Mallory Square as well as assist the other passengers from our disastrous sunset cruise.

"Can you text Miss Gloria and let her know I'm coming?" I asked Nathan. She would have heard about the accident on her personal police scanner and would be worrying already. "Let's go," I said, taking my mother's hand. "Okay to drop off my mother and Sam on the way?" I asked Officer Ryan.

"Of course."

"Thank you for understanding," Nathan said, hugging me hard.

* * *

By the time Officer Ryan's cruiser reached Houseboat Row, Miss Gloria and Mrs. Dubisson were waiting in the parking lot to walk me to our floating home. I headed directly into the shower, scrubbed off the salt and muck with a pounding stream of hot water, and pulled on sweats that on a normal May night would have felt too warm. Then I tied my hair up into a loose knot and slathered my face with lavender-scented cream.

"Sit here," my friend said, as I emerged back onto the deck. She pointed to the most comfortable lounge chair and once I'd settled, wrapped me in a quilted blanket. All three cats—two of hers and one of mine—jumped up to arrange themselves on my lap, as if they knew I had survived something terrible. Ziggy, Nathan's min-pin, sprawled on my feet. Then my friend handed me a piping hot mug of something that smelled strongly of rum. Her famous hot toddy.

"Double shot of Cuban rum in there, so sip slowly." She grinned. "I know it's over eighty degrees, but you are probably in shock."

I took a big gulp of the drink and felt the welcome warmth of the alcohol flood my throat and trickle down to my stomach. "I thought you were at the birthday dinner party?" I said, pushing a hank of damp hair off my forehead.

"We heard the news on my scanner, which I've got set up to feed to my Apple watch," said Miss Gloria, showing me the large black disk on her wrist, "and then Nathan texted so we rushed right home. You need to rest; we can talk later. I'll sit over here and read the paper." She gestured at another lounge chair a few feet away. "I brought my elderly iPad for you to use until you get the new phone. It might give out at any moment though."

"Thanks." I realized that my teeth were starting to chatter; I was shivering as if I'd fallen into a frozen Michigan lake instead of the warm bath that was the Gulf of Mexico. Once I'd downed the strong drink, I drifted off to sleep but was quickly startled awake by my own scream. Flashes of the explosion and my horror and surprise and terror at that abrupt landing in the water had begun to cycle through my dreaming mind.

"Nathan's here," Miss Gloria announced, relief in her voice. "With friends."

Nathan and Chief Brandenburg and Steve Torrence, KWPD police officer and dear friend, were tromping down the finger to the houseboat. Nathan leapt aboard and hurried over to me. The boat rocked as the others boarded, too, cramming a lot of testosterone onto our little deck.

"She's a little freaked out," Miss Gloria told him in a stage whisper. "She just woke herself up screaming."

"Are you sure you're all right?" my husband asked, his expression worried. "We should have insisted you get checked out by the medics." He crouched beside me and took my hand.

"I'm sure," I said, squeezing his fingers and managing a grin. "I'm perfectly fine. I mean, I will be. But what about all the others? The guests and the crew?"

"A few were transported to the hospital for evaluation," said the chief, his voice grim.

"Including the man with the bloody head, who said you saved him," said Torrence. He was grinning, trying not to scare me, I suspected.

"I wouldn't go that far," I said, "but thanks. I must be a VIP survivor to have warranted a visit from all three of you." I glanced at each of the men in turn, looking for hints about their purpose here.

"We need to ask some questions about what you remember and what you noticed before and after the incident," said the chief.

"While your memory is still fresh," Nathan added, patting my hand. His knees creaked as he stood.

I nodded. "I get that." For sure, they were worried about me. But more important, people had been injured and property damaged, so they had to understand what happened. If it wasn't an accident, they needed to know who was responsible. I had proven myself to be a good observer in stressful situations over the past few years.

"Obviously," I began, "either it was an accident or someone who was on the boat caused the explosion. Luckily," I added, "no one was seriously hurt or killed." I fell silent when I saw them exchanging glances. The glances that meant that they already knew a lot more than I did, and I wasn't going to like that information once it was shared. If it was shared.

"Let's start at the beginning," the chief said gently. "Tell us about the event, as if we knew nothing about it."

"That won't be a stretch for some of us," said Torrence with another grin. He was still trying to lighten the mood, which was pretty darn glum.

"I'll give you some background first." I explained that the party had been Palamina's brainstorm, a way to move our e-zine into the community spotlight and encourage people to think of us when they had news or wanted to advertise their business. "*Key Zest* is not only about food, though as you know, that's my main beat. But we want to compete with the other magazines in town—and online sites—as the best source for local news, along with more detailed articles about the politics of our town and more serious issues, from affordable housing to the homeless to stray cats needing to be neutered."

Miss Gloria's orange tiger cat T-bone, an SPCA rescue, lifted his head to glower at me and then turned away as if to say, "this doesn't concern me."

"Go on," said Nathan, picking my hand up and stroking each finger. "Tell us everything you can remember. Was there anything that felt out of whack? Anyone behaving in a strange way?"

I thought that over. "When we booked the *Pilar Too* at the office, we were told there was a second kitchen down below the main cabin. For us, that was a selling point. But then the captain insisted it was reserved for his special passengers and their private chef, so we shouldn't use that area."

"Did you use it?" Nathan asked.

"Of course not," I said. "We'd planned on storing some ingredients there, and maybe even doing some staging, but once he made it clear that this was off-limits, we crammed them into the bigger kitchen instead."

He chewed on his bottom lip for a moment. "What can you tell us about the passenger manifesto?"

That made me giggle a little hysterically. "It was much less formal than that, more like a chicken scratching guest list than a manifesto. Some people declined or changed their minds at the last minute, and some never responded. We were forever adding names we hadn't thought of. We had a paper copy but of course that's at the bottom of the deep because I'd brought the folder with all my notes into the cabin and left it with my mom's catering stuff. My phone's gone too." I felt a surge of panic, stricken with a sudden loss that surely had more to it than losing a fully replaceable iPhone. Twenty-four hours disconnected from the e-world was not going to kill me.

"We'll take care of that soon. I know you're lost without it." Nathan tried to smile and squeezed my hand. "Let's try that again from a different angle. What do you remember about who was on the boat? Had any obvious conflicts already surfaced among the guests? Tell us about the captain and crew members if you can remember any details about them."

My husband looked pained as though he hated to put me through this, and probably hated that I had gone through it even more. He despised knowing that I might have been injured or was scared or most of all, that he might have lost me. I was determined to act strong, in order to reassure him. Maybe I would start to feel that way again in the process.

I told them more about the names on the list, free-associating the restaurant owners and local politicians that I could remember. "We certainly have an earlier draft on my mother's computer—she was charged with keeping track of the count, though maybe I have a printout of an early version at the office. We can probably reconstruct everything between me and Palamina and Danielle and my mother and Sam. I'm sure we'll come up with most of the names."

Palamina! I couldn't remember seeing her at all after the blast. "Is my boss OK?" I asked, my gaze searching all three faces in case one or more of them would be loath to tell an unfortunate truth.

"She'll be fine," said Torrence, nodding with reassurance. "She's in a little bit of shock so they're keeping her at the ER for the time being."

The Mango Murders

"Danielle's fine too. She was slightly hysterical and definitely wet, but otherwise in good shape. Her husband took her home." Nathan would know that would be my next question.

"Thank goodness." I nodded and swallowed and started again. "The captain gave his safety talk." I paused to think. "He was a bit of a showman, telling jokes about how he hoped the poor swimmers didn't get a life preserver with a hole in it and so on. Not really all that funny if you were a little nervous to begin with. I was pretty busy greeting people and filling champagne glasses, so I can't remember every detail, but that's the gist. Then he began to describe the route he would be taking, passing Wisteria and Sunset Key. We'd asked him to linger a bit in front of Mallory Square so we could feel like part of the sunset party action, then head away from shore. Early on as we sailed, I overheard snatches of unhappy discussion, people squabbling over who really owns Wisteria Island, and whether it should be developed. I can't think why that would lead to arson though."

"Ridiculous," said Nathan under his breath. "Go on."

The chief made a note in his phone.

"My mother was passing around a tray of shrimp puffs, or was it the spicy cheese wafers?" I pressed my hands to my head. "Oh god, everything feels jumbled up." The men were looking edgy and impatient, so I tried to focus. "I was right behind her with a champagne bottle in one hand and a pitcher of mango daiquiris in the other to refill glasses as needed." I could imagine the weight of the pitcher straining my forearm as I described it. But was that real or was I only carrying champagne? My memories were getting muddled.

"Then someone yelled 'fire,' and one of the crew announced we should abandon ship. Finally, the captain came on the address system asking people to remain calm and grab life jackets. It was kind of too late for the staying calm bit. Actually, it happened too fast for those life jackets too. Next, there was a loud noise like something blew up, and the next thing I knew I was in the water." My eyes filled with tears again, but I worked hard to blink them back and cover my distress by pressing my fingers against my cheekbones. Nathan crouched down beside me again and took both of my hands.

"Tell me everything you can think of right before you heard the noise. Who was around you? Anyone who was not behaving like a guest? Can you remember anyone hovering near the cabin other than the captain and other crew members?"

"It's a big cabin," I said, squeezing my eyes shut so I could visualize accurately. "There's a kitchen inside with a regular refrigerator and a small oven and sink and acres of counter space. Sam had the auxiliary bar arranged there so he could whip up refills of the special cocktails quickly and carry them outside. It turned out there was lots of room under the counter so we could roll Mom's carts underneath to get them out of the way. In other words, we didn't miss the extra kitchen. We had a table in the middle of the living area to display our food, and we could also stage platters for those of us who'd be passing the nibbles around. The captain told us there were two heads, one inside for ladies and one at the front for men. We were to go down the ladder backwards. He said, 'Toes grip and heels slip.' That little maxim was to remind us of his safety tip." A flash of memory came to me.

"Most people were outside on the deck all around the boat, but I did see one man enter the cabin as I was coming out. I assumed he was feeling seasick and going to the head—I guess the ladies' room was closer. Although the water was calm, and we hadn't gotten very far from shore. Besides, I know from experience he would have been better off out in the fresh air." My eyes flew open, and I looked at Nathan. "Actually, I don't think he went down the ladder to the head and the bunk. He went down the further steps that lead to the office and maybe the engine room? I didn't get a chance to explore that far. It was restricted to the crew anyway."

"Who was the man?" asked my husband. "He wasn't a member of the crew?"

"I didn't recognize him," I said slowly. "But most of the crew were girls—maybe in their teenage years or early twenties and all adorable and wearing short shorts and nautical caps. Why do you ask? Are you thinking someone sabotaged the party for some reason? Like he went downstairs and messed with the engine?" I felt a flicker of hysteria. Americans had grown inured to the news about mass tragedies in the country unless they happened very close to home. Even with all the difficult events I'd been witness to lately, I honestly had never considered that I'd be involved in one. Maybe even the target.

"We won't know for sure until we recover what's left of the boat and piece everything together," Nathan said, all business. "It's too early to assume anything."

"If you could," said the chief, "please describe what the point of this party was. Tell us what kinds of people were invited and whether you expected any conflicts. Start from the beginning as if I knew nothing about it." He'd already used that line, but it felt like a warm invitation for a witness to share everything without feeling threatened. I took a big breath and tried to organize my thoughts in a way that might be useful to the investigators.

"As I said, my boss, Palamina, feels very ambitious for our magazine. She wants more people to reach out to us as important news occurs, because we don't have a very big staff so we can't go chasing every story. Also, on the food criticism front, there have been some complaints about whether my reviews are either too soft or too harsh. Ha! They should read some of the things that real critics from big newspapers write. Like Robert Sietsema describing one dish from someone's menu as looking like a small dead animal. Or Sam Sifton. If you want tough, Google some of his older reviews. He once described a *Vitello tonnato* as tasting like sliced shoe, with a tuna sauce that carried a Miracle Whip tang."

"Hmm." Nathan rubbed his chin. "I can't quite picture someone sabotaging a whole party by blowing up a ship because of the way you wrote a review."

"On the other hand," I snapped back, "you don't care what you eat. Other people including me, care deeply."

The three men eyed each other nervously, and Steve Torrence said, "I think she needs to rest. We know where to find her if we have more questions."

My husband looked chagrined. "I'm sorry if it sounded like I was haranguing you. I'm worried about everything. But especially you."

"I know," I said, patting his forearm, suddenly flattened by a wave of post-excitement exhaustion. "But I would love to take a real nap."

"Great idea. I'll be going back to work if that's OK," Nathan said.

"That's perfect," I said, my eyes fluttering shut for a blissful moment.

"Do you want me to stay?" Miss Gloria asked.

"I'll be fine," I said, "and I might need you later." I stood up to give them all hugs.

Once they'd left, I headed into the houseboat to rest on our bed. I woke up who knows how much later at the cheerful sound of a phone. I groped around for my cell phone, finally remembering that I'd lost it in the incident. The ringing came from the landline that Nathan insisted we keep in case the cell towers went down some day. He always wanted to be prepared for future disaster. I snatched up the receiver, wincing as the quick movement tweaked my shoulder. My mother's number scrolled over the small screen, and I punched accept.

"Are you OK?" I asked. At the same time, she said, "how do you feel?" We both laughed.

"Shocked," she said, "horrified. Disappointed but grateful. I'm physically fine and Sam is too." She lowered her voice as if someone would listen in. "The cops were here. Asking all kinds of questions. I get the feeling they think we are at the center of what might have been the crime of the year in Key West."

"Same," I said. "I got the bigwigs, my husband, the chief, and Steve Torrence. Looking back, do you think you saw anybody doing anything suspicious?"

"I was so focused on getting the food out and making sure everyone was having a lovely time with something to nibble on and full champagne glasses. I wasn't watching for criminals." Her voice sounded sad. This promised to be a showcase for her business as well as my e-zine.

"Yes," I said, "I'm sorry. It was going to be such a lovely party. Plus, you've lost a lot of your catering equipment."

"Insurance will cover it," she said. "We're alive and well, that's all that matters. Did you come up with any leads for them?"

"I mentioned that there were a lot of people from the local food world, and that some of them would not have been happy about my reviews. Nathan made fun of that, and we had a little mini spat."

"Tension is inevitable in a crisis," she said. "He adores you and he respects what you do. But he feels responsible for a lot of trouble right now, and I know he worries about all of us." She paused, and I could hear the click of her fingernail on her phone. "I wonder if it would be worth us doing some informal interviews with a few folks in the foodie world. People who the police might not necessarily reach out to. Even if they did, they might not ask the right questions because they can never truly understand what drives our passion."

It was a wonderful idea, and it would give my mother and me a chance to go out for a couple of meals and decompress. "I know where we could start," I said. "I saw on Facebook this morning that Lola's Bistro has openings for tomorrow night, last minute cancellations. Their chef was on our cruise. Hopefully he won't be too distraught to cook." Although truthfully, I'd never known a chef who was too upset to cook. Drunk maybe, or hungover, sure, but usually cooking calmed a person down. You couldn't worry too much about the rest of life's problems when you were focused on a souffle or a bechamel sauce.

"Count me in," she said. "Sam has bocci tomorrow, so he won't miss me. We can go over the details of Miss Gloria's party while we're at it."

I called Lola's to make a reservation in the name of Janet for the early seating. Then I emailed Palamina to check in on her

The Mango Murders

and report that I could fill in some of the empty space left open by the truncated sailing expedition with an extra review. *Unless you want me to write up the crash from an insider POV? By the way, how are you feeling?* I added. She didn't like a fuss made over her, but it seemed ridiculous not to make an exception in this case.

Sounds good, the review I mean, she answered. *I'm fine. Staff meeting day after tomorrow at 9 am.*

Next, I checked in with Danielle, who seemed to be enjoying her unexpected day off, catered to by her handsome new husband. I scrolled through the stories about the incident in our rival news sources, but nothing new seemed to have surfaced. At least not publicly. I noticed a Facebook message had come in from Lorenzo.

Worried. Can I bring you lunch tomorrow? I am assuming you are fine because I felt no negative vibrations in the universe. But fine in body does not mean fine in mind, so I'd like to lay eyes on you in person. Sandwich from Frenchie's? Takeout from the Café? Toasted bagel with chicken salad from Goldman's? Your choice. Noon OK?

I messaged him right back.

You're on! Anything you choose will be fine. I didn't say it, because I wanted the trip to be convenient for him, but the sound of that creamy chicken salad contrasting with the crunch of a toasted bagel made my mouth water furiously. Poppyseed maybe? Or sesame?

His mention of lunch and the food visions it brought up made me realize I'd missed dinner and was starving. I puttered around the kitchen, slicing Irish cheddar for a grilled cheese, adding arugula, avocado, and a muffuletta olive spread I'd recently fallen in love with. Once the sandwich was sizzling in hot butter, I fed Evinrude, who was purring loudly and winding between my legs. Then I shook a few chips onto the plate (from a stash I'd designated as emergency-only), added a pickle, and sat down to enjoy every buttery, oozing bite. With my stomach full and the dishes washed, I took Ziggy out for a quick walk and climbed into bed with my laptop.

The Key West locals Facebook page was full of the news of the sunset cruise gone bad. The theories ranged from a Cuban missile meant for the military base but gone astray, to a rooster flown into the engine. That made me giggle—the scenario would have been physically impossible unless the rooster had stowed away on the boat and flung himself into the engine compartment once we got moving. I heard our front door unlock, and Ziggy woofed and jumped off the bed with narrow tail whipping as he ran to greet Nathan.

"How's my patient?" Nathan asked, coming over to the bed to kiss me.

"Pretty good," I said. "Maybe still a teeny tiny bit freaked out, but I'll get over that. I talked to my mom, we're all disappointed of course, but it could have been a lot worse." I shivered. "Supposing that oil slick caught on fire?"

"Best not to imagine all the possible disastrous scenarios," said my husband, perching on the bed beside me and taking my hand. "Let the professionals do that." He paused. "We're puzzled about why this happened. Assuming it wasn't an accident, which we are assuming for now." Another pause. "Was there anyone on the expedition who had a grudge against you? When you think about it," he said, "you've been on the sidelines of quite a few crimes. Sometimes more front and center than sideline."

I started to protest but honestly, I couldn't disagree. He was making me pretty nervous. Chad Lutz, my ex-boyfriend, was the first name that came to mind. I briefly considered not mentioning him but realized that could lead to trouble later.

"Chad," I said, "but I think he's long since gotten over me. We didn't have a lot between us to begin with. Though he was mad about the time I helped put one of his clients in jail, remember?" I snickered. Sometimes he represented bad actors, and it didn't bother me a bit to see them get what they deserved. "On the other hand, he wasn't anywhere near that boat. As far as I know."

"I'll kill the rat bastard," Nathan muttered.

"You're sweet," I said, "but I don't think that will be necessary. He's not worth the bother. He probably still holds a grudge, but he doesn't have the gumption to do anything about it. He'd delegate it to his assistant, Deena, and she's my friend." We both laughed.

"What about Wally?" he asked.

I was sure it pained him to talk about another one of my ex's, although that relationship had been even briefer than the one with Chad.

"No way," I said confidently. "Wally ended up being a milquetoast—not at all the kind of guy who'd nurse a grudge and blow up a boat. Besides, he's the one who dumped me, so he could hardly blame me for taking up with you."

"You'd be surprised at the way people think, the way they twist endings to fit their own version of the truth. The cops see this all the time. Anybody else who might have it in for you?"

I let my mind rove over the incidents I'd been involved in over the past few years. It wasn't like I was a police officer who could arrest murderers and make sure they were jailed. I was just a curious citizen, with an above average propensity for stumbling into trouble. "There were a couple of bad guys I tangled with, but they are definitely in jail."

Nathan stood up, took off his shirt, and fired it into the hamper. "Could it be that the perpetrator of the explosion resents someone else in your magazine?"

I considered this while he went into the bathroom to wash his face and brush his teeth. "Everyone loves Danielle," I said when he came out. "I don't think her husband is senior enough in the police department to have really angered any criminals."

"Probably not," said Nathan as he slid into bed next to Ziggy, who was snuggled against my ribs. Ziggy bared his sharp little teeth and growled. "Knock it off pal," he told the dog. "I found her first." He had a pained look on his face, probably thinking there might very well be bad guys who would harm me, in order to punish him.

"Palamina?" he asked. "What do you know about her background?"

"Not a lot. She came from New York. That's pretty much what I know because she's super reserved. In case you're wondering, she's very invested in the e-zine, and this party was her brainstorm. She would never ever have blown this thing up. She was counting on these people giving the magazine a great big boost. She's very ambitious."

A bad feeling swept over me. "You wouldn't be asking all these questions if someone hadn't been killed. Am I right?"

Nathan dipped his chin. "You know I'll tell you when I can. You can guess that the experts have a lot to do if there is a casualty, studying the remains and searching for personal effects."

I gulped, absolutely sick to my stomach. "Can you give me a hint about who it is? What kind of effects might have been left behind?"

"I can't say more yet, Hayley," he said, his expression fierce, "but I will when I'm able. There was an explosion and a hot fire."

I knew what that had to mean—a person who had been *alive at our party* was now dead, possibly burned beyond recognition. "You think this had something to do with *Key Zest*?"

"Possibly. We're looking into every angle." He kissed me. "Try not to worry too much about it. That's my job."

"Is it OK if I talk with some of the foodie people who were on the trip who might have seen or heard something?" I hated the idea of sitting tight and waiting like a hapless duck while they explored possible explanations.

After some back and forth about how I would report to him (often) and how far I would go to get information (not far) and how I would never ever put myself in a dangerous situation, he agreed.

Nathan dropped right off to sleep, but it wasn't going to be that easy for me. For one thing, my body ached, especially my left shoulder, which must have hit the water first. The whole experience had been completely unnerving. The news that someone was missing and possibly dead and that someone else was possibly resentful enough of me or someone else at *Key Zest* to sabotage the event made it feel even more unnerving. Tomorrow I'd look back over all my old reviews to look for clues to anyone who might still be annoyed with me. More than annoyed, angry enough to possibly kill me and a lot of other random people.

Lucy Burdette

Like others who watched the news in this country, I'd come to realize that many of the tragedies and mass casualties we suffered were caused by someone with an unreasonable grievance and a screw loose. Plus, access to weapons. And probably in this case, enough knowledge of boats to understand what might have caused one to catch fire and blow up.

Chapter Four

No matter: Bad is bad, and it's a critic's central function to point out the vile as well as the wonderful.
　　　　　—Robert Sietsema, "Sietsema's 10 Worst Dishes of 2023." *Eater New York.*

I woke later than usual, having slept like the dead, to use an expression that gave me the creeps. Nathan had left a note on the kitchen counter saying he didn't want to wake me because I looked so peaceful, and I'd been through so much. Please check in with him later. He had fed both the animals, in case they tried to pull a fast one and demand a second breakfast. I made myself a quick cup of strong coffee and went out to the deck.

As my brain and body woke along with sounds and sights of marina life, the memories of the night before sifted in. It was nothing short of miraculous that there hadn't been more injuries, or God help us, deaths, during or after the incident. I tilted my neck toward one shoulder and then the other, feeling a sharp pain running down my neck to my left shoulder. I had definitely wrenched something that I didn't notice right away while my adrenalin was surging.

With my phone out of action, I opened my laptop and began to peruse the news. *The Key West Citizen, Konk Life,* and *Florida Keys Weekly* all had stories about the incident, but their reporting told pretty much what I already knew: the yacht hosting a sunset cocktail party sponsored by *Key Zest* and catered by my mother's company had either caught fire or blown up or both around 7 p.m. Passengers had been thrown off the deck into the water, and the *Pilar Too* was decimated by the explosion. Reporters had added a few conversations with and quotes from bystanders who had been enjoying the sunset celebration on Mallory Square before it was ruined by the boat disaster, but nothing that shed any light on what caused the incident. Nathan seemed to think the perpetrator might be related to my foodie world, uncomfortably close. Neither one of us would be able to leave this alone until we knew the truth.

I began to pull up all the articles that I'd written over the past few years, including restaurant reviews, both negative and positive. My idea was to scroll through them in case any suspects popped out—anyone who might have a lingering grievance with me. As I'd mentioned to Nathan and the other officers, the worst of the criminals that I'd helped "put away" were in jail. Unless there had been a sudden move by the Florida State legislators to release the criminal population out of the prisons and into the world, it seemed doubtful that any of these would have cared enough about my role to harm me. Would incarcerated prisoners have the wherewithal to set up an explosion 500 miles away? Seemed unlikely.

My reviews had evolved over time, as I adopted a balanced and more confident approach to doing my job. I tried to be tough, but always fair. Key West was essentially a small town with party trappings that sometimes disguised the real-life people behind the scenes. Restaurant staff were hard-working people who weren't earning big salaries as they scrambled to feed both visitors and locals. The few restaurants I'd panned in the beginning had gone out of business or changed owners. I was convinced the failures were not my fault, even if I'd been a small cog in that wheel. I didn't carry that much influence, so I couldn't believe any of those would harbor enough ill will toward me to spark this disaster. On the other hand, humans weren't always logical.

Next, I googled my boss and watched the pages load. There were articles she'd written for her gigs at the *New York Post* and *New York Magazine*. Further down on the page, Palamina was featured as an up-and-coming newcomer at a recent Key West Chamber of Commerce meeting. I also found links to several dozen filler pieces she'd written for our magazine. At the very bottom, I was most astonished to discover a story in the *New York Times* style section about her wedding seven years ago to Damian Wayne McIlroy. In the photo of the happy couple, Palamina was wearing a stunning oyster-colored, trumpet-style gown overlaid with lace that suited her tall, slim figure perfectly. Her new husband, attired in a flawless black tux with his dark wavy hair marked by one silver streak, looked like Italian royalty.

But she had never mentioned a husband to me. Not once, even in passing. Even when I was engaged and quickly married, all through Danielle's engagement and elegant wedding, she'd never mentioned her own marital status. My impression had been that Palamina saw our romances as something that could only interfere with our jobs. I made a note to double-check that

Danielle hadn't heard this gossip and failed to pass the information on. She wasn't usually one to keep juicy bits to herself.

Again, it seemed unlikely that an ex, no matter how rancorous the split, would have cooked up such an elaborate "accident." Was Palamina still married? If not, who had called it quits, and why? I remembered that she'd scheduled a staff meeting for first thing tomorrow morning. Would I have the nerve to ask her about this fascinating nugget of private history?

I sat back, trying to imagine the big picture—who else might have been involved with or responsible for our disaster? As I'd told Nathan, I simply couldn't believe that Danielle herself would be the target of any attack. She had lived in Key West all her life and was well loved, as was her family. Conchs, as people born in Key West were called, were treated differently than the rest of us—easily trusted and beloved by other natives. I could understand this even if I didn't like it, as over the years the island had been flooded with people who either wanted to exploit its resources (turtles, sponges, real estate, and more) or claim the beauty for themselves.

Next, I googled Danielle's husband, Jeremy, who'd also been born and raised on the island and was a fairly new recruit at the Key West police department. His name did not come up in any mentions of Major Crimes or criminals. Would someone who was given a ticket for reckless driving or public drunkenness have the interest or wherewithal to blow up our party? It seemed unlikely.

I spotted Miss Gloria out on her deck and waved at her to come over for a chat. Her face looked worried as she came aboard.

"How do you feel this morning?" she asked. She rested her palm on my forehead, like a mother checking for a fever in a child.

"Better," I said. "Stiff and sore but nothing major." I rubbed the side of my neck. "I feel like I yanked something, probably when I was thrown off the boat. But I'm sure it will get better."

"Don't wait too long to get it checked out," she said. "These little aches and pains tend to add up and become chronic. I have a fantastic masseuse and also a bar tab with the best physical therapist in town." We both broke out laughing. "She knows just about everyone in Key West and has probably already solved the boating mystery. Her name is Heather—I think she won the Miss Tennessee title a few years back. She's tough, but adorable. Just like you."

"Aw, thanks," I said, grinning.

She scrolled through the contacts on her phone until she found the therapist. "Want me to use my phone to set up an appointment?"

I cricked my neck to the right and then over to the left again. Ouch. An appointment seemed like a good idea. Miss Gloria left a message requesting a visit for the earliest opening in Heather's schedule next week, leaving both her phone number and my mother's, and then patted my knee. "Since we have that all settled, and if you're not otherwise a basket case, is it OK if we talk about next week's party? I'm feeling slightly overwhelmed."

"Of course," I said.

When we'd discussed a celebration for her eighty-fifth birthday last year, we'd started small, but plans had mushroomed. Many out-of-town relatives and friends had insisted on receiving invitations to the party. We hadn't gotten the expected number of regrets, either. That meant that her sons and their wives were coming, along with my father, stepmother, and half-brother, and both of Nathan's parents. They were divorced, but fortunately had gotten to the point where they could be in the same county without poisoning the well water in order to target their ex. Even the scone sisters from Scotland, Bettina and Violet, had threatened to make a surprise appearance. I thought I'd convinced them that visiting sometime after the party would mean more quality time with their friend. This was shaping up to be a mob scene. I opened my laptop, which I'd closed when Gloria came over to chat.

"I'll pull up my spreadsheet. Then you can tell me what you're concerned about, and I'll fix it. Talk to me."

"A fair number of these people on the guest list are prickly, wouldn't you agree?"

I snickered. "I can't disagree."

"Some of them have never met. Take my sons and their wives. Please." She paused and grinned. "I can't picture them connecting with Nathan's family, for example."

"We aren't running a weekend session of family therapy," I said in return. "It's a party. A series of parties to be accurate. We won't have icebreaker exercises meant to force people together, I promise. If some of them don't hit it off, they don't have to hang out together."

My friend heaved a big sigh. "I can just picture my daughter-in-law Henrietta throwing a pall over every gathering. She's not a team player, and I can't trust her to be polite. Then James's wife, Tonya, falls in with her, and it begins to feel like a critical mass of negativity. I'm also worried about Annie Dubisson." She paused for a moment, and I waited, too. Mrs. Dubisson was a darling elderly woman, Miss Gloria's best pal for going on forty years. I couldn't imagine her causing trouble and I finally said so.

The Mango Murders

"No, it's not that. It's that we're celebrating her birthday this week but without the same trumpets and swans and fuss and general pizzazz you've planned for me. Is the difference going to make her feel bad? Since she lives at the end of the pier, she's going to see every bit of excitement and all the people visiting me. Will she feel alone and unappreciated? I would hate for that to happen."

I opened my mouth to reassure her, but she barreled on.

"What if the family starts lecturing me about how I'm too old to live on a houseboat, and that my body's failing, and my mind is addled, and they won't be able to stop worrying as long as I remain on this island."

"We will cut that dead, right at the roots," I said. "You know that my mother and Nathan and I and Sam will all speak up for you. We can present a plan for hurricane season where the minute any big storms appear on the horizon, we drive you north with all the animals. Safe and sound."

We went round and round with another list of her worries, but none of the party details seemed really worth stressing over. All the guests had places to stay, and we had the menus planned for the two big dinner parties. I had to think her anxiety was based on the cumulative effects of so much planning, and so many visitors all at once. She would want to be the best hostess possible, including skipping naps and eating at unusual hours and giving up activities that provided her purpose and pleasure. Many of us received a lot of visitors on this island paradise, and we loved seeing them, but they brought their own brand of stress, interrupting the comfortable flow of everyday life.

"I feel a tiny bit better," she said finally. "I'll leave you to your work."

Lorenzo arrived on the dot of noon with a big bag of food. I knew this had been a sacrifice for him because he was not an early riser. His 12 noon was probably equivalent to my 6 a.m.. I beckoned him inside where I'd set the banquette with utensils and glasses of iced tea with lemon. Even with the sun umbrellas up, it had grown uncomfortably hot out on our deck. Besides, I wanted to talk to him privately without the denizens of the pier possibly listening in.

"I got your favorite from Goldman's Deli—a toasted poppyseed bagel loaded with chicken salad," he said after greeting me with a kiss.

"That sounds heavenly. Thanks." My mouth was watering, and I tore open the bag he offered, and moved the sandwiches to plates. As we dug into the lunch, he quizzed me ever so gently about my mental and physical well-being.

"I feel fine except I must've wrenched my neck and my shoulder because it's been slowly tightening up and now I can hardly move it. Luckily, it's the left side so I'll be able to write and cook and everything else. I'm hoping to set up an appointment with Miss Gloria's physical therapist early next week."

"The world won't stop spinning if you take a few days off," he said, his forehead creased with worry. "How's your mother?"

"She's fine, too," I said, tucking a stray bit of chicken salad onto my bagel. "She and I are going to dinner later. You were there at Mallory Square last night," I added, looking up from my plate to his troubled face. "How did it unfold from your vantage point?"

He finished chewing and laid his fork on the table. "I didn't have a clear look at your boat when it arrived, because my table was set up along the little alley that runs perpendicular to the

The Mango Murders

water. You know how the crowd clusters at the edge of the pier as the time for sunset gets closer. The whole place is a madhouse."

I nodded my agreement and nibbled at the top of my bagel. "I wonder whether some of the details around you might become clear if you describe the reading you were doing at the time? Eric always says that traumatic memories can be stored in our senses—smells, sounds, sights." Eric was another good friend, a psychologist who also brimmed with compassion and common sense. "Maybe imagining those cards would jog loose something else you didn't consciously notice at the time?"

Lorenzo looked thoughtful. "I'll try." He closed his eyes as I'd seen him do so many times when he read cards for me. Minutes later, they fluttered back open. "My customer at the time was very upset. Needy," he added. "Her boyfriend had called things off with her recently. This was supposed to be their 'juice up the relationship' weekend, but he opted out at the last minute. Pretty much told her there was no juice left."

"Sounds so distressing," I said, patting my mouth with a paper napkin. "I bet she wanted you to tell her whether he was coming back."

"Yes, and believe it or not, I get a lot of this kind of request. All that to say, I wasn't really focused on what was going on around me, my energy was directed at her."

I was nodding vigorously. "That's exactly why people who need help love you: they get all of your attention."

"Thanks, I try. This woman was frantic. She started to tell me about how her beloved had left, and I asked her to please stop, that it was better if I looked at the cards and interpreted what I saw there. If I know facts about someone, it can color my mind and muddle the process." He sorted through his well-used deck of cards and pulled out four: the ace of swords, the fool reversed, the four of pentacles and the three of pentacles.

"What did you tell her about these?"

He folded his hands on the table, studying the spread. "The cards said that her situation was teaching her something profound, and that this reading would help push her into making a decision that she needed to make. That message came from the ace of swords. Then she'd drawn the fool, reversed. When this card is reversed, it's all about fear. She had so much apprehension and this fear was blocking her from making a good decision. The four of pentacles told me that she was giving too much outside. I told her that she needed to regulate her energy. She was drained. That she needed to value herself and her life, rather than give herself away so easily."

"I bet she found all that super helpful even if somewhat disturbing," I said.

He smiled. "Isn't it always disturbing to find that it's your point of view that needs to shift rather than the world around you? However, right at that moment as she was about to respond, we heard the big noise that must've been your boat. So, I never had the chance to follow up on how she felt about what I saw in those cards."

"Did you realize right away that something was wrong?"

"You know how it is on Mallory Square, it's noisy all the time. I've gotten very good at tuning this out because it all starts to seem normal, crazy normal for sure, but not fraught with danger. I need to focus on the person in front of me. So it took me a couple of minutes to recognize that we had a huge problem. By then all the bystanders were rushing to the edge of the water. It definitely wasn't business as usual. My customer got spooked and left the table. I hate that I dumped all that news on her with no time to digest it. I never even got to the three of pentacles."

Like a good therapist, he stayed with his clients until every question was answered. Or at least until he'd helped them sit with the mysteries of their life.

He closed his eyes for another moment and then they flew open. "Tobin might have seen it happen," he said, "because he was up on that ladder right as the boat blew up. I remember how nimbly he and his partner dropped down once they heard all the emergency vehicles."

Tobin and his partner performed athletic and acrobatic stunts that included balancing upside-down on a ladder. The sheer strength it took to do a handstand on your partner's shoulders while teetering on a ladder had always astonished me. He might have seen something from that vantage point, but on the other hand he would have needed to be focusing hard on what he was doing. Sometimes he played tennis at Bayview Park in the morning. It might be worthwhile buzzing over there later this week to ask what he'd seen.

Lorenzo's face was alert with a sudden idea. "Do you know by any chance Robert Jensen? He ran a disaster management company for years. Not to say that he would have been on the scene at Mallory Square, but it's possible that he could point us in the right direction as far as understanding how to think about this kind of event. Maybe you saw his op-ed a couple of weeks ago about how Key West should get prepared in case of a cruise ship disaster? This isn't that, but it's in the same ballpark."

I wasn't sure how helpful this would be, but how could it hurt? "What did this company do?" I asked.

"If there was a big event like a plane crash or terrorist activity that resulted in fatalities and injuries, his company would be called in. They helped organize the site and retrieve the personal effects of the victims and then deal with the bereaved families. You can imagine how stressful and painful that job must've been."

"I can't really imagine. I've dealt with survivors after a murder, and that was hard enough. Could you text an introduction, and maybe he'll meet for a coffee?"

After my friend left, I cleaned up the kitchen thinking about what Lorenzo had told his client. What had she been able to absorb, without him helping her to understand?

You never finished telling me, what does the three of pentacles mean? I texted him.

Competence, encouragement, collaboration. Especially collaboration and planning, though it would depend on the circumstances too, he texted back.

Collaboration and planning, that's what our party cruise had entailed, lots of it. All of that blown to smithereens in moments. According to Nathan's hints, someone was missing, probably dead, leaving only personal effects behind. What an odd turn of phrase for the leftovers of someone who was no longer with us.

Chapter Five

Hunger is not how our family mourns.
—Melissa Clark, "On Mother's Day." *New York Times: Cooking*, May 11, 2024

Everything about Lola's Bistro was quirky, from the lack of online reservations to the two seatings to the lack of paper menus. I was glad I had my mother with me, rather than Nathan. Not only would she appreciate the food, but she also wouldn't be bothered by the quirkiness, she'd be intrigued. She knew one of the wait staff who moonlighted for her catering company. I'd mentioned his name in my phone message, and he'd promised we could be seated near the chef so we could watch him work.

The restaurant was a small storefront on Simonton Street; the door was painted black with Lola's written on the window in elegant script. You could miss it if you weren't looking for it. We were the only ones in line at 5:45—the first dinner seating began at six. But the door was locked—because of course we both tried it—and the outside lights were turned off. We peered in the front window and saw a man on a ladder, lighting small tea candles one by one and placing them in holders that dotted the wall.

"That's the chef," my mother said. "What a labor-intensive decoration, though it's going to look gorgeous. I would not allow Sam to get up on a ladder right before we were making and serving dinner to a restaurant full of people."

"Imagine what happens if he falls off—no dinner for anyone," I added. "Or what if he sets the wall on fire?"

"Leave it to us to imagine the worst that could happen in any situation," my mother added with a chuckle.

Though it made sense, given the disaster we'd narrowly escaped. Those awful events would echo in our memories for a long time.

From what I'd heard about this restaurant, there was only one chef, and only two waiters. I surely hoped they had some people in the back kitchen doing the dishes and some of the prep work, as it looked like the tables were set for about thirty diners.

When the tea lights had all been lit, and the tables arranged, a young, energetic man who introduced himself as Rhett came out to call the names of diners with reservations. Then he beckoned us in one by one and settled us at tables. "As you may know, there is no menu," he said after we were seated with a view of the open kitchen area. "Your waiter will list the dishes the chef has selected to feature this evening, including appetizers, main courses, and dessert. You are not obligated to choose one of each."

He brought us a bottle of water, filled our glasses, and then opened the bottle of rosé that I'd brought with me. Both my mother and I had decided we deserved a glass or two of wine—we'd taken Ubers to the restaurant, so I didn't have to worry about wobbling home on a scooter, nor she driving their van.

The Mango Murders

For dinner, we chose artichokes, Florida lobster tails in a sweet and spicy sauce, gnocchi in a cream sauce, a ribeye for my mother and hogfish with shrimp for me. It would be a lot of food, but since I would be writing this up for the e-zine, we needed to taste as many dishes as possible. I clinked my glass against my mother's.

"To not drowning," I said, with a grin.

"To no one getting hurt, at least seriously," she added. "At least everyone except for that poor man with the bloody head."

"Nathan did tell me that somebody might be missing," I cautioned. I didn't dare tell her it was probably much worse than that.

She frowned, pulled a copy of the almost final guest list out of her big bag, and handed it to me. "One mayor, a former mayor, two commissioners, a developer, a few businessmen, and a smattering of journalists and food people and artistic types. I'm going to assume that Nathan and the police department will be interviewing the bigshots, right?" asked my mother.

"Probably. Is there anyone on the list who's unfamiliar to you?" I asked.

"I marked those in yellow," she said. I skimmed her notes—most of those she'd highlighted were political types.

The waiter brought our appetizers, and we dove into the food, exclaiming to each other over every bite of the sweet and spicy lobster sauce and creamy gnocchi.

"I'm stopping here," said my mother, pushing her plate away with a few bites left on it. "I want to save room for my main." She glanced over at the chef, whose face had grown red as he moved in double-time. "His job is so much more exhausting than mine. For one thing, I don't have all my guests looking on while I cook. Plus, after the general concept of the menu is commissioned by the party giver, I pretty much tell the guests what they're eating. I don't have to deal with them telling me."

The chef appeared more and more flustered as he worked. We watched as the waiters returned a few dishes that were apparently not what the customers had ordered, including a pork chop that neither of us had chosen.

"I wonder," said my mother as the waiter scurried away, "whether he should have taken another night off? What we went through was very stressful."

The waiter returned with my mother's ribeye paired with perfectly browned potatoes and a roasted tomato. "Our apologies for the mix-up."

"It can happen." My mother smiled warmly. "I'm Janet Snow and this is my daughter, Hayley. When Chef Richard is done cooking, do you suppose we could chat with him? We're in the food business too and wanted to compliment him. And we were on the same boat that he was yesterday, the one that caught fire off Mallory Square."

His eyes bugged wide. "I can ask." He bustled back over within minutes with word that we could join the chef at the bar for dessert.

Once we'd finished our main courses, we shifted over to the two stools placed in front of the bar.

Chef Richard nodded hello. He had striking blue eyes and wore a white chef's coat and a pork pie hat. "I'd like you to try one of all the desserts. I'm sorry for the error with your steak. I'm afraid I'm not at my very best," he said. He pushed three plates in front of us. "Mango upside down cake with a dollop of whipped cream because it's the season, bananas Foster because it's simple, and chocolate cheesecake with caramel sauce, because the superfans demand it. We made extra caramel sauce to serve on the side of the mango cake, should that appeal to you."

"Yes, please," we said in unison. "It very much appeals to us," I added.

The phone on the counter to his left buzzed. He rolled his eyes and pushed it away, but it continued to rattle and fuss. Finally, he wiped his hands on his apron and moved over to look at the screen. The color drained from his face, and he muttered an expletive in a hoarse whisper.

"Are you alright?" my mother asked, leaning toward him over the counter.

"A friend texted me earlier that someone on that boat died." He lowered his voice. "Now he says they think it was murder."

"Murder?" I said. "How? Why? Who died?" My mind was whirling with possibilities, none of them good. Was the boat set on fire in order to cover a crime that was even worse? I was getting ahead of myself, imagining the worst.

"They don't know yet, or if they do, they aren't sharing with my friend. Certainly no one told me anything this afternoon. The authorities were here for hours when I was trying to get prep work done for dinner. What did I see? What did I hear? Did anybody have it in for any of the other guests as far as I knew? I was just trying to have a relaxing evening on the water." He tipped his head toward my mother and grimaced. "Enjoying someone else's food for once."

"I'm so sorry it turned out like that," my mother said at the same time as I said, "We had hoped for that too." This conversation made me wonder how many other chefs and restaurant owners in town were suffering from PTSD from our outing yesterday.

"You're certain they didn't hint anything this afternoon about a possible murder?"

Chef Richard looked at me as though I had lost my mind. "These were cops—aren't you married to one? You know they aren't going to tell civilians anything. Especially if they think you might be involved in some way."

My mother reached out a comforting hand to the chef. "Surely, they don't think you had anything to do with this death. If anything, it could be us," she waved at me and her. "After all, we're the ones who invited everyone on that darn boat. For all they know, we could've set it up in order to cover up a murder that we had commissioned."

Now it was my turn to look like she had lost her marbles. "Mom, even if a thought like that crosses your mind, it's a really bad idea to say it out loud." I rolled my eyes in the direction of the other diners, who appeared to be watching us and trying to listen in, at least the ones nearest to the open kitchen.

"I certainly didn't mean that we intended for this murder to happen. I was just saying it could be anyone." She turned her attention back to the chef. He'd begun to furiously chop the bananas in front of him on the cutting board.

"If you'll excuse me now, I have to turn out 30 desserts, and then get ready for the next seating."

"I'm so sorry for distracting you. Your dinner was delicious. We especially adored those lobster tails," said my mother. "We'll go back to our table, so we don't bother you."

It was quarter to eight by the time we finished sharing the desserts. I'd done my best to try several bites of everything, but my gut was roiling as the latest news about a possible murder sank in. It made sense if someone had in fact sabotaged the boat.

"Do you want to go with me to check out the scene at Mallory Square? Maybe we could catch Tobin after his show. Lorenzo suggested that he might have seen something when he was up on his ladder. I'm sure the cops will have canvassed all the performers, but it never hurts to get another point of view."

"I would not miss it," she said, already tapping her phone to call a ride.

Her face had a grim set, and I'm sure she felt the same way I did—what had begun as a relaxing and triumphant evening yesterday had turned out anything but.

Chapter Six

But this is terrible news for me. If Word gets out, it will ruin my career. It will haunt me. Everywhere I go they will point at me and say, "this is the chef whose food killed a man."

—Rhys Bowen, *The Proof of the Pudding*

As we rode across town in the back of the Uber, I began to feel more and more upset, and then angry. "I wish I'd asked the chef who his texting friend was, and who he thought had been murdered. Do you think it was a cop who told him that? Why did Chef Richard learn something that we didn't know? I can't understand why Nathan didn't tell me what happened. Does he not get that we are into this up to our necks?"

My mother looked instantly worried, pointing to her ear and then the Uber driver who may or may not have been listening. "Nathan certainly knows we're involved and interested. Maybe he didn't know this additional information yet, or he wasn't at liberty to tell you all the insider police facts," my mother said in a low voice, stroking my hair as she'd done when I was a girl. She often tried to calm down my hotheaded tendencies, encouraging me to think twice or even three times, especially before lighting into my husband.

"Also, consider that this is secondhand or thirdhand information. You know how rumors spread in this town. This guy's information could be totally off base. Let's wait and see what we find out for ourselves."

I took a couple of deep breaths and tried to absorb her calming words. I knew that part of why I was so upset had to do with the way the entire disaster had unfolded. We'd all staked a lot on this event—my mother and Sam with their catering reputation, and the rest of us, with our place in Key West journalism. Plus, it had been terrifying to be thrown into the water. The further I got from the situation, the more the frightening details crept into consciousness. The strong smell of gasoline, or was it diesel? People screaming, the man's bloodied head. A question popped into my mind. If the boat was mostly a sailboat, would there have been enough fuel on board to blow it up? Had the captain lied as he bragged about the features of his craft?

None of this was reason to be angry with Nathan. I leaned my head back against the seat. "You're right, again. I'll wait to hear what he says before I go on the attack."

The Uber driver left us off at the entrance to the alley that ran past the sculpture garden memorializing historical Key West characters, and then past the Waterfront Playhouse and out to Mallory Square. The hours of the sunset celebration varied with the time of year, of course. Visitors generally came here for cocktails and predinner entertainment but left to continue their nights once the sun went down. I could tell by the chattering crowds that were streaming away from the pier that we had just missed the sun slipping into the water.

Lorenzo had his usual space staked out fifty yards away from the edge of the square, and he was deep in conversation with a client who was peering at the cards on his table. The soft light from his large electric candles flickered over the deep blue cloth that covered the surface. TAROT was spelled out in glittery silver and gold on the sides of his tablecloth.

Tobin and his partner, David, wearing their trademark bright red pants, black shirts, and black shoes, were finishing up their performance. This time they'd included a little girl in pink leggings and a blue shirt studded with hearts—she stood in the center of the crowd, who was chanting "Thea, Thea, Thea!" Tobin thanked her for her assistance and tucked a ten-dollar bill into her fist, then thanked the spectators and encouraged them to drop tips into a glass jar. He was drenched with sweat, so I figured this might have been the third or fourth performance of the night. This meant he would be tired but wound up too. He was much like Lorenzo in that his work took a lot of concentration and energy, though Lorenzo's was more mental and Tobin's physical.

We waited to approach him until the last of his admirers—the smiling girl who was holding the hand of her father—moved away. I introduced my mother and me and explained that we had been on the boat that had blown up the night before.

The cheery smile fell from his face. "Sorry to hear that, hope you're OK."

"Pretty much, just a few postcalamity jitters." We all laughed, a bit hysterically in my case. "I know it's unlikely, because you were working hard, but I wondered if you might have seen anything unexpected in the water or on a nearby boat before the fire started and all those emergency vehicles arrived? Apparently, the police haven't yet concluded what caused the accident." If it was one, I thought but did not say, mindful not to spread rumors of my own.

Tobin absorbed my question carefully, rasping his knuckles over the stubble on his chin. This made me wonder whether he had pregame rituals, such as eating certain food or not shaving until after a performance, like some professional athletes did.

"You've probably reviewed all of this with the authorities," my mother added, "but might it be helpful to talk about what you noticed before the incident occurred?"

He nodded at her. "We were in the middle of one of our shows when all the shouting started and we heard the boom. A precarious point," he added, with a small grin, "because I remember us bobbling a little on the ladder. I was upside down at that moment, balanced on my partner's shoulders. Everything looks different from that perspective."

"Can't imagine," my mother murmured, nodding with encouragement.

"Nothing out of the ordinary sticks out that I can think of. It was a pretty good crowd for this time of year. It looked like smooth sailing on the Gulf; I saw nothing that would have caused me to predict trouble. Oh." He stopped for a minute and rubbed his chin again.

"It's possible someone dropped off the edge of that sailboat and swam to a nearby dinghy. It didn't register at the time, and maybe I'm making the whole thing up, but it's possible that it happened this way. It would have been ten minutes or so before the incident."

"A man? A woman?" I asked. "What were they wearing?" It wasn't often that people swam off that pier, or dove off a boat into those waters, especially at this time of day. Aside from the occasional leaking fluids and trash from visiting ships, the busy traffic made it downright dangerous.

Tobin shook his head. "I was concentrating so hard on our routine, that I can't answer that."

We were both disappointed, but nothing would come of pushing him to recall something he hadn't seen or registered well enough to remember. I handed him my *Key Zest* business card, thinking maybe he'd remember more later.

"Uh-oh," my mother said, grabbing my elbow. "Looks like Lorenzo could use some backup."

Three men were clustered around Lorenzo's table, and his client gathered her belongings and quickly scuttled away. Two of the men were police officers in uniform, the other I recognized as a plainclothes detective in a tweed jacket that looked way too warm for the evening. We thanked Tobin for his help and drifted a little closer to my friend.

"What exactly do you remember from those moments before the explosion on the harbor?" the detective was asking Lorenzo.

"As I am certain I told the officers who interviewed me, I had a client who was quite distraught. I had just finished telling her the outline of what I saw in her cards—three out of four, anyway, when the crowd began to rush the edge of the pier. By the time I turned my attention back to my customer, she was gone."

"What was her name?" Now the detective had a pad out, preparing to take notes.

"I have no idea. I do not ask anyone's name unless they specifically offer it, and she did not." Lorenzo was beginning to look pressured and frazzled. "She might have mentioned that her boyfriend's name was Peter."

"Last name?" asked the detective, poised to jot the information down.

Lorenzo shook his head. "Sorry, I have no idea."

"What did she look like?" asked one of the uniforms.

Lorenzo's eyes darted over toward my mother and me. He gestured at my mother. "She was taller than my friend here, reddish hair with some light streaks, like the way Bonnie Raitt developed that dramatic streak of gray in her early singing career."

The men looked puzzled, which I took to mean they had no idea who Bonnie Raitt might have been, and certainly no familiarity with her fashion choices. The detective pointed at my mother. "Was this your customer?"

A look of horror spread over Lorenzo's face. "Absolutely not, I was just trying to say there were some similarities between her and my friend, Janet. This other woman was younger. Very fit. I think she was wearing stripes." He had started to sweat a little, beads of moisture gathering along his hairline. It was hot here on the plaza, but I thought he was also very nervous. I hoped he wasn't making things up.

I took a big step closer. "I'm Nathan Bransford's wife, Hayley, and this is my mother, Janet Snow. We were on the boat that exploded, so neither one of us could've been here on the pier, talking with this man."

"Exactly," said my friend, puffing out a breath of relief. "My client was very jittery, both upset about some events in her life and also, I believe about the cards that she had been dealt."

"Did you see where she went?" asked the detective.

Lorenzo shook his head. "It was mayhem after that, complete chaos. I gathered my cards up and tucked them away and walked over to see what was happening, and whether I could be of any assistance."

"And could you?" That question came from one of the uniforms, and I hoped he wasn't smirking.

"No," said Lorenzo. "By then they were asking all the bystanders and performers to clear the area. So I packed up my things and left. I have a cart that I use to roll my equipment across the pavement to the car. I was so upset; I threw everything in topsy-turvy. Everyone was rushing back to their cars and all those emergency vehicles had arrived . . ."

He looked genuinely distraught at this point, and I imagined it was almost as hard for him to remember the scene as it had been for those of us on the boat. I doubted they were going to squeeze much more useful information out of him.

The detective seemed to come to the same conclusion. "We'll probably need to speak to you again," the detective said, handing my friend a business card. "We'll be in touch, and you should do the same, if you remember details you've forgotten to report."

I thought they had made one mistake, not asking my friend both what was on the spread of cards and what his interpretation of them was. But in my experience, police officers were not familiar with tarot and probably wouldn't have believed they could find anything useful in those cards.

"Try not to worry," I said to Lorenzo once the police had moved out of earshot. "It seems possible that someone died in the explosion, and so they feel a lot of pressure to find out what happened. I doubt they think you were involved." I paused for a minute. "Could it be that your client had some connection with the boat?"

My mother looked alarmed. "She wasn't wet, was she? Tobin mentioned that he saw someone drop off the side of the boat into the water."

"I would have noticed that for sure," said Lorenzo. "Nor did I see anyone dripping wet who was running from the scene. Which would be the next logical question if one was a detective, correct?" We all three laughed a little.

"Correct," I said. "Would you mind summarizing the interaction with that woman and her cards and then send the notes to me? I could share them with Nathan just in case he's interested. That might spare you more grilling by Key West's finest."

He nodded gratefully and confirmed that he would send me something later tonight. My mother looked as though she was seriously drooping, and I felt the same way. She held up her phone. "I've called an Uber. They'll be here in five."

We each hugged our friend and started back down the alley to our ride.

"Why are they pressuring poor Lorenzo now?" my mother asked. "Didn't they already interview him?"

"Good question," I said. "They must have some new information." I texted Nathan from Miss Gloria's old iPad as soon as we were settled in the back seat to explain the highlights of what we'd seen and heard this evening. I was getting tired of carrying the bulky device around, but I hadn't had time to buy a new phone, and I had needed to take photos of the food in Lola's for a possible review in the future. "Any news from your end?" I asked.

"Be home shortly and will tell all," he texted back.

We dropped my mom off in front of her home in the Truman Annex, with promises to stay in close touch. Then I was whisked up town toward Garrison Bight. Nathan was pulling into the houseboat row parking lot just as I arrived in my Uber. I gave him a big hug, happy as always to have his strong presence in my life. I linked my arm through his, and we padded down the dock to our home.

"Tell me what you heard at dinner and Sunset," he suggested, after returning from a quick walk with Ziggy.

I had already washed my face and brushed my teeth and changed into a cozy flannel nightgown. The temperature wasn't anywhere near chilly—in fact I had the AC running, but again I felt in need of comfort. I slid in between the covers and told him about the meal and the chef at Lola's and my conversation with Tobin. "He thinks he might have seen someone slip off our boat and into the water, but he isn't sure." I ended with the cops' interrogation of Lorenzo. "He's going to send me a summary of what he remembers of the boat disaster night, and also about the cards he was reading at the time."

"We won't overlook anything," Nathan said with a shrug. "Even tarot cards. In case you should worry that the officers were being too hard on him, things have gotten very serious. The authorities were able to tow the boat to the military base and have started investigating what's left of it." His face was very serious. "Unfortunately, they found a propane tank among the equipment in the kitchen. It looked as though it had been brought in on or stashed in one of your mother's carts. It was almost empty, as though someone had left the gas regulator open."

The Mango Murders

I gasped. "No way!"

"That's when they discovered the remains of the body."

This had to be the same information that Chef Richard had somehow gotten before I did. The Key West Coconut Telegraph was always hard at work, especially for the bad stuff. In this case, it began to seriously look like my mother was to blame for the explosion.

Chapter Seven

"Even your hot dishes are cold."
—Diner to the chef in *The Menu*.

I woke up early, and took my coffee out to the deck, mulling over the bits of information that Nathan had been able to share with me the night before. The local Key West Facebook groups were abuzz with speculation about what had happened.

Even though Nathan had attempted to reassure me that much work needed to be done before they understood what happened, it worried me deeply that an apparent cause of the catastrophe was a propane tank found amongst my mother's equipment. That, along with Lorenzo's suggestion that his troubled customer looked like my mother, brought a wave of anxiety that I was having trouble containing. I didn't understand how these bits of information fit together, but I needed to do something to help. I wasn't due at our staff meeting until nine, which gave me time to visit the Old Town harbor.

After taking care of the animals and downing a bowl of cereal with fresh berries, I buzzed across the island to the harbor on my scooter. Unable to resist the siren call of a café con leche,

The Mango Murders

I stopped at the Cuban Coffee Queen to pick one up. One of my favorite baristas, Paulina, was working the window. While the milk for my large drink steamed, she returned to chat while I paid.

"Hayley," she said, "I hear you've had a lot of excitement in your life."

"Unfortunately," I said glumly. "Any news from your end?"

"Everyone's talking about the body in the hold. Have you learned who it was?"

"No idea," I said, taking the first glorious sip of the coffee she'd slid to me. "They can't identify a burned body without a name. As far as we know, no one from our guest list is missing." That last was from a quick scan of my memory, and it could have been wrong. Did we actually know this? At this point, it could be super important. I hated to think of anyone trapped below in the boat by the fumes or the fire. Claustrophobia at its very worst.

"Have you heard anyone speculating?" I asked. Paulina was perfectly positioned to hear gossip from the locals, and it often turned out to be true.

"Nothing specific or credible," she said. "It's almost like the dock crowd has closed ranks."

This left me more determined than ever to speak with people along the dock to ask about the owner of our doomed boat. Did he have a beef with someone who would be willing to destroy his craft and his livelihood? I walked to the dock in between the Half Shell and Schooner Wharf, where we had boarded our cruise two days ago. Of course, the *Pilar Too* was not at the dock, because according to Nathan, its remains had been towed to the military base for investigation. I approached the catamaran docked nearest the empty space. A youngish man with a short ponytail, dressed in khaki shorts and a bright pink and yellow shirt was swabbing the entrance to the deck. As I got closer, I could see he was older than he first appeared.

"Hello!" I called out. "I was hoping to speak with the captain."

"Speaking," he said.

I grinned. "Wonderful. I was on the boat that was involved in the accident off Mallory Square the other night. I'm doing some informal investigating into the possible causes of that event. I gather that it's very rare for that kind of thing to happen, and I wondered if you could point me to toward any possible theories?"

He turned off the hose and coiled it up, looking disgusted. "I have no insider information."

"Understood," I said, bobbing my head in a friendly way. "But since you are an experienced sailor, perhaps you have ideas?"

He took a deep breath, narrowed his eyes, and leaned against the railing. "For one thing, sailing a wooden boat is asking for trouble in my opinion. If we had had a fire here," he pointed to his fiberglass catamaran, "it would not have spread like a proverbial wildfire. It could have been easily contained to the few flammable objects aboard."

That made sense to me, though I understood the other captain's desire to emulate Hemingway's gorgeous hand-hewn wooden boat.

"Second," said the captain, "we changed everything on our craft over to electric several years ago. Yes, you can get unlucky and have a fire in the engine room on any boat, that's always a possibility. But we do not carry propane on board, which I gather is what propelled the small fire into a big explosion. What was your role on this excursion?"

"I'm with the magazine *Key Zest* which sponsored the event. But also, I assisted my mother, the caterer."

"Her propane then."

Oh lord. My stomach sank with a great big thunk. This news was everywhere. "Here's the rub. She was only heating her nibbles in the electric oven upstairs. But a large propane tank was found in the hold on a cart with some of her other equipment." I knew it was not a good idea to spread this piece of data around the island, but I wanted to stick up for her. Plus, I didn't see how I would squeeze much else from him if I didn't offer him something first. "We did not put it there," I added, with all the certainty I could muster.

"I figure you know everybody in this boating world, am I right? Can you think of a reason why someone might have wanted to sabotage Captain Roche's craft?"

"I can think of more than one reason—he wasn't that well liked."

"Because?" I fell silent, hoping he'd fill in the blanks. Before I could press him further, my watch beeped telling me I was due at the office in fifteen minutes. I wanted to ask him more, and I thought he might be about to spill some beans, but the interruption must have quelled his urge to talk. Plus, one of his crew members was calling from the prow.

"Gotta get to work," he said.

"Thanks for the chat," I called after his retreating back.

Chapter Eight

> LOVE—*If you really love someone, you want to know what they ate for lunch or dinner without you.*
> —Amy Krouse Rosenthat, *Encyclopedia of an Ordinary Life*

Although I'd insisted to Nathan that I was 100 percent recovered from the shock of the disaster at sea, I could feel in my legs that wasn't exactly true. As I trudged up to the second floor *Key Zest* office, my thighs were quivering like jelly and my neck hurt like heck. Danielle was at her desk, but she didn't look that perky either.

"How's it going?" I asked her. "You look a little peaked."

She smiled, but it was a pale imitation of her usual friendly grin. "I guess that whole incident was a bigger shock than I realized. To make things worse, Jeremy says the police department is on edge because they don't know who the deceased was or why they were targeted."

"Or even if they were targeted?"

"Yes, that's a possibility. Maybe she was an ordinary citizen, like us, who'd gone down to use the head."

The Mango Murders

"True," I said. "Nathan and I have gone over all the people who might have wanted to do me harm, but realistically, I'm not much of a threat to the average criminal. Same with my mother and you." I tipped my head in the direction of Palamina's office. "Any word from the boss?"

"If possible, she looks worse than we do. She asked for fifteen minutes alone before we come in."

We shook our heads in tandem. She never wanted time alone, because that was time wasted when she could be cracking the whip to generate new ideas or more expansive goals for the magazine. On the other hand, the boating disaster had to be a big letdown for her. She'd spent the last several months laying the groundwork to get our guests excited about the catamaran expedition. She had expected the advertising dollars to come rolling in after she gave her talk about the vital importance of a thriving local press. Instead, she hadn't gotten to speak to the gathering, not one word.

"Did we have any calls or emails this morning about advertising?"

"Nothing. Nada," she said, wagging her head sadly. "A few press inquiries about our role in the explosion. Other than that, people are keeping their distance like we're a collective Typhoid Mary."

Exactly as bad as I'd feared. "On a different note, take a look at what I found." I showed her the digital copy of Palamina's wedding announcement from seven years ago that I'd sent to Miss Gloria's iPad.

"Holy Toledo!" Danielle said. "What universe did that come from?"

I put a finger to my lips. "I think we have to call her on it. What if the explosion was related to *her* past rather than any of us or our guests?"

She grabbed the iPad from me and studied the photo. "You've definitely, definitely piqued my curiosity."

"I'm going to do some more digging." I walked back to my little office overlooking Southard Street and pulled up the notes I'd been making on my computer. Forget working, we needed to figure out who had ruined the outing and why, endangering a lot of people and killing a citizen along the way.

Danielle pinged me a few minutes later. "She's ready for us."

"I'd like to get back to business as usual," Palamina said as soon as we were settled on our folding chairs. She had more space in her office than I did, but with three people in the meeting, we could almost hear each other's hearts beat. Danielle and I exchanged a glance.

"We'd love to do that, boss," said Danielle, "but it's hard with an elephant stomping through the room."

"What elephant would that be?"

"Somebody either wanted to destroy one of us or destroy our business or destroy someone on that boat. Any of those choices suck, to be frank. Hayley and I thought we should spend some time brainstorming about what might have happened. She's made a list."

I presented them each with a copy of what I'd written when I should have been working on a story, any story. "We know there was a victim, but was she the target?"

Danielle nodded vigorously. "Jeremy says that isn't clear at all."

"It could be someone from one of our pasts," I said. "Or someone from one of our presents. I suppose it also could have nothing to do with us, and perhaps be related to someone who wanted to destroy our boat captain's business. It's also not impossible that it could be politically motivated—we did have some local politicians aboard. Or, because our attendees were heavily foodie related, it could be someone wanting to wreak havoc in the food world."

Palamina looked a little shell-shocked, as though she'd lost control of the staff meeting. Which she had. I barreled on. "I thought it would be a good idea to start out leveling with each other. We need to trust each other to tell the truth in order to move forward."

"Agreed," said Danielle.

"I have no idea what you're getting at," said my boss, slumping back in her chair.

"Here on the list," I tapped the paper on my lap, "are some of the people whom I might have angered over the years. Long shots, mostly. I would make a list for you as well, except I hardly know anything personal about you. So, to be perfectly honest, I googled you yesterday. I had no idea that you were married. Featured in the *New York Times* style section no less."

"Wearing the most stunning lace gown I've ever seen—it made my dress look like a rag," Danielle added, her eyebrows arching high. "Wow, and the venue looked amazing. Those flowers, oh my! Here the whole time I was planning my wedding, you acted as though you couldn't have been less interested and barely agreed to attend. I felt guilty even mentioning what was the biggest event in my life so far. We figured you weren't married and therefore weren't interested."

"I'm not." She pressed her lips into one grim line. Then she burst into tears.

I looked at Danielle who shrugged her shoulders and widened her eyes but leaned over to pat Palamina's hand. Neither one of us had ever seen our boss cry. Not even close.

"These last few days have been an awful shock," I said, trying to be as sympathetic as I thought she'd allow.

"So you're divorced?" Danielle asked her.

"Separated," said Palamina. She retrieved a tissue from the box on her desk and patted her cheeks and eyes. "Though I honestly hold out no hope for getting back together. It's been five years since I moved down here, and he pretty much despises me at this point."

"Do you mind telling us what happened?" Danielle asked.

I was glad she was taking the lead, tiptoeing across the thin ice of Palamina's emotional landscape. She had a lighter touch than I did.

Palamina covered her face with her hands. "I wouldn't consider that this is any of your business except that Hayley has a point. Someone on that boat targeted one of us passengers with catastrophic results. It could have been me."

"Do you think your ex or almost ex has it in for you?" I asked.

"No," she said. "I said he hated me, but the truth is I don't think he cares enough to bother with me. But I've had a stalker. A woman I was involved with briefly before I fell in love with my husband. She didn't take my rejection well, and she's caused more damage than you can imagine, including informing my husband that I loved her and not him." She took the list lying on my lap and scribbled a name on it. "There you go, prime suspect. Athena. Ha ha ha."

"Athena?" asked Danielle. "I've never come across anyone with that name. It's lovely though. What nationality is it?"

My eyes twitched as I wondered what this had to do with anything.

The Mango Murders

Palamina sighed. "Who knows? She renamed herself after the goddess of wisdom and war when she had the life-changing realization that she was 'woman-facing', as she called it."

"Is she here in Key West?" I asked.

"I certainly hope not," said Palamina in a breezy voice. "But one never knows with her." She frowned. "Chances are, this has nothing to do with her. It would be more productive to think about the professionals on that cruise. I am aware that we had some guests with opposing and strongly held opinions about our town—"

A text message appeared on the borrowed iPad, which I was still lugging around until I had time to get to the T-Mobile store for a new phone. This one was from my stepmother.

Landed in Miami. We should arrive at the airport by two. LMK if not convenient to pick us up, otherwise see you soon!

I'd completely forgotten my father and his entourage were arriving today.

Chapter Nine

Sorrow is food swallowed too quickly, caught in the throat, making it nearly impossible to breathe.
—Jesmyn Ward, *Sing, Unburied, Sing*

Without a lot of enthusiasm, the three of us finished planning the upcoming issue of our sagging magazine. I had promised a roundup of events in town, focusing on mango madness. There was a wonderful exhibit at The Studios of Key West showcasing many local artists, all incorporating mangoes in their artwork. There were, naturally, full course dinners at a couple of the fancier restaurants in town, including mangoes in some form in every dish. I remembered that my mother and I had agreed to work out a couple of mango recipes to act as filler. Those would have to wait.

After we sketched out the issue, and I had edited my mango article for completeness and sent it over to Palamina, I rushed home to neaten up the houseboat, take care of the animals, and retrieve Miss Gloria's Buick for my run to the airport. My friend was not at home, so I left her a note telling her I'd gone to pick up my father's family and would be back later to escort her to the preparty at Salute on the Beach.

I parked in the small, short-term lot used for passenger pick up and headed toward the terminal. My father, Jim Snow, stepmother, Allison, and Rory, my half-brother, were just emerging, dragging big suitcases behind them. I felt a rush of affection for all three of them, but especially Rory. He was the same sweet guy, but he'd shot up a good six inches taller than last time I'd seen him, with a shadow of a beard and sharp edges where his round boyish face had been. We'd had a complicated relationship as I was growing up. I was distressed by the finality of my parents' divorce, and the forced new stepfamily, and finally the new baby who stole my thunder as an only child. Rory had only adored me throughout my neurotic wanderings and those problems had faded over time.

My father had mellowed as well, no longer seeming to feel that it was his responsibility to correct my life choices. Allison, my stepmother, had been good for him and was good for all of us. Rory had just finished his second year in college, majoring in social work, with good grades and a lot of enthusiasm. He hadn't been back to Key West since he was a troubled teenager, when he had disappeared into the Key West party scene and scared the rest of us half to death. He'd ended up tagging along with a group of homeless kids and that experience had affected him deeply.

I rushed forward and hugged each of them in turn. "I am so glad to see you, and I know Miss Gloria will be thrilled as well."

"Are you kidding?" asked Allison. "Not a chance we would miss her birthday party!"

I helped them load the suitcases into the trunk, and then drove right on South Roosevelt Boulevard, and along Atlantic to the Casa Marina. This hotel had been built by Henry Flagler and opened to great fanfare in 1920. It had recently been completely renovated, and I couldn't wait to see their suite, though the cost of a three-night stay was eye popping. I'd checked.

We caught up on the surface basics on the short drive to the hotel. My father was considering retirement, though not in the next ten years. That made my stepmother giggle.

"Thank goodness he won't be underfoot at home for a while!" She was deeply invested in her charity work with the Friends of the Library, and a homeless drop-in center, inspired by her son's experience.

"But enough of all that, how are you doing? And Miss Gloria and your mother? And Nathan?"

"All is well with everyone," I said, glad that the news of the boat accident didn't seem to have reached New Jersey, though a little sorry that I had to broach the subject myself. It was going to come up, so I might as well get it over with.

"Let's get you settled and then I'll buy you a drink and tell you everything."

"Fine," my father grumbled, "but since I'm paying a fortune anyway, I'm buying."

Everything about the Casa Marina had been recently refreshed, though the ambience and historical weight of the design had not been changed. It remained a gorgeous white stucco building with a red tile roof and a series of arches leading into the reception area and other public spaces. My family had reserved a Key West view, king suite, with a private bedroom and a pullout couch for Rory in the living area, according to the clerk at the desk.

My father jerked a thumb at his wife. "I convinced her that for $200 less, we could step outside and see the ocean for ourselves easily enough. We didn't need a view from our mattress." Allison and I laughed and rolled our eyes.

The suite was stunning, with a brown and white checkerboard tile floor, comfortable, beige upholstered and wicker furniture, whitewashed ceilings with brown wood beams crossing. The artwork was tasteful, and mostly featured local artists.

"This is glorious," I said.

"Heavenly," added my stepmother. "Do you know you can book a cabana on the beach for a personal massage? I couldn't convince your father"—he snorted—"but I booked time for two, hoping you'd be tempted."

"Maybe," I said. "Things have gotten a little hectic and crazy around here." The iPad's alarm beeped—time to head back, get ready for the dinner, and transport Miss Gloria to the restaurant. "I promise to fill you in on every detail tonight."

* * *

I began to get a little worried when I arrived home, and Miss Gloria had not returned to her houseboat following her shift at the cemetery. Most of the time she preferred to walk home, but sometimes she called for a ride. Maybe I'd missed that because of my phone problems. At eighty-five, she was old enough that I couldn't get settled with the idea of letting her take care of herself completely. She did forget things from time to time. Or maybe she'd felt it was too hot to walk and was waiting for me to pick her up? I grabbed my helmet along with my spare and hopped on the scooter to head toward the cemetery—the scooter was much easier to park in this town than the hulking Buick. I took the route that I thought she would be walking, in case she had gotten held up or worst-case scenario, hit by a car. With the huge influx of visitors on our island who weren't paying attention to their driving, these things did happen.

I stopped at the office and called a cheery hello to the pretty, dark-haired sexton. "Hi, it's Hayley Snow here. Did you happen to see Miss Gloria leave?"

"I saw her come in but haven't seen her leave. The folks on her tour left about an hour ago. I've been busy on the phone and computer, so it's quite possible she slipped out without me seeing her. Or went out the Frances Street gate. But she almost always checks in with me on the way out." Now she looked worried too.

This was making me very anxious. I moved my scooter off the sidewalk and set out to look for her. The cemetery was a big space right in the middle of Old Town. It was laid out in a giant grid, identified with street names, and contained the resting places of many Key West residents, along with elaborate family crypts and various celebrity graves with oddball inscriptions. "I told you I was sick," was a very popular destination, along with "I'm just resting my eyes" and "I always dreamed of owning a small place in Key West." There were more serious gravesites too, of course, including the section devoted to the victims of the U.S.S. Maine, and a trove of local eccentrics and heroes. A tall, black metal fence surrounded the cemetery so it could be locked up at night, leaving only iguanas and chickens as company for the dead.

I hurried down the biggest street, headed toward the Jewish section of cemetery that I knew my friend favored as a place to sit and think. She liked the idea of visitors leaving stones on a grave, as she thought it must remind the inhabitants they weren't forgotten or alone.

Minutes later, I spotted her perched on a concrete bench under a big gumbo limbo tree. I breathed a sigh of relief and tried to gather myself so I wouldn't appear like a worried and hovering mother. She looked sad, and that made me feel glad I had come.

I sat beside her on the bench and tucked my arm around her shoulders. "I got a little concerned about you because we're due at Salute in an hour or so. I hope you don't mind that I came to give you a ride home."

She looked at me, seemingly puzzled, her expression a million miles away.

"I thought you might have been hit by a car or one of those crazy people drinking beer in golf carts with the right-hand turn signal permanently on." That was a joke she loved to tell about how some tourists behaved on our island.

Miss Gloria smiled briefly and patted my knee. "We can't really know when our time is up, can we?" she said in a wistful voice. "I don't think mine is anytime soon. Though with a murder or a freak accident, those are impossible to predict." She paused and I suppressed the urge to fill the silence. She needed to talk, and I needed to listen. "The one thing I don't like about getting older is remembering and missing all the friends and relations who've passed before me. I love my life and my new friends, but I miss the old ones too."

"Of course you would, that seems only natural." She had a melancholy look on her face that I'd rarely seen. I wondered if she was thinking about her husband, Frank. He'd been gone for many years, but they'd had a happy marriage full of adventure and love, and I knew how much she still missed him.

"Are the plans for big gatherings and parties this week wearing you out before they even happen?" I asked. "We could call the whole thing off, it's not too late. I can tell the influx of relatives and friends that they should consider this a vacation rather than a birthday party, that you are feeling indisposed. People will understand."

"Some of them," she said, with a wry grin. She shook her head. "No, these are my people, the people who love me. Let's shake it off and carry on."

Chapter Ten

Sally is a great orderer. Not only does she always pick the best thing on the menu, but she orders it in a way even the chef didn't know how good it could be.
— Nora Ephron, *When Harry Met Sally*

Forty-five minutes later, Miss Gloria emerged from her houseboat, looking refreshed, almost her usual, perky self. She trotted up the finger to collect her friend, Annie Dubisson, and we headed out to the parking lot and her Buick. Lately, she'd given up pretending that she was going to drive us somewhere, and automatically went to the passenger side. Another sign that her age was catching up with her? I hated to think it.

"We better hustle," I said, "because I try not to leave my mother and father entertaining each other too long without a buffer."

"I thought they were doing so much better?" asked Mrs. Dubisson.

"Oh, they are for sure," I said, "though not bosom buddies. I still worry that things could blow up. Plus, I'm not sure when Nathan's parents are arriving. That's a pair that I wouldn't want to leave alone."

"You must remember to fashion your marriage after mine or Annie's, and not those divorced folks," Miss Gloria said with a grin.

"Don't worry," I said, grinning back. "I've been watching and admiring you for years." Though I did not wish to join their widowed wives club, not for years and years anyway.

I pulled into the parking lot that ran alongside Higgs Beach and the Atlantic Ocean. There was a band playing on the small pergola on the beach; luckily, not so loud that I thought they would drown out conversation. Salute was the perfect place to bring out of town guests who were just getting acclimated to the island. The doors and walls of the restaurant were open to the outside—and the beach. There was always a breeze, reminding people why the pains and annoyances of traveling were worthwhile.

The staff had set up a long table with twelve places at the front of the restaurant directly overlooking the water. My parents were seated across from each other with their new spouses—new, relatively speaking—and they seem to be talking and laughing in a friendly way. I took a deep breath in and let my shoulders relax, reminding myself that it was not my job to keep the peace with every odd relative. Hopefully they were all mature enough to remember that the point this weekend was celebrating our friend. Old grudges and unspoken hostilities could be left to the side. In fact, why not let them go permanently?

We stopped at the host station and explained that we were part of the group gathering at the front of the room. "Gloria!" said the host, his multiple diamond studs twinkling as he smiled and hugged her, "we have been waiting for you, darling."

The Mango Murders

At that moment, Nathan arrived with his parents in tow. Skip and Helen. They were the ones I worried about most, other than Miss Gloria's daughters-in-law. Each was intimidating and gave the impression of volcanoes close to blowing. I greeted them both with a big hug and kiss and welcomed them into the restaurant. I raised my eyebrows at Nathan, inquiring silently about how it was going so far.

He pulled me close and whispered in my ear. "The knives have not come out yet. But it's early."

Once we were all settled with drinks and appetizers, Miss Gloria said, "Wait till you hear the latest excitement in our crowd."

Then she described the boat incident, with my mother and me correcting her exaggerations, such as that this had been *the disaster of the decade.*

"It wasn't that bad," I said, smiling at her. "Scary, yes, and distressing for the passengers." I didn't want to overwhelm our families when they'd just arrived, so I teased my friend. "She's mostly unhappy that she missed the excitement."

"But didn't Nathan say that today they found a body in the debris of the boat?"

"My word," said my mother-in-law, looking at Nathan, who was grimacing. "How tragic. Who died? Have the police figured out what happened? Who would be in charge of a possible criminal investigation at sea?"

"That's just it," said Miss Gloria, "It could be any number of organizations who should take the lead, but nobody seems to know anything."

Nathan cleared his throat and stared her down. "That's not exactly true. We don't share every step of every investigation with our civilian friends, even someone as clever as you. It's definitely a police department matter, with assistance from our partners."

"What *can* you tell us?" asked Helen, looking straight back at Nathan.

Nathan gave me the briefest nod. So, I explained how the trip had been designed as a public relations coup for both the magazine I worked for and my mother's company. "We had a splendid guest list of the city's movers and shakers, and the most amazing menu. You guys may not realize that it's mango season, but it is, so we designed a heavy mango theme."

"Always with the food," said Nathan's dad, but he added a smile to soften the words. "How often has food solved a criminal case?" He had been in law enforcement his entire life and was the kind of man who ate to live, preferring steaks and burgers, hold the vegetables, and don't offer any strange but tasty condiments, pickles, or spice-heavy garnishes. We didn't have a lot in common, but we did both love Nathan. In him, I could see glimpses of my husband's future older self—I thought he'd inherited the best of his dad.

"Let me think about that," I said, tapping my chin. "Every poisoning case in the history of the world likely involved food."

"But was this an accident? Or sabotage?" That was Nathan's mother again. She and I had solved a murder a few years back, including a kidnapping which proved her to be both curious and a dogged force to be reckoned with. She was not one to gloss over details or accept the surface explanation.

"Unlikely to be found as an accident," Nathan said. "It's very frustrating because who set it up and why is not obvious. In addition to all the injuries and near drownings, one person did die. But so far, no one has been reported missing, and that makes identification impossible."

"I keep thinking that he could have been collateral damage," said my mother. "That sounds terrible, doesn't it? What I meant was, this person went to the bathroom at the wrong time."

"I'll say," said my father.

"What have you figured out?" asked Helen of me and Nathan. "Can you share any theories that the police are either considering or have cast aside?"

The waitress appeared at our table to take orders for more drinks and dinner. Waffling between the gold-standard grouper cakes or more comfort food lasagna or even a bowl of garlicky mussels with crispy toast points for dipping, I ended up choosing a bowl of bean soup and a shrimp salad. This way, I'd have two delicious dishes plus room for a homemade ice cream cookie sandwich.

Once everyone had ordered, Nathan nodded at me, and I told them the bits and pieces that I knew. "It's possible that the perpetrator was someone connected with my boss, Palamina. Arguably, she had the most at stake for this event." I looked around the table. "This is all in the cone of silence, right?" I waited for their nods, feeling a little guilty that I was sharing her most private moments. With a big table of my family and friends. "She's very secretive. I never would have known she was married if I hadn't stumbled across an announcement in the *New York Times* Style section from seven years ago when I was randomly googling."

"Palamina is married?" exclaimed Miss Gloria. "I would have guessed she was gay, but probably still in the closet."

"It's complicated," I said, and further explained the woman who had destroyed her relationship with her husband by stalking her. "Maybe because she was rebuffed. But her coming to Key West to blow up a boat seems like a long shot."

"Who would take out an entire ship and all the people on it just to punish one passenger? That sounds like an awkward and clumsy way to plan a murder," said Helen.

"True," said my mother, "though I've heard about stranger motives. Unfortunately, it's also possible that I might have been the target of this attack."

"You?" I asked. "I can't think of anyone more unlikely than you." I did not like the direction this informal dinner-table investigation was taking, and I wished she had not announced this to the entire group. My mother could not have been involved with this, no matter what the evidence pointed toward.

She shook her head sadly. "Not everyone loves me as much as you do Hayley."

I realized I was shutting her down with my disbelief. "Tell us, then, how could this possibly be connected with you, best caterer in town, creator of meals that leave people feeling like they've been folded into a warm hug, kindest person in the universe."

My father cleared his throat and looked hard at my mother. "Seems like I remember you telling me something about a grudge held by another chef. Or was it the entire Key West community of chefs who resented your arrival on the island?" I knew he was mostly razzing my mother. He and my father-in-law shared this trait, never convinced that food was important enough to take a stand over, never mind murder someone. My mother was getting her feathers ruffled.

The Mango Murders

"Believe this or not, it's very galling that someone from outside who is relatively new is doing so well in what is a very competitive business. Money and prestige and reputations and livelihoods are on the line."

"I think we can all agree that Janet's culinary success as a murder motive is grasping at straws. More likely," said Nathan, "there is an addict who was fired by one of your chefs. Or someone entirely unrelated to the food world."

"I know how stressful that mayor's job can be," said Miss Gloria. "I suspect our former mayor has angered a lot of citizens and lowlifes over the years."

"That's definitely true," I said. "There's so much history burbling under the surface of island life. Sorting through all that is a job for the police." I added that last bit as both a sop for Nathan and a redirect for the table conversation.

As the waiter arrived to deliver our dinners, Allison turned to Miss Gloria. "How are you feeling about your big day?"

I winced, worried that would send my friend back into a tailspin. I'd seen her crumpled on that cemetery bench earlier. This big birthday business wasn't all hearts and flowers.

"Ask me tomorrow after my family arrives," she said to a big laugh. "Actually, the truth is it's mixed. I love that you're all here, and I'm honored that it's because of me. But good gravy, as my friend Hayley might say, eighty-five is getting old."

"I'm even older," said Mrs. Dubisson, breaking into a wide grin. "It's a cakewalk."

"How did you two meet again?" asked Helen.

"We came down with our husbands around the same year and ended up neighbors," said Miss Gloria. "When the gentlemen passed, we became closest of friends." Her smile lit up her face and was mirrored in the face of her dear friend.

We all began to eat and chatter independently. I felt relieved that the conversation had ducked and weaved around any number of emotional landmines.

"What's everyone got on the agenda for tomorrow?" asked my stepfather, Sam, as we finished up our ice cream sandwiches. "Janet and I have some prep work to do for the cocktail party we're hosting. Reminder, we will expect all of you at 5:30."

"My father wants to play golf," Nathan said, looking as if he was headed toward a hanging rather than the golf course.

"We'd like to fill out the foursome," said my father-in-law to my father. "We were hoping we could entice you to play with us."

A look of horror bloomed on my father's face. He was not a fan of golf. Nor was he a yuk-it-up sportsman who could pretend to be best friends with a group of men over what would feel like an interminable four hours.

"That sounds like a wonderful idea!" my stepmother exclaimed. "I have plans for the spa and the beach. But maybe Rory would like to go along as your fourth?"

If possible, Rory looked more horrified than my father had. He wasn't an accomplished golfer, either—had probably only played half a dozen rounds in his life. That aside, he would not want to spend his days in paradise with three curmudgeonly older guys.

"Perfect," said Nathan's mom, clapping her hands. "That means Hayley and I can bum around together, get reacquainted."

Yikes, whatever she had in mind, I'd find out tomorrow.

Chapter Eleven

You know those people who say, "Huh, I forgot to eat today"? And are telling the truth? I basically consider them aliens.
—Frank Bruni, *Newsletter* August 1, 2024

"So does the department really have no idea how this happened, or you just can't tell the civilians yet? Were we getting warm with any of our theories?" I was standing outside our little bathroom with a cup of coffee, watching Nathan get ready for the day, and hoping to coax some new insights from him.

He wiped a bit of shaving cream off his chin and smiled at my reflection in his mirror. "No civilians yet. We can't identify a body until someone is declared missing. If we have a missing person, we can compare their dental records or bone DNA to confirm."

I opened my mouth to protest, but he was looking frustrated. "It's just this simple, if the authorities don't know who's missing, they have nothing to compare to the burned victim. I can say it was likely a woman, based on height and approximate weight."

"So the man I thought I saw going into the hold before the explosion wasn't involved?"

"He wasn't the victim," Nathan said. "Don't know much else."

"OK then, can you tell me why three of your guys were quizzing Lorenzo at sunset the other night? He was having a panic attack when we stopped by afterward to talk to him. He doesn't do well with authority figures."

My husband sighed and stashed his razor and toothbrush in the medicine cabinet. Since everything about our floating home was small, we tried to keep things tidy. "It's not him specifically who's in the spotlight. It's the customer he was seeing right before the incident."

I followed him from the bedroom to the kitchen. "The woman whose spouse had run off? Surely that one man's betrayal didn't set off a maritime chain reaction of disaster?"

He pulled me into a quick squeeze, smiling as he poured coffee into his to-go cup. "You know I will keep you posted the minute I know more. Meanwhile, I'm going to dash into the office before trudging off to the golf course." He grabbed at his neck as if he was choking. "I'm ambivalent about golf on a good day. This foursome doesn't make it more appealing. I wouldn't do this if it wasn't for Gloria."

I grinned. "We'd all do a lot for Gloria. Anything, really."

I checked my computer, where I had received a note from Helen. If I wouldn't mind swinging by to pick her up at the Casa Marina, she would love to have breakfast with me at Harpoon Harry's. This seemed like an odd choice for my mother-in-law who was more concerned about health and wellness than omelets oozing cheese and bacon and served with crispy hash browns. But I loved their breakfasts, so I didn't try to talk her out of it. That aside, nothing Helen did was random, so I was certain she had a reason for this choice, too.

I scrolled through Facebook for a few minutes hoping someone had more information than I did, or even the police department. There were more random musings about the explosion, but no real facts. I hated to think that if I went missing, no one would notice. But somewhere, someone didn't go home that night. So why weren't we hearing about it?

I finished getting ready and settling the animals, then zipped over to the Casa Marina to pick up Helen on the way to the restaurant. After claiming a bright orange booth and ordering breakfast, Helen and I exchanged pleasant chitchat about the family. Nathan's sister was threatening a trip to the United States in the summer and hoped to make a Key West visit part of it. "I will keep you posted on that. If she can't make it down, maybe you'll pop up to my house?"

"For sure," I said. I'd met Nathan's sister and her husband during our honeymoon to Scotland and liked them very much.

"You and Nathan are doing well?"

"Very well." I smiled and nodded firmly. I couldn't imagine what issues she thought we might be dealing with, but I sure didn't want her poking around in my marriage.

"Excellent." She took a sip of coffee from her white china cup. "Tell me again exactly what happened with this boat trip the other night."

I gave her the short version, explaining what we were doing on the big catamaran and why I thought it might have been related to competition in our Key West food world.

"No offense," she said slowly, "but it's hard to picture someone blowing a boat up because someone else's food was better than theirs and therefore they were losing business. Why not just upgrade the chefs or the menus or the ingredients and fight back by becoming superior to the competition?"

The waitress swept in with our plates and my mouth watered at the sight of my omelet. "Anything else, hons?" she asked.

"All set for now, thanks so much," I said, and turned back to my mother-in-law. "That would make sense, but I don't think we're dealing with a normal person here," I said. "Who blows up a boat with a bunch of people on it anyway? Psychopath? Someone with a deep rumbling grudge that's existed for a long time, growing uglier and more pressing in the depths of someone's psyche until it finally breaks free?"

"Exactly." Helen had picked up a fork to tackle her poached eggs with wheat toast, no butter, and a side of fruit, and now she pointed it at me. "I'm afraid we are thrashing around a bit and grasping at straws that are long shots. It makes more sense to me that the attack or incident or whatever it was would be related to the captain of the boat, than the passengers. If I was in charge of the investigation, I would want to know as much as possible about the captain of this craft, as well as the woman who was below deck when the explosion occurred. Was she actually a target, or, as your mother suggested last night, just unfortunate baggage?"

"You're right on both counts," I said, biting into a strip of bacon so crisp it snapped in my mouth. "I don't know much about either of them. Hearsay, that's the extent of it."

She punctured the remaining egg on her plate with her fork and dabbed a piece of dry toast into the yolk. "We're quite near the docks, aren't we? Could we pop over after breakfast and make some inquiries?"

The Mango Murders

"Why not?" I asked, breaking into a grin. Once we'd finished eating and tussled over who was paying, we left my scooter where I'd parked it and walked the block to the water.

Captain LaRue, the man whom I'd interviewed yesterday, was polishing his catamaran again this morning. I leaned over to Helen and whispered: "I asked him about how a boat might be blown up. He was quite dismissive—said it couldn't happen on his catamaran."

Helen marched toward him, her silver curls glinting in the bright sun. "Good morning," she said, putting her hand out to shake. "I'm Helen Bransford."

"Buddy LaRue," he said, then gestured at the woman scrubbing the side of the boat. She was medium height and muscular, with reddish-blonde hair pulled into a low ponytail. "My first mate, Louise Wardell." I thought I recognized her as the one of the folks who'd watched us launch the big party the other night, looking very glum.

Helen moved forward to shake her hand too. "We are investigating the incident that occurred off Mallory Square the other night. The *Pilar Too* docked right here," she pointed to the empty slip where'd we boarded the boat for the party. Then she opened her wallet to flash what looked like a badge. Was she snowing him completely? "As his close neighbor, you must've known Captain Roche rather well. From what I hear, he wasn't universally liked nor half the sailor that you are." She flashed a blinding smile.

He grimaced, evaluating her through narrowed eyes. "I did. If you're asking my theory about who might have sabotaged his boat, it could take me a long time to list all the possibles. He was aggressive, unafraid to grease political palms, and also unafraid to steal the business of other boat captains. On top of that, he was completely full of himself." Behind him, his first mate covered a smile.

This unattractive description made me wonder how my mother had chosen the *Pilar Too*. Had she gotten a recommendation from another caterer? References? Had Sam come down to the dock to talk with potential venue owners? Honestly, my stepfather was better at the business end of my mother's business that she'd ever been. Or had someone approached her and talked her into it? Even perhaps the captain himself.

"Was the captain involved in local politics?" Helen asked. "Did he spearhead something unpopular for example?"

"I couldn't tell you," said Buddy LaRue. "We were not friendly. However, I noticed several politicians boarding his ship that evening. If you're investigating the incident, you know how much conflict there is in this town. In some eyes, the Tourist Development Commission continues to bring in more traffic than a small island can reasonably handle. Not that I'm complaining as a businessman, but as a local resident, yes."

The TDC had been established to promote tourism in the Keys, in the name of supporting long-term economic security. Unfortunately, considering the crowds and prices on our island, some residents (including me) thought they might have done their job too well. "Agree completely," I piped in.

He glanced at me but focused back on Helen. "The question you might want to ask is who makes those decisions, and how might Captain Roche have been involved? You'd certainly want to talk with the city commissioners, including the new mayor. He is all about increasing revenue regardless of the cost in livability."

Helen didn't appear completely satisfied with his explanation. She said, "I know it's hard to describe, but looking back, could you say that you saw anyone boarding the ship who didn't belong there?"

He squinted at her. "You'd have to ask the person who developed the guest list, wouldn't you?" Then he turned back to his work, along with his mate.

"He's not wrong there," Helen said to me as we walked away. But did she realize that meant me and my mother and my coworkers? It had been so chaotic that none of us had a clear answer to Helen's questions and observations.

We walked a little further north along the docks, so I could show her the culvert where manatees sometimes gathered to drink fresh water. "I'm obsessed with them," I told her. "Somehow, to me they represent everything good and fragile in the world. If my spirit animal isn't a cat, it's a manatee. I can hardly bear to see one with propellor scars on its back."

I dropped down on the cement wall bordering the sidewalk. We were in luck, there was a pair sipping from the water rushing from the culvert, one old and weathered and one a baby.

"Hmm," Helen said, peering into the murky water. "You're obsessed with those gray blobs?"

"Wait a minute," I said. "They might come closer." As if on cue, the bigger one floated to the surface to look at us, showing a manatee smile, big nostrils, and whitish-rheumy eyes. I felt instantly teary. "On a day when I see these guys," I explained, "especially one with a baby, I can't help feeling hopeful about our little Key West universe. Even if everything else around us feels like it's literally or figuratively on fire, these guys have showed up."

I couldn't tell if she was interested in my manatee musings or thought I was a nut case. Even though I'd felt near tears after the manatee encounter, I took a deep breath and pointed out the dock where the ferry to Fort Myers left daily. Then we started back down Caroline Street in the direction of the scooter.

"So, what have we got Hayley?" my mother-in-law asked. "Nothing's jumping out at me, which makes me think we should cast the net wide for solutions. What should we be following up on?"

I told her about visiting the Mallory Square performers and how Tobin the acrobat noticed that someone had possibly dropped off the boat as it entered the harbor.

"You were on the boat at the time, right?"

I knew she must be wondering why I wouldn't have noticed such an obvious aberration. "Yes, correct. However, I was flitting about filling up peoples' champagne glasses and making sure the hors d'oeuvres were piping hot. I wasn't really paying attention to the bigger surroundings. We certainly weren't anticipating disaster."

She nodded gravely. "Who else might have been paying attention?"

I closed my eyes and pictured the rescue attempts. A flotilla of boats had swarmed ours after the explosion, ranging from the coast guard to tourists on Jet Skis to one tiki boat. "Have we taken you over to the community on Sunset Key? I can't remember. They have a lovely restaurant that sits right on the beach, and we often have lunch there with out-of-towners. You have to make a reservation months or weeks ahead and then take the small ferry over to the island. They don't want people coming onto their island who aren't property owners or renters."

The Mango Murders

My mother-in-law was wrinkling her nose, and I imagined she was wondering why *why why* I would be talking about lunch when we had just finished breakfast and furthermore were in the thick of a murder investigation.

"I tell you this because I know the captain of one of the boats that transports passengers to the island. Becky. She came over to help fish our guests out of the water. Having been that close to the scene, she may have noticed something before the explosion."

"Have you spoken to her?"

"I only just thought of her right now."

"What are we waiting for?" She slung her leg over the back of the scooter seat and gripped my waist as we took off toward Mallory Square.

I parked at the very western end of Duval Street near the Ocean Key resort, so we could walk all the way around the dock starting at Sunset Pier, and in the process, maybe jog other memories from the boating disaster. As we rounded the dock along the iconic pier with its multi-colored umbrellas and stage for musicians, I pointed out the exact spot where Nathan had proposed. "I never realized he was so soft-hearted and romantic," I said, describing the box he'd given me and the song he'd arranged for a local musician to play. I could feel my eyes filling as I told her, surprised at how emotional I'd felt ever since the frightening boat accident.

"He didn't learn that from his father," Helen said, scowling.

"You did a good job with him," I told her. "He's tough on the outside and sweet inside."

She made a noncommittal noise, but her expression was pleased.

We walked along the edge of Mallory Square, and I pointed out exactly how our boat had cruised into the harbor, and where we were when it blew up. We crossed the little bridge that led toward the Opal Key resort. I noticed that huge white tents had been erected along the water past the beehive of activity on Mallory Square. A wedding no doubt, as at least one was scheduled weekly in the high season. The tents alone had to cost a fortune, with plastic sides that could be lowered in case of rain, not to mention a dance floor, a live band, multiple open bars, and a phalanx of caterers carrying in food. I bet they'd even hired a drone service to record the activity from the air. These days, photographers and a videographer and a photo booth were not enough for some brides. Or their mothers.

I felt a flash of envy, thinking about my own unfancy, unscheduled wedding. Though the food had been amazing, and most of our loved ones attended, a small part of me still dreamed about this kind of party from time to time. But in truth, as my grandmother would have said, the proof was in the pudding of the marriage. Who cared how big the party was if the union only lasted a year or two? Then all the time it took to plan and the money to pay for it became dirty water circling the drain.

Finally, we reached the hut where the Sunset Key boats docked. Becky, who was chatting with waiting customers, was an athletic looking woman who wore a daily uniform of khaki skirt and white shirt unless it dropped below 70. She had a sailor's tan and wore her blonde hair in a top knot.

"I don't know her well," I said to Helen, "but she's always kind to animals and very competent on the water. She fished several of our customers out the other night, without a thought of whether she ought to be deviating from her trip to the restaurant on Sunset Key." As we approached, I introduced her to Nathan's mother.

"We're asking some questions about the incident the other night. Since I was in the thick of the action, I wasn't really registering anything that seemed out of place. I wondered if you might have?" I would tell her about Tobin's noticing someone dropping off the boat before the explosion if she didn't bring it up herself. But she did.

"First of all, on my trip over to Sunset Key I saw someone slip off that very boat and begin swimming toward the square. I tried to wave him down, but he didn't respond. I even yelled out, 'This is a dangerous time to be in the water.' I dropped off my passengers and started back here because more diners were waiting. That's when I saw the explosion. I roared over as quickly as possible to pitch in as I could until the authorities arrived."

"Are you certain the swimmer was a he?" I asked.

"Not entirely." She paused, folded her arms over her stomach. "I guess I assumed because the person looked like such a strong and muscular swimmer."

"Have you heard anything on the grapevine about how this happened?" I asked. I'd witnessed her camaraderie with other workers and passing strangers, both on the pier and the island. She would absolutely have her ear to the conch shell and would likely be privy to a stream of theories and gossip.

"I've heard everything. Vandalism, careless boating, love triangle, your mother's carelessness, sabotage. Take your pick, but I have no idea which if any are correct." She looked genuinely mystified, not cagey like she was holding something back, like the captain of the catamaran at the Key West Bight had.

We thanked her and asked her to contact me—and of course the police—if she heard something new. As we'd chatted at the Latitudes boat dock, a giant cruise ship docked at the pier had begun to discharge its passengers. Helen watched with dismay as a hoard of tourists disembarked from the ship. The ship had at least seven layers of cabins with double glass doors leading to individual balconies, and below that, smaller cabins for both the staff and people with less disposable income.

"Good God," Helen said, "that's a behemoth. It literally looks like an apartment complex. What are they thinking, letting that monstrous ship onto this island?"

"It's complicated," I said. "And controversial. The residents of Key West voted to reduce the size and frequency of the cruise ships because of the damage they were doing to the environment. Not to mention that people aren't convinced that passengers spend a lot of money in Key West because their meals are already provided on the ship. However, the results of our referendum were overturned by the state. And that's that. I sort of see some of the other sides, people have to earn a living. Plus, not everyone can afford an expensive vacation, and cruises can be quite reasonable. But on the *other* other hand, the people of Key West spoke about preserving our fragile ecosystem, and we were batted down like mosquitoes."

We started winding our way through the tourists toward my scooter. They eagerly pushed along the sidewalk, chattering in a rainbow of languages, headed toward the joys of Duval Street. I hoped that they would see more of our town than those dirty sidewalks and noisy bars, but often visitors didn't know what else was available, such as the cemetery, the two bookstores, the Custom House Museum, the Harry Truman Little White

The Mango Murders

House, the historic Key West Woman's Club. Most of these places were within easy walking distance of the cruise ship port, but not well known to cruisers. As we gawked at a gaggle of young woman wearing thongs ineffectively covered by see-through skirts, I heard the roar of an engine. A motorcycle burst through the crowd, aimed right at us.

"Look out!" I cried, grabbing my mother-in-law's elbow and diving to the pavement. But she dodged in the wrong direction, darting right in front of the noisy bike. Before I could push her out of the way, I heard a distressing thunk. The bike had knocked her to the ground and then roared off. Blood began to ooze from her forehead, and she looked disoriented and shocked. People were screaming and shoving toward us to gawk or squeezing away from Helen, to avoid the bullseye of violence. The gash on her head was bleeding faster, and I could only think that Nathan was going to kill me for allowing his mother to be damaged. I scrambled over on hands and knees to help her.

"Are you OK?" I asked, grabbing her hand. "Where's your phone? I'll call 911."

Before she could answer, a middle-aged woman with a neat bob arrived at the scene, extracted a T-shirt from a plastic bag emblazoned with the Saltwater Angler logo, and knelt to press it to Helen's head. "Are you her daughter?" she asked, looking over at me. "With a head injury, we should definitely call the EMTs."

"We don't need the EMTs," said Helen firmly, in her executive voice. She pulled the T-shirt from her head and stared at the blood. "How does it look?" she asked me, struggling to sit up. She glanced around and pointed at a few gawkers who were filming with their phones. "Could any of you identify the motorcycle, or the driver?" she asked in a fierce voice. One by one, they began to slink away.

"How does it look?" she asked me again. A rivulet of blood was dribbling down her face.

I'd begun to feel a little queasy. "It looks like it's going to need stitches, and it looks like it's going to hurt like heck and so is your hip. You hit the sidewalk hard."

The T-shirt woman tried again. "I'm a nurse, and I think we should call an ambulance."

"No, thank you. Not necessary," said Helen. "My daughter-in-law can take me to a doc in the box. Or the hospital. No problem." She pushed herself up from the sidewalk to her knees, wincing. "Our car is right nearby."

Except our car was not nearby, and aside from the distance we had to walk to reach it, it was a scooter, not a car. I didn't relish driving through town to the next island with her bleeding from her who-knows-how-serious head injury. But Helen would not change her mind. I pressed my *Key Zest* business card into the nurse's hand. "Text me and we'll pay for your t-shirt."

"Don't be silly," she said.

"Did you see who was driving the motorcycle?" Helen asked. "Could you identify him?"

"It all happened so fast." I circled my arm around my mother-in-law, and we began to shuffle slowly to the scooter, calling back more thanks as we walked. This felt like a terrible idea.

"Did you not recognize that driver?" Helen asked. "Do you think you were the target?"

I felt my eyes go wide. Had she not seen that the bike was aimed right at her? At that moment, one of her knees buckled, and she bobbled and almost went down to the pavement again.

The Mango Murders

I grabbed her around the waist. "Are you sure you can manage? Are you woozy? In pain? Please let me call Nathan. He can pick us up and drive us to the hospital."

"I'm sure," she said, still holding the bloody t-shirt against her forehead. "Not necessary to bother Nathan. While I'm getting stitched up, you can go talk to the captain of the damaged ship. Didn't Nathan say he was admitted to the hospital?"

She was unbelievable.

She wasn't bleeding as much but she looked a little pale, which gave me the slightest window into what she might be like as an older woman, more frail, less indomitable. I did not welcome this glimpse into the future, and I suspected she would not either.

Chapter Twelve

> *It was redundant, while at the same time, discordant. It's kind of like putting pasta on pizza—they're both related, but they have nothing to do with each other.*
> —David Lebovitz *Newsletter,* April 1, 2024

I worried the entire ride north to Stock Island, where the hospital was located, that Helen might pass out and drop off the back of my scooter. Then we'd truly have an emergency on our hands. I also worried whether she might have been deliberately targeted. Another reason why it would have been good to call the police. I parked in the large lot behind the hospital, and we started slowly toward the sliding glass doors. Despite her protests that everything was fine, Helen was definitely the worse for wear.

There was a sign posted outside the entrance that read: *Please pardon our dust while we remodel. Thank you for your patience.*

"It's never fun to be here, but it looks like it's going to be more grim than usual," I said. We stepped into the tiny waiting room, with its gray-green walls that I swore reminded me of

The Mango Murders

vomit. Who would choose a drab color like that for a space that was already chock full of pain and worry? Why not a nice sunny yellow or a cheerful pale orange? Every plastic seat in the room was taken, filled with every kind of patient, from screeching infant to confused elderly.

Helen leaned over to hiss at me. "You don't have to wait. I don't need a babysitter. I suggest you go pay a visit to the captain of your ill-fated ship before they release him. He'll likely have more to say if he's a captive audience."

It sounded like she'd taken my comment as a complaint. "I didn't mean to suggest anything . . ."

"Seriously," she said, gripping my arm. "You'll be a lot more use interviewing that man than sitting around here cow-eyed, worrying about what germs we're contracting."

I could tell she was dead serious, plus the whole series of events had left her grouchy. She most likely had hatched this plan once she realized that she was going to need medical attention of some kind. As usual, she was several steps ahead of me. "You'll text me the instant you have news here?"

"I will."

I walked around the outside of the little hospital to the main entrance and approached the visitors' desk. "I'm here to visit Captain Amos Roche," I said to the clerk, adding a big smile. "I'm his niece, and I brought him some things he requested." I showed her my ID and held up my backpack, which contained my own personal flotsam and jetsam, absolutely nothing he might want.

The clerk scrolled through some screens on her computer and then looked up. "He's being discharged today, but probably not until this afternoon. Chances are he would welcome some company." She gave me a blue marker and a paper visitors badge. I scribbled my name in illegible script and pasted the tag on my T-shirt.

"Third floor, room 302."

I took the elevator up, thinking of maniacal fictional captains, Captain Hook, Captain Nemo, Captain Ahab. Did this man hold a similar grudge that called him to destroy his own boat? That seemed absurd. Still, I'd need to approach him gingerly and kindly to see what he might reveal.

Captain Roche sat in a chair by the bed, looking out the window toward the road that ran alongside the community college. He was wearing blue cotton medical pants and a T-shirt, with his arm in a sling and head bandaged. His roommate was in the bed nearest the door, in a johnny coat, with the television blasting a game show rerun.

I tapped on the open door. "Captain Roche?"

The captain scowled when he saw me, but I was determined to be friendly. I approached with my hand out to shake before realizing his right hand was the one in the sling. Standing beside him, feeling foolish, I introduced myself, explaining who I was and that I'd been on the boat at the time of the explosion. "You can imagine that I'm very invested in finding out why this occurred."

His scowl deepened. "Does it matter who did it, when my boat is gone and along with it, my livelihood?"

"It kind of does, since someone perished in the explosion." Besides, wouldn't he himself want to know if someone had targeted his valuable boat?

The man in the next bed had perked up as we talked and now reduced the TV volume. I leaned against the air conditioning vent and lowered my voice to ask a series of questions about whether the captain had noticed anyone unfamiliar in the engine room or one of the cabins before the boat sailed.

"Almost everyone was unfamiliar, as you'd expect," he said. "I'm not usually catering to fussy food people. I prefer fishermen. I do very well with that crowd—they seem to like the idea that they're emulating Hemingway. I'm hired more often than most of the other boats of my size. I have no beefs with my usual clientele. If they bring food aboard, it's sandwiches and beer." His nostrils flared, which I took to mean he blamed my mother and me for what had happened. This didn't exactly jibe with what we'd been told about private chefs using the lower kitchen.

"Have the authorities come here to interview you?" I asked. "Do you get a sense that they have theories about what caused the explosion, or the victim's connection with the cruise? Or with you?"

"They've asked a million questions, but they haven't said a word to me about who did it," he replied. "They clearly haven't even gotten so far as to identify the deceased. If that doesn't give you a clue into the incompetence of the so-called professionals, don't know what would."

I didn't figure it would do one bit of good to argue. After a lot of coaxing, the only new information I gleaned was that someone had made a delivery—possibly more than one, earlier in the afternoon, supposedly on my mother's behalf. He hadn't inspected any of the cargo, because why would he? His business was based on mutual trust.

"One last question," I asked. "Can you take a wild guess about anyone who might have targeted you in the explosion? Someone you owed money to, or something like that?"

All I got was a flat no.

"No," he said a second time. "It wasn't my problem. I've never had issues with customers before."

By the time I arrived back at the emergency room, my mother-in-law was waiting outside. "They don't like head wounds," she said, adding her dry chuckle. "They cleaned the area and stitched me up but wanted to keep me there overnight. I insisted that I hadn't hit the pavement very hard so there shouldn't be concern of concussion or bleeding into the brain. If I had symptoms, they could be sure I'd come back. In the end, I had to take full responsibility and sign out against medical advice."

Concussions and brain bleeds were outcomes that I hadn't even considered. If I'd been thinking straight, I wouldn't have agreed to ferry her on a scooter across town with a fresh head wound. Or leave her alone in the ER while I went nosing into Captain Roche's business. The better daughter-in-law behavior would have been to stick with her, even if she protested. Nathan was going to literally kill me.

"I'm to ice it faithfully—they seemed to think I'd look like a bit of a Frankenstein for a while. But no one's looking at me anyway," Helen added. "What did your captain say?"

I told her that he remembered a delivery, probably several, but could not describe the people delivering. He denied any reason to suspect the incident happened because of something related to him. "Are you certain you feel up to a scooter ride back to the hotel?"

"Of course," she said, her voice steely.

I drove across town, pulled up in front of the Casa Marina, and grasped her elbow to help steady her off the scooter. "Nathan is going to be furious about this whole episode," I said.

The Mango Murders

"He'll be even madder if you drive yourself to the party. Maybe it would be a good idea to stay home, order room service and rest tonight?"

"I came here to celebrate Gloria, and I plan to do exactly that." She handed me her helmet and walked away.

"Then we will pick you up," I yelled after her, matching her steeliness with mine. "No discussion. See you at 5:10 right here."

Chapter Thirteen

Cooking came to me as though it had been there all along, waiting to be expressed; it came as words come to a child when it is time for her to speak.
—Marcella Hazen, *Amarcord: Marcella Remembers*

All the way home, I worried about how to tell Nathan that his mother had been in an accident. I could spill everything ahead of picking her up and take the brunt of his wrath. Or I could warn him with a soft-pedaled version, admitting we'd been in a little accident, but insisting his mother wanted to tell him the details. Or I could mention nothing at all and wait for him to see the bandage on her head. For sure, he'd be maddest about that last. I circled around and around the possibilities.

I had a text from Helen on my computer when I reached the houseboat. "I'd rather tell Nathan myself what happened. Can you drop a hint, maybe something nondescript about how we had a little incident and that I will fill him in?"

I felt a whoosh of relief. Now the only thing I'd have to explain were the abrasions on my knees that I'd noticed after the adrenalin about Helen's so-called incident had receded. I could bypass those questions by wearing either a long dress or capri pants. I popped into the shower and carefully soaped the raw patches of skin. I didn't want a big infection from scraping the sidewalk where thousands of dogs and tourists had walked or worse.

* * *

"I'll wait here," I told my husband as we pulled into the Casa Marina parking lot at 5 p.m. "She had a little accident today and she insists on telling you the story herself." This was a chicken move, but if she wanted to tell him what happened, why did I have to be the witness? I moved into the back seat to leave the roomier passenger side seat open for her.

He returned to the car, gripping his mother's elbow like the tiller on an outboard motor, his face resembling an angry white-capped sea.

"I'd love to hear your perspective on this," he said, glaring at me once he tucked his mother into the front seat and helped her fasten her seatbelt like a toddler in a car seat. "I am really, *really* unhappy about the fact that you didn't call me right away. Never mind that you were nosing in police business in the first place," he said, now glaring at me in the rearview mirror.

I expected his mother to snap back with something about how we could take care of ourselves, and that I, Hayley, had every right to ask questions about an incident that Helen was injured in. Or something. But she was quiet. As I was about to speak up, she finally broke the silence.

"It's possible that we should have called you. But when you've been mowed down by a motorcycle and have blood dripping down your face, chin, boobs, and so on, and you're angry as hell about it, maybe your thinking is not as clear as it could be. Although to be fair, Hayley asked several times if I wouldn't consider calling the EMTs or at least you, Nathan. I refused. I had in my mind that they could clean me up, and we could talk to the captain of the boat that was blown up if we went directly to the hospital. Which we did."

He thunked his forehead with his palm. "Now you're not only putting your lives in danger but interfering with a murder investigation." He glanced back at me again. "What did you notice about the motorcycle and what do you think is going on here?" Before I could answer, he added, "Why the devil didn't you call me even if she didn't want you to?"

My mother-in-law's lips were set in a pinched line. "May I remind you, Mr. Detective bigshot, that we have unraveled some situations that flummoxed the police in the past. I have extensive training in criminology as you know perfectly well, and your wife is gifted, nearly a whiz at amateur sleuth investigations."

I was grateful that she was sticking up for me, not so happy that she was poking Nathan like a kid who'd come across a nest of wasps. I leaned forward and touched each of their shoulders.

"If we could possibly continue this conversation after the party, I would appreciate it. There is going to be enough drama just by the fact that Gloria's family will be here."

Nathan took a big breath in and let it out slowly. "Can you remember any identifying characteristics of the person on the motorcycle?" he asked us.

"It happened so quickly," I said, closing my eyes and trying to bring up a picture of that moment. "I was focused on getting us out of danger. Either a smallish man or a large-ish woman.

The Mango Murders

The person was wearing a big helmet with one of those plastic flaps, and the plastic itself was colored like dark sunglasses." Nothing very useful there. "We parked at the end of Duval near the Ocean Key and walked toward Mallory Square, and then on to talk to Becky." My eyes went wide. "In case you're wondering, there is absolutely no reason why she'd want to run us down. She was as helpful as she could be. Like Tobin, she saw someone drop off the side of our boat."

I looked over at my mother-in-law. "Can you do any better than that?"

She shrugged and sighed. "As Hayley said, it happened fast. Plus, the pier was mobbed with tourists. One minute we heard the roar of the engine and a lot of people yelling, and the next minute I'd banged down onto the pavement. By the time I thought to take note of what the driver looked like, the bike and its rider were long gone."

"I hate to harp on this," Nathan said after a pause. "Were there not any police on the scene? I'm surprised I didn't hear about this."

"Your mother was very definite about not calling for help," I said, now feeling guilty and embarrassed about the way we'd handled it. Helen must have been addled by the blow to her head and not thinking clearly. I should have insisted. "We heard some sirens as we were leaving the scene, and I know some of the bystanders filmed it with their phones. It might be possible to follow up on that. But as you know and I know, if the officers learned that no one died or was bleeding heavily or putting someone else in danger, they probably moved on to other problems."

"Probably. I'll check the log and see what the guys on the ground might have reported. This is difficult since you can't seem to describe the attacker, but did you get a sense of whether this was random? Or, were you targeted?" Nathan asked.

Helen shrugged, adding, "We don't know."

Wasn't that always the question in the aftermath of a disaster? It had been asked in various forms over the last few days about the boat fire and explosion. Did someone mean to damage the boat, the passengers, one passenger? Did someone mean to injure Helen or was she collateral damage, like the person who'd died in the hold? None of it was clear.

Nathan drove through the big white pillars flanking the entrance to the Truman Annex and parked on Noah Lane behind a few other cars. We trooped into my mother and Sam's lovely home. I often felt a small jolt of longing in their house—the surroundings were so peaceful and green, and the home itself much more spacious than our floating houseboat. They had room for a big living area, and an even bigger kitchen, and a porch outside that provided a glimpse of the Truman Waterfront Park, and beyond that, the Navy basin where they could sometimes watch dolphins or even Navy Seals during training exercises. I adored our neighborhood and our home, but for sure there was more room to breathe right here.

Nathan escorted his mother out to the porch, the two of them arguing about whether she should chance a glass of wine. I hung back, hearing Miss Gloria's family troop up the steps to the front porch in a small gaggle. I returned to the front door so I could greet them, happy to distance myself from the squabble between my husband and his mother. The Peterson family was dressed in dark clothes that would've been comfortable in a Michigan spring but were not suited to the tropical vibe and moist heat of Key West. I hurried to welcome them, not wanting them to feel the way they looked: absolutely out of place.

The last time I had seen Miss Gloria's sons, they had arrived in Key West intent on moving her to an assisted living place up north, regardless of her hopes and desires. We had fended that off, at least in the short run, but I was certain they would be watching carefully for signs of her deterioration. Nathan and I and our friends, Connie and Ray, who lived up the finger, had promised we would treat her like our own family and keep her safe on Houseboat Row. Her biological family would be alert for lapses in our care and attention. Perhaps lapses such as a boat explosion or motorcycle-driven head injury. With a little bad luck, Miss Gloria could have been involved with either of those.

Connie and Ray arrived right behind Miss Gloria's relations, mutually giddy about having secured a babysitter for the evening. I introduced everyone around and showed them through the living area to the back porch where Sam was pouring champagne, the usual selection of beer and wine and soft drinks, and his special cocktail of the night, a mango daquiri.

Miss Gloria rushed over to hug Helen, then peered at her face, which was beginning to discolor under the makeup she had used. "My goodness, what in the world happened to you? Hopefully not a prize fight?"

I stepped back waiting to hear what she would tell them. Motorcycle run amok, that was the gist of it. Knocked down but bounced right back up. She certainly didn't tell them about the scooter ride to the hospital on Stock Island.

"Somebody knocked you down on purpose?" Miss Gloria asked.

"We don't know," Helen said. "But I'm really fine."

Annie Dubisson approached. "Do you think it could have been as simple as an accident, someone a little careless but not ill-intentioned? I'll tell you why I say that. I was in the Publix parking lot last week. It's always a mob scene there, and the parking spaces are so close together. People walk right behind cars with their groceries without even checking to see if anyone is backing out or what."

Nathan's mom looked a little glazed but nodded politely.

"My point is," said Mrs. Dubisson, biting her lip, "I did notice a little thump last week, but I thought nothing of it. It wasn't until I was waved down on North Roosevelt by one of Nathan's colleagues that I realized I'd hit a person."

"What?" asked Frank's wife, Henrietta, in a loud voice that bordered on a shriek. "You knocked someone over and didn't recognize that it had happened? Did they fall under the car? How did you not see them?" She shot eye daggers at her husband. "This is why they should have a road driving test for all seniors over 70. In my opinion, no elderly person above 80 should even have a driver's license."

I laughed with forced gaiety and moved to cut her out of the pack and direct her to the view of the water from the edge of the porch. "That would never gain traction in Florida. *Seniors Are Us* in this state. Look—" I pointed to the Navy basin, "I think we're going to get a show of Navy Seal practice maneuvers tonight. If we're lucky, they'll be working with their dolphins. Did you know that they possess the most sophisticated sonar known to man—and that's naturally. In other words, they are born with it."

Thank goodness my mother arrived on the deck to announce that dinner was served, because who knows what random subject I might have blathered about next. "We are serving a mango themed dinner tonight because it's the season. We made a few dishes minus mango in case someone is allergic or simply loathes tropical fruit. Sam and I had a lot of back and forth about which recipes to choose. Shrimp and mango skewers, that was a no brainer. Sam, of course, insisted on the mango daiquiri—the same drink he was serving on our excursion the other night. Unfortunately, no one got to sample much of that batch."

"What's for dessert?" I asked, trying steer conversation away from the touchy subject of the torched catamaran.

"For dessert, we have a chocolate cake as well as a mango upside down cake."

"Remember, Frank, when we went to that lobster-themed dinner at what was supposed to be a fancy three-star restaurant?" asked Henrietta. She rolled her eyes and mimed grabbing her throat. "Believe me by the time we got to dessert, lobster was the last thing I was hoping for. I had to literally choke that dish down."

"That's why we chose to make the chocolate as well," my mother said. She had a gracious Buddha smile pasted on her face, but I guessed she was probably thinking, as I was, that this woman was the rudest person currently inhabiting our island. Plus, to be rude myself, skipping one dessert would not have hurt her a bit.

"But you may want to try the upside-down cake. Hayley's magazine printed it in the last issue, and they've gotten a lot of positive comments on their website. Of course, if you drown anything in butter and brown sugar, it's going to be delicious." She laughed, a tinkly, cheery sound that I knew was meant to be inviting and happy. Underneath that, I heard the tension she was feeling from the gathered families too.

She clapped her hands together. "Dinner is served!"

* * *

As the Michigan guests got ready to depart after dinner, taking Miss Gloria and her best pal home with them, I heard my friend tell her sons and their wives, "You must come over to Houseboat Row tomorrow!" I hustled over to the little group so I could help decide what outing she was planning next.

"Hayley bakes the most amazing scones, well, only second to those that we had in Scotland. We'll give you the whole tour of life on houseboat row. Unless you've had too much mango this and mango that, I'm sure she would rustle up some mango scones. And Nathan, he's the coffee brewmaster! I'd love to show you all around our little neighborhood. It could be like a progressive dinner, only it would be progressive houseboat tours. With snacks."

"We would love to host you," I said. "Scones are easy."

There were more eyerolls but finally Frank agreed that the visit sounded fine, and we settled on them arriving between 9:30 and 10. They would text to confirm once they left the hotel. Miss Gloria headed to their car, chattering with her two sons. I could see the daughters-in-law grimacing as they trailed behind. If they did not realize by now what a treasure of a mother-in-law they had, no scolding I was tempted to give them would make a difference.

As Nathan made a move to follow, I insisted on staying a bit longer to help my mother and Sam with the cleanup. "You can take your mother home; I can handle things here." It would actually feel like a relief if he went ahead, as he had barely said one word to me over the last three hours. His silence felt like being tethered to an iceberg. If that was the tiniest bit too harsh, a granite boulder. In winter.

"My father is already signed on for that," he said. "He nearly came to fisticuffs with your father, fighting over who could be the biggest gentleman."

I muttered under my breath, "You would not be in the running for that title tonight."

"Excuse me?" he asked.

"You showed unnecessary roughness, interrogating us in the car," I snapped.

He was breathing a little faster, I imagined trying to keep control of his temper, same as I was. "We can talk more about this later," I said. "We're all tired and I'd love to help mom and Sam clean up." I felt beyond tired, boneless with exhaustion, but my parents had to be feeling just as bad if not worse.

"I'm staying to help and will take you home when we're done," he said, already heading toward the kitchen.

The clean-up was finished quickly with four people working. Then Sam suggested we adjourn to the deck with glasses of wine to relax.

"I'll trade you my wine for another piece of that mango cake," I said, flashing him a smile. I knew I didn't need more alcohol, but caramelized butter and sugar sounded like the perfect fortification.

"Just water for me please," Nathan said.

Once he'd returned from the kitchen to the porch with the drinks and the cake, Sam said, "Nathan, I respect that you don't like to discuss your cases with nosy civilians, but we are very much connected with this situation. We were paddling in the salt water off Mallory Square with the rest of the victims. We have no idea who the actual target of the fire was, but maybe by now you do?"

Nathan said, "I'm sorry, we don't have answers yet." Then he relented and glanced at me. "It might be helpful to go over what happened today again with that motorcycle incident. Let's be systematic as we think this through. A, the rider could have been pointed at my mother," Nathan said. "She's the one he hit and maybe he meant to do that."

"That's possible," I said. "He or she."

He grunted, ceding my point. "B, the rider might have meant to hit you, Hayley, but you jumped out of the way," said Nathan.

"I certainly wasn't trying to put Helen in the path of danger," I protested.

"I'm not suggesting that," said Nathan. "I'm trying to figure out what might have been going on in the mind of the assailant. Which would've been made easier had there been any police officers on the scene."

"I believe you already made that point, Nathan," said my mother.

I flashed her a grateful smile.

"Possibility C," Nathan continued, "it had nothing to do with either of you. Nothing personal that is. The driver was drunk or otherwise impaired and out of control. Either they meant to inflict some damage, or they were stupid and careless. Any thoughts about whether one of those feels right?"

I sank back into my lounge chair and closed my eyes to think over the possibilities. "I think maybe he was aimed at Helen," I said, slowly. "The motorcycle wasn't wandering, but more pointed at her. I yelled for her to move when I heard the engine and then saw him coming. She jumped out of the way, but in the wrong direction." I stopped for a moment to really picture whether the rider's path toward Helen seemed incidental or purposeful. "Trouble with that theory is I can't imagine who would have it in for her. She only landed on the island yesterday."

"Yet ever since she arrived, she's been involved in snooping around about the Mallory Square incident." Nathan put his water glass on the table and crossed his arms over his chest.

I ignored that comment, though it wasn't wrong. "I have a question," I said to mom and Sam. "How did you end up choosing the *Pilar Too*? That captain didn't seem like much of a prize to me, though the boat was handsome. To be fair, I wasn't seeing him in his best moment in that hospital room. He was grouchy and ungracious and decidedly unhelpful. But I figure you guys must have gone through a selection process. There was something about him and his boat that helped him rise above the other candidates, like the guy docked right next to him."

They looked at each other, both faces a little puzzled. "From what I can remember," Sam said. "We left the final decision to Palamina. She told us about several options and asked our opinions, but we were so busy, we both agreed whoever she chose would be fine. As long as there was some kind of kitchen to heat up the hors d'oeuvres and stage the food, we could make it work." My mother was nodding but she looked droopy, barely suppressing a major yawn.

I pressed the tines of my fork into the plate, gathering up the last buttery crumbs of cake. A sudden question jolted my foggy brain. Who else had submitted recipes to *Key Zest*, outside of my mother? Could a baker who was not chosen have been angry enough to ruin our party? Seemed absurd, but I could do that research tomorrow at the office to rule it out, without worrying my parents.

"We'll talk more tomorrow," I said, standing to kiss each of them. "Thank you for putting on a lovely spread for Miss Gloria and her not-so-lovely family."

"We'll gossip about them in the morning," my mother said with a laugh. "Meanwhile, we will remember our mantra: anything for Gloria."

Once Nathan and I were back in his car driving out of the Annex, I said, "I should have another talk with Palamina. Don't you think it seems important, figuring out why she chose that boat? Also, I'll ask her if she really believes her ex might be in town, causing a lot of trouble for all of us, as it turns out. Probably won't hurt to talk with Lorenzo again too, because he'll have been putting a lot of thought into what he might have noticed unconsciously the night of the incident. And the recipe contest, now I'm worried about that."

Nathan pulled over to the side of Southard Street right before the Truman Annex guardhouse, put his vehicle into park, and turned to face me. "Seriously?" he asked. "My mother is run down by a madman on a motorcycle and suffers a head injury in an incident that could have been aimed at you, and you still don't understand that this is police business?"

I couldn't have felt more shocked if he'd slapped me. I had a strong urge to burst into tears, but I pushed it back. "Must we relitigate the same issue about how sometimes I have useful things to contribute every single time we disagree? It's exhausting and painful and feels like we're moving backward in this relationship, not forward."

"I can't argue with that," he said, his expression stony. "You provide some interesting insights that might not occur to me. But as long as you are blasting off doing things that put you and people you love in danger, I can hardly sit back and say nothing. Do you think that would be fair or wise?"

I had a powerful urge to fling myself out of the car and storm home by foot. But I knew he'd follow me, creeping along behind me until I got back in, even if it took walking across the entire town with a police vehicle trailing me.

"Like I said, relitigating." I leaned against the headrest, arms planted over my chest.

With his face looking as hard as mine felt, he started the car up and drove us home.

Once we were back inside the houseboat, I took a deep breath, scooped up Evinrude for comfort and protection, and tried again. "I thought maybe we had developed a different level of trust between us than we had at the beginning. I had hoped that you weren't always going to assume I was insanely shooting off to court danger. Then I wouldn't have to assume that you're a big bully wanting to squash every good idea that comes along. Every good idea that doesn't come directly from you, I mean." I stalked toward the bedroom, the cat squeezed close to my ribs. He gave a small meow of protest.

"Really," Nathan said, "you think I'm a big bully."

"Duh." I slammed the bathroom door shut, sank onto the toilet seat, still clutching Evinrude, and began to cry. Evinrude licked the tears off my cheek with his rough tongue as fast as they trickled down. In the kitchen, I could hear my husband calling to Ziggy to take him on his final walk of the night. I washed my face and brushed my teeth and fell into bed with my back toward his side, Evinrude cuddled on the outside, sure sleep wouldn't come.

Ten minutes later, Nathan and Ziggy followed me to bed. "I'm sorry to come across as a bully," he said. "I admit there are things you can do that I cannot. But I don't want to lose you to some madman."

"Apology accepted," I said, though I still felt mad. "It's just that I'm certain Lorenzo will clam up if more police show up to talk to him without me as a buffer. I would not be the least bit surprised if Palamina does the same thing."

"Message received," he said. "How about you have those two conversations and then report back to me?"

"Fine," I said.

"I love you."

I gave him the barest grunt in reply.

Chapter Fourteen

I dissect mangoes with ease now, licking the juice from my fingers, looking with sadness and panic as each day the supply wanes.
—Jaya Saxena, "Just Another Member of the Diaspora, Writing About Mangoes,", *Eater*, May 7, 2024

I woke up later than usual, with memories of the last few days' violent adventures swirling in my brain. Nathan had already gone to work but had left a note with a second apology and a big pot of coffee, both of which helped boost my mood.

"Maybe we're not doomed to be a broken family," I said to the cat, giving him a few extra treats as a reward for his comforting presence last night. The idea of making the mango scones requested by Miss Gloria felt appealing—the familiar rhythm of putting the dough together would be soothing. Maybe while I was measuring, chopping, and kneading, some new ideas would rise through what felt like sludge in my brain.

Since I'd finished mixing and patting the dough into shape by 8:30, I had time to walk Ziggy before popping the scones into the oven. This way they'd be piping hot when the guests arrived, and I could quickly zap them with the cream cheese frosting after we toured the other boats. Ziggy and I jogged over the Palm Avenue Bridge and then crossed the road to walk back through the more peaceful Meadows neighborhood. The mostly historic homes here felt like they composed a real neighborhood, without the hustle-bustle of Houseboat Row. I waved at a thin woman with a brown bob and tortoiseshell eyeglasses sitting on her porch in a rocking chair, then recognized her as our former mayor, Teri Johnston.

"You look quite relaxed," I said, smiling at her from the bottom of her stoop.

"Retirement suits me so far," she said with an answering grin.

"I hope you didn't suffer any ill effects from that dunk in the harbor the other night?"

"I'm fine." Her brows furrowed. "I'm so sorry that happened to your cruise event. It looked like you'd spent a lot of energy and money getting it arranged, and you had a gorgeous night."

I nodded. "We were devastated. Probably makes you glad you didn't run for a third term." Which was kind of a dumb thing to say, because it wouldn't have been her problem anyway, other than expressing concern for her citizens. "What I meant to say is, I'm sorry you aren't still our mayor."

"Thank you," she said, adding a broad smile. "I loved doing that job, working for this town. But it was time to take a breather, let someone else lead." She paused for a moment. "I miss some of it," she added. "But not the politics."

We both laughed because what else was there in that job?

"I went in all dewy-eyed, thinking we could change some intractable problems, because I'd been in business in this town

The Mango Murders

for years and thought I knew the players and how to get them working together successfully. But connections feel different these days. People have grown angry and seem willing to lash out rather than talk things through."

"Is that what you think happened on our cruise?" I asked. "Maybe someone who had a grudge against the new mayor who might have gone on the attack? He was on the boat with us, so he could have been the target."

I could hear the squeak of her rocking chair as she pondered my question.

She took a sip of coffee from a white mug with the city of Key West's seal engraved on it. "I don't mean to suggest that someone was out to harm him, even though Mayor Tom and I disagree on most subjects, including overcrowding Key West. I think we have about as many residents and visitors on this island as we can manage, and he's all about keeping the income stream flowing and growing regardless of the costs."

I nodded, as this sounded very familiar. Lorenzo had warned me many times that, odd as it might sound, the city of Key West was created a Capricorn, and thus very focused on money. Bringing money into business coffers at the cost of our water quality and wildlife and the land itself was a huge bone of contention.

"You had some rabid environmentalists on the boat," said Mayor Teri. "Could one of them have been the target? You know the mayor is very close with two men who own most of the businesses along the harbor. You set up a pretty good conflict right there with your guest list."

"We didn't think that one through," I said ruefully. "But surely a person wouldn't blow up a boat if they themselves were a passenger. Would they?"

"It wouldn't seem logical," she agreed. "Very risky in fact. Are the authorities talking about what happened?"

"Not much," I said. "A lot of different agencies helped with the rescue and are now involved in the investigation, so that complicates what they feel comfortable making public." I paused. "You didn't notice anything that felt off before the accident occurred?" I wanted to ask her if she'd noticed any of her own enemies, but that felt too fraught.

"No," she said. "I wish I'd been paying closer attention, but I was enjoying the champagne and the gorgeous evening and old friends without worrying about saying too much or too little."

"Have you heard of any locals who've been reported missing?" I asked. "The police are having trouble identifying the victim."

"Tragic!" she said, her forehead wrinkling in concern. "I haven't heard of anyone missing, but I'll call them if I do."

I wondered how to push on this a little harder, but my Fitbit beeped, announcing that I had paused my exercise and should keep moving. Besides, I needed to bake the scones and put on some clothes fit for fancy company. I said goodbye and hurried home.

Minutes before ten I heard the high-pitched voices of Miss Gloria's family arriving on the dock. I drew in a calming breath and went out to greet them. This time it was only the wives, pecking Miss Gloria's cheeks like hungry chickens.

"Frank Jr. and James have gone for a run and will join us a little later," Henrietta explained.

"Neither one of them really needs the extra calories in your baked goods," Tonya added with a smirk, patting her waistline for emphasis.

"Scones and coffee first?" Miss Gloria asked, after a quick eyeroll in my direction, "or would you like the tour and then relax on Hayley's deck?"

Nobody answered.

"Let's do the tour first," I suggested. "That will give the scones time to cool so the icing doesn't run off them."

Miss Gloria clapped her hands. "Wonderful! Warm scones slathered with frosting! Should we start with your place?"

As I urged them in, I told them about the ruined tub of a boat that had been abandoned here for years, and how Nathan and I had it stripped down inside and out. "I was worried at first—you know what they say about a silk purse and a sow's ear—but it turned out to suit us perfectly, even if it's tiny." I led them into my kitchen, with its clever storage everywhere, only the most frequently used workhorses of my cooking projects on display. A full plate of golden scones studded with bits of orange mango posed on the counter, releasing the irresistible smell of butter and sugar and cinnamon. I waved them across the kitchen and stepped aside so they could peek into our bedroom.

"We only have one bedroom and you've seen my husband. He's a strapping guy. Luckily, he doesn't snore because there's no place to send him if he did." Miss Gloria's daughters-in-law snickered. "The architect and the builder did so much to maximize our space. With the vaulted ceiling and the double doors looking out on the water at both ends, it never feels as small as it actually is."

Once I'd showed them everything and introduced them to the animals, we headed to Miss Gloria's boat. I stayed outside because three people in that little space all paneled in dark wood would already feel congested, and I wanted my friend to show her beloved home in its best light.

"Imagine what it was like with Hayley and her handsome police officer husband, Nathan, and three cats and a dog living in here together with me. Now that was a crowd!" I heard her tell them. A few minutes later, she led her relatives back onto the finger of the dock. "Next up, Annie Dubisson's home."

This time I did troop along behind because it had been a minute since I'd seen the inside of her best friend's place. Mrs. Dubisson appeared delighted to show us around. We toured the larger boxy living area, with a faded red Tibetan rug, a multitude of plants, and workmanlike kitchen. I knew the ladies liked playing mahjong here because it felt more spacious and lighter than Miss Gloria's place.

"We love living here on the water," Mrs. Dubisson told the guests. "That little bit of wave action at night always makes me feel like I'm being rocked to sleep in my mother's arms." She paused. "There are surely drawbacks—it's damp out here and everything tends to rust, and it's more trouble to schlep back groceries and what not. This life wouldn't be for everyone. Maybe someday we'll retire to one of those homes." She glanced at Miss Gloria—two weathered old women who would be bored silly without something to do—and they howled with laughter.

Miss Gloria's sons arrived as we emerged onto the dock.

"What did we miss?" Frank asked.

"Your mother's chatter." His wife blinked her eyes open and shut. With a cat, I was pretty sure that meant *I love you*, but I doubted the same translation worked with her.

"Speaking of mothers, next up, Connie and Ray, and their delightful children! We won't go inside because both kids are

The Mango Murders

napping," Miss Gloria said, pausing in front of their blue home. "They've been very creative with a small space. Even Hayley lived here for a bit."

"Have you lived on every boat in this harbor?" asked Henrietta.

Miss Gloria ignored her question with its rude inflection. "That was at the beginning of her Key West existence. Well, not the very beginning because she moved down here to be with this dreadful man who threw her out after six weeks." She turned to face me with a broad grin. "Am I right, Hayley?"

I snickered. "You are right." What else could I add? It was the most embarrassing moment of my life so far. I didn't especially love her sharing it with the daughters-in-law, but it was an integral part of my Key West origin story. Everyone who lived here had a story about how they came to land on this most unlikely of homes, this fragile string of islands extending into the ocean. Plenty of people were running away from something, so they found the distance from mainland to the Keys as the perfect prescription for sorting out life confusion. I wasn't the only one whose story sounded a little ridiculous.

"Luckily for Hayley," Miss Gloria said, "her college roommate, Connie, was living right here on this dock." She pointed to the adorable blue floating home, its deck lined with herbs and tomato plants. "Connie took her in because that's what good friends do. Then one morning, Hayley stumbled upon a heap of something right here on these wooden planks. That heap turned out to be me!" She looked at the horrified faces around her, grinning like a crazy woman. "Can you imagine? She thought I was a bag of old rags. Instead, she saved me, and we've become tight friends, more like grandmother and granddaughter than anything else."

I blew her a kiss, wondering how her offspring-in-laws felt about that description. I honestly did seem closer to her than her biological family appeared to feel. I adored her. "You are so right. I was definitely guilty of underestimating you."

Miss Gloria piped up again. "Oh, I forgot to show you the secret compartment in my boat. That was where Hayley found me when I'd been trussed up and left for dead. Everyone thought that would be the end of me, that I'd be too frightened to go on. But you know what, when someone threatens you like that, you get mad and fight back." She clenched her tiny hands into fists and squinted her eyes, looking as fierce as an elfin woman could look.

I tried to catch her attention to signal that maybe she'd be better off keeping this kind of reminiscence to herself.

James's wife, Tonya, muttered, "What's next on the tour? The place where she was slashed across the neck and left to bleed out? Or run over by a motorcycle? Or blown up on a party boat? This is not a safe place for an old woman."

"Agreed," said Henrietta.

"Oh, how you do go on," said Miss Gloria waving a dismissive hand. "Didn't James Taylor sing a song about the secret of life being enjoying the ride as you go along? That's how I take things, and it's worked very well for me so far."

"We'll talk," said the daughters-in-law, almost in unison.

By now I wanted to wring their necks but instead I smiled pleasantly. I invited them all to take seats on my deck, which was bigger than Miss Gloria's outside space, where I would serve up coffee and the scones. I dashed inside to slather on the icing. The scones had turned out very well, if I said so myself, especially with that cream cheese frosting. More like a treasured dessert than a dry breakfast item.

The Mango Murders

Once everyone was settled with their food, Frank turned to his mother. "I have a question," he said, "after hearing about your nautical disaster. Do these houseboats have engines? In other words, could your homes blow up like that catamaran did?"

I put my half-eaten scone on a plate. "If I might answer that? Nathan and I renovated this place from the studs up," I said, "so we were able to discuss whether our floating home even needed an engine. He was concerned about carbon monoxide poisoning from a potential gas engine or generator. Everything else, like our stove and heat, is electric. In the end, we agreed that we weren't going to be motoring anywhere because we're docked right here permanently for better or worse. Or until the rent goes so high that we can no longer stomach it. At that point we can either sell it or have it towed." My mind jogged over to the conversation I'd had with the catamaran captain next to the *Pilar Too*. He'd been proud about deciding to renovate his boat to all-electric to avoid problems that gas engines might cause.

"Really?" asked James. "They raise the rent here when it isn't even physical property? And that drives people out?"

"Sooner or later, most people can't afford life in Key West." That was Miss Gloria, and her voice sounded sad. "This is partly a legacy of the pandemic. People were afraid to fly out of the country, but Key West feels like a Caribbean island, even though you can drive here. Hence, we got very popular. Too popular, really. Besides that, we advertise all over the country, even if we don't really need more tourism. Even if that's the last thing we need."

She was rambling a little, as this was a pet peeve.

"But you do have an engine," I said to my friend. "So you could leave if you needed to."

"Yes, though we haven't gone anywhere in ages. I don't even know if there's any fuel in the tank."

The Michigan relatives were exchanging meaningful glances that I took to mean that she was giving them more ammunition about the ways she couldn't handle living alone in Key West. I wished I hadn't said anything about her engine.

Nathan texted Miss Gloria after her relatives had departed, as we were cleaning up from the breakfast party. "Please let my lovely but phoneless wife know we're holding a press conference this afternoon around one. She'll probably be interested in attending."

I figured he was trying to make up for being so hard on both me and his mother yesterday. Whatever his reasoning and however annoyed I still was with him, I wouldn't miss it. Meanwhile, I had time to motor over to the *Key Zest* office to organize my work for the week, and hopefully have a good talk with Palamina.

Chapter Fifteen

Anyone—ask a six-year-old with a granny—can bake a cake. All you need (give or take) is eggs, flour, sugar, butter, and patience.
—Elisabeth Luard, *Cookstory*. July 12, 2024

I wrapped up the leftover scones, tucked them into the freezer, and zipped down the island to the office. As I'd hoped, Palamina was at work in her office. "Do you have a couple of minutes?" I asked.

She nodded and I took the seat cattycorner to hers.

"Any word on the disaster?" she asked. "I still can't believe that happened. If *Key Zest* was a boat, she went from America's Cup yacht to derelict vessel in the blink of an eye."

She looked beaten down and sad, I noticed now, without the usual careful attention to make-up and dress. She was wearing yoga pants and sneakers with her hair in a messy ponytail, for heaven's sake. Not a whisper of makeup. I wished I had something uplifting to tell her, some kind of insider info from Nathan. But I didn't.

"Nothing definite yet that I've been told, although the authorities are holding a joint press conference at city hall at

1 p.m. I'll be there, of course." I paused and nibbled on my lip, deciding that since she was feeling vulnerable, direct was the best approach. "Is it possible that your ex—and I don't mean your husband—is in town? Would she do something crazy like sabotage a boat? Could she even have been on the boat with us?"

"Not a chance," my boss said, looking shocked at my questions. "I would have known if she was one of the guests. Why would you even think this way? I would've had her thrown off instantly. Weren't you and Danielle checking everyone in?"

"Yes, but we didn't know who she was. We didn't know she existed. She could have pretended to be another guest, and we wouldn't have known the difference. To be honest, the launch at the end was kind of chaotic, with a big rush of guests."

I let that last sentence linger as I examined my boss's face, reflecting a pained combination of regret and anger.

She glanced around the office as if checking for an eavesdropper or even a bug. "Let's take a walk." She stuffed her phone and her keys into her leather crossbody purse and started down the stairs, assuming that I would follow. I dropped my backpack on Danielle's desk and hurried after her. She marched down Southard Street at a brisk pace, all the way to the Truman Waterfront, with me dogtrotting behind in her wake. She turned right into the park, passing the former Coast Guard ship, and settled on a bench facing the water, under the mottled shade of a coconut palm tree.

I sat next to her, huffing from the pace she'd kept. She turned to face me. "About your question, to be very, very clear, there's no way she could have been a passenger on that boat. If I'd seen her name on the list, I would have crossed it off. Ditto if I'd actually *seen her*. She'd have been tossed off that boat before she could get a word of protest out. She was toxic, as I discovered early on. As I mentioned, she ambushed my husband to tell him about our relationship. She did that at the wedding reception—it was an unbearable scene."

"At the wedding reception?" I asked, feeling completely appalled. I wanted to hear the details, but I was afraid to ask. My mind was going crazy with the possibilities—did Athena rush up to the microphone as if she was going to make a toast? Cut in on the bride and groom's first dance? Slam the wedding cake into Damian's face? Or Palamina's? Thank goodness none of this drama had been documented in the *New York Times Style* article.

Palamina continued, "I've never been so embarrassed. To my mind, she was fully intending to blow the marriage up, before it even had a chance to get started. I told her before the wedding that I had made the biggest mistake of my life, getting entangled with her, and that we had absolutely no future. My father had her thrown out, and we carried on with the party. But the guests streamed out soon after that. My husband was absolutely livid, both with her and with me. My unfortunate confusion and her complete lack of appropriate boundaries had turned him into a block of quartz. I got a restraining order against her the following week. Obviously, the beginning of that marriage was also the end, thanks to her."

Now she studied my face, and I imagined that she was looking for understanding.

"A scene like that would be hard to survive," I said.

Palamina continued, "Perhaps you yourself have had a boyfriend whom you regret getting involved with. Perhaps you ended the relationship after realizing you'd made a horrible misjudgment, and the other person couldn't live with that. It's a terrifying feeling. I thought I was in control and found out I had none."

"It sounds possible that she could have come to town then, intent on doing you harm again. Maybe in the guise of luring you back into the relationship?" I asked.

"That question right there tells you how twisted her thinking is. She was very, very angry with me the last time we spoke." She pinched her lips together and gazed out over the water.

"When was this last conversation?" I asked.

"A few weeks ago," she said. Yikes! I felt shocked. "Why would she keep coming back when I'd rebuffed her so clearly? Who in her right mind would do that? I haven't seen her or heard from her since. Thank God. You're fishing in an empty pond."

I sat back, remembering what had happened with me and Chad several years ago. I was probably more on the stalker side of the equation, although nothing like the extreme territory that Palamina's girlfriend had staked out. But I could understand the sense of desperation, the sense of being left, feeling alone, and not knowing how to handle that. At least I was psychologically sturdy enough to allow friends and relatives to help me through that awful time, so I would grow into a person who could choose a healthy relationship and then thrive in it. Even as mad as I got with my husband's hair-trigger temper and occasional overprotectiveness, he was never crazy. Not even close.

"Again, is she capable of sabotaging a boat to get your attention? Or get even with you over your perceived slight?"

She shook her head vehemently.

"Do you have photos you could share, to be on the safe side?" I asked.

Palamina dropped her chin to her chest and covered her eyes with her hands. "OK, anything's possible with this woman," she mumbled. "But that scenario remains extremely unlikely. Photos are overkill, Hayley. Empty pond. Hard stop."

I felt a surge of annoyance. How did she not see it was important to share what she knew about this possibility? "I think you need to either tell me the dates and details of everything you can about that relationship and send me photos of her to forward to the authorities, or else you need to go to them yourself. She might be a reasonable suspect in the sinking of our boat, that's what I hear you saying. To get back at you."

She leaned back against the bench, her face crumpling. "I can't go to the police station. I just can't drag all that dirty laundry out in public again. Besides, there isn't enough evidence for them to be interested in her."

"OK, I'll ask you some questions then." I reached for my phone to take notes, feeling a spike of panic when realizing again that my usual pocket was empty, and I had yet to replace the lost phone. "Let's assume it's possible that this woman in is town right now—even if you think it's a long shot, we need to find her, to rule out whether she was involved with the disaster. Did you and she ever come to Key West, before Damian, I mean?"

"Early on," Palamina said. "She loved it here. We both did."

That was news to me, as I'd been under the impression that Palamina wasn't familiar with our island when she arrived from New York to take over the e-zine. "Can you imagine where she might be staying or with whom? What's her real name by the way?"

Palamina shook her head sharply and shot up from the bench. "I have to get back to the office, I have a meeting in ten minutes." She hurried through the park and back up Southard Street with me in her wake.

"Another question on another topic," I called after her as she dashed up the stairs. "Do you have the list of cooks who competed to have their recipes placed in *Key Zest* the week that my mother's mango upside down cake recipe won?"

As I came huffing up the stairs to the second-floor office, she turned to face me and whispered hoarsely, "She called herself Athena Flanagan, but she was born Eva. Yes, on the recipes, I'll send you those names."

Then Palamina greeted the man waiting in the vestibule, telling him she was running a few minutes late. "Do you have Athena's photo?" I asked her in a low voice as she headed to her office.

She paused for a minute at her door and punched a few things on her phone. Then I heard the whirring of the copy machine. She pointed down the hall at the copier, pasted a big phony smile on her face, beckoned to her visitor, and then disappeared into her office.

I grabbed the printouts from the machine and retired to my small space to study them. The woman in the first photograph with her arm thrown around Palamina's shoulders had a lovely narrow face with full cheeks and an impish look in her brown eyes. She was smiling in this photo, revealing the tiniest overlap of her incisors onto her two front teeth. I could imagine her either hating this, considering it a design flaw, or embracing it as offbeat and slightly sexy. A person who accepted herself as she was. Knowing Palamina, I was betting on the second. I could not picture her with someone who lacked self-esteem. They wouldn't last long with my boss. Though according to her, their

The Mango Murders

relationship *hadn't* lasted long, as Palamina ended up feeling ambushed and smothered.

I studied the second photo, just Eva aka Athena herself this time, standing at the kitchen sink with a vegetable peeler in one hand and a carrot in the other and a big grin on her face. She reminded me a tiny bit of my mother, though probably ten to fifteen years younger and quite a bit thinner and taller. If I'd had my phone, I would have taken a photo and texted it to Lorenzo to see if he could confirm that this was the woman he was doing the reading for the night of the disaster. If she had been sitting with him, she couldn't have been a passenger on our boat. Instead of texting, I'd have to make a point of zipping over to meet him at his home or visit him later at Mallory Square so I could show it to him.

Next, I looked at the file pages from the mango contest that Palamina had sent. The recipe contest had been a last-minute brainstorm, so we hadn't had much time to advertise or even decide how to judge submissions. In the beginning, I'd panicked about how slowly the recipes were coming in and begged my mother to submit something. She agreed but didn't tell me which recipe she'd chosen. My boss had collected the emails and sent them to us with names removed so that Danielle and I could choose the winner anonymously. I reviewed the names of the cooks and bakers who'd entered. Half a dozen people had submitted recipes and photos, including Nan Copley, who'd been a mainstay on the island over the last fifteen years. She was a caterer/chef like my mother, but with more traditional training and long-time business ties to Key West. There was no love lost between them as they competed for the same jobs over and over. This time, she'd offered a towering vanilla cake layered with mango puree, topped with a swirling cream cheese frosting patted with coconut flakes and decorated with fresh mango.

Honestly, her contribution was a stunner, and from the outside, might have looked like it should have been the winner. This was bad, as it made it appear that my mother could indeed have been the target of the someone's anger—attacked by a chef who felt she should have won the publicity. Maybe she felt that the honor was stolen out from under her through the time-honored petty crime of nepotism. Had her anger and disappointment led to her getting involved in the disaster in some twisted way? But why would she be on the boat if she was planning to set it on fire? I felt so confused about the possibilities. Surely there was a simpler explanation.

I skimmed over the batch of recipes again to remind myself why we had chosen my mother's upside-down cake. Several of the submissions were mango smoothie recipes, containing little more than mango and ice cream or mango and almond milk and ice. Danielle had nixed those as too plain, and a waste of calories. "If you are going to eat something fattening," she'd announced, "you should know that it's fattening, and that cost should be worth every single bite. Don't try to hide a fat bomb in fruit and pretend it's a health drink." She was right about that.

There were several salads, mostly involving chunks of mango and avocado that looked fine, but not exciting. Plus, mango chia seed pudding (good for you, but let's face it, homely and unappealing,) and a whole grilled and blackened fish sitting in a pool of mango and three kinds of peppers that we determined would be impossible to replicate and probably too spicy to eat. Looking back at what had unfolded since the contest ended last week, I still believed that the homey mango cake was the best choice of the lot. The vanilla coconut cake looked splendid, but it had too many complicated steps for the average home cook. We honestly hadn't realized the mango upside down cake came from my mother until after the contest was decided. Once the winner was announced, why didn't one of us recognize that outsiders might have seen this contest as hopelessly rigged from the beginning?

Reading about all that food was making my stomach growl with anticipation, even though I'd eaten more than my share of scones after the houseboat tour. I needed something more substantial, such as a big sandwich loaded with meat and cheese and fixings. I glanced at my wall clock. Lunch would have to wait as it was almost time for the press conference at City Hall.

I tucked the photo of my boss's ex-girlfriend and the print-outs of recipes and their authors into my backpack. Palamina called to me as I headed down the hall.

"This is in no way related to our event, but I know how dogged you are on the scent of a mystery. So . . ." She hesitated. "Eva comes to court me every year on what she claims is our anniversary. This week," she added, looking and sounding entirely glum. "She always writes me first, and I always tell her not to come. I tell her in the firmest way that it is over. This relationship is dead to me. It was dead before I got married, and if it hadn't been, her behavior at the wedding would have killed it."

"What does she say when you tell her not to come?"

Palamina sighed, looking down at her desk. "She comes anyway. She shows up at my place, and I tell her to go away." She glanced back at me. "That's it, end of story. You can stop digging."

"In other words, she could have snuck onto the *Pilar Too*."

"Oh, for god's sake, she could have tried, but I would have noticed and repelled her instantly." She was angry now, and I wasn't going to get another word from her.

"Thanks for telling me. I'm off to the press conference and will keep you posted."

* * *

Our beautiful white stone City Hall had served as a Key West school for many years before it was completely renovated for town business. The wide steps sweeping down from the entrance to a wider sidewalk and gathering place made the perfect backdrop for official press conferences. The building was located conveniently on White Street, not far from the White Street pier that extended into the Atlantic and served as a hub for tourists, fishermen, and dogwalkers.

I could see from the crowd that had already gathered around the steps and on the sidewalk that I was almost late. There was a podium with microphone set up at the top of the stairs and behind that, several law enforcement officers were conferring. Nathan was there, of course, along with the police chief, several deputies from the Sheriff's Office, and several other officers wearing uniforms from the Coast Guard and the Fish and Wildlife Commission. Even if I hadn't known this already, I would have to assume this press conference was a big deal. Several local journalists, in addition to staff from a Miami television station, waited off to the side of the podium. Nathan stepped forward, a host of bright lights snapped on, and members of the press and some unofficial citizens held out their microphones and cell phones.

The Mango Murders

"Good afternoon," said my husband. "I am deputy chief Nathan Bransford from the Key West Police Department. As you know, four days ago a commercial vessel, the *Pilar Too*, suffered an incident resulting in an explosion, multiple injuries, and destruction of property. We were assisted in the rescue by the Coast Guard, the Fish and Wildlife Commission, the Fire Department, the Sheriff's Office, and various good Samaritans who were in the area at the time. As you can imagine, we are taking this incident very, very seriously." He looked around at the gathered crowd, glowering fiercely.

"With our partners' assistance, we are in the process of investigating the circumstances fully. Once we identify the perpetrator or perpetrators, we will take the appropriate action," he added. "We have always pledged and strived to keep this community informed of significant events that occur in this town—good or bad. This one is bad."

So far, he was reporting nothing new. I wiggled a little closer, hoping to read the expression in his eyes that might tell me what he wasn't telling us. He looked a bit trapped, and maybe defensive, too. He hated showing weakness in public, weakness such as the fact that authorities seemed to be flummoxed.

"We are in the process of interviewing witnesses and compiling psychological composites of possible perpetrators."

What did that even mean?

Nathan continued, beads of sweat popping out on his forehead. Yes, it was a warm and sticky day, but he was also nervous. "If members of the community have information that might help us solve the mystery of what occurred on the *Pilar Too*, we ask you to come forward as soon as possible."

People in the audience began to pepper him with questions.

"We've heard that a woman died in the accident, what can you tell us about this?"

Another said, "What are you doing to follow up? Even though you had dozens of professionals on the scene, we are getting spotty information about root causes. This does not give us confidence about going about our business."

Someone else shouted: "Many of us have boats. How do we know we are going to be safe? How can we assure our customers that they will be safe on our vessels?"

"Yes, we understand that people are worried," Nathan said. "We appreciate your concerns and are working hard to answer these questions." He gestured at the group behind him and then stepped back to confer with Chief Brandenburg. After a moment, he returned to the microphone. "I can confirm that there was one casualty, and we do have a tentative identification. We will hold that name pending notification of next of kin."

He cracked what I'm certain was meant to be a reassuring smile, but it looked strained to my eye.

"Now we'd like to recognize several citizens who were instrumental in rescuing the passengers from the *Pilar Too*." He read off the names of Becky from the Sunset Key launch boat, and the owners of two other small crafts whose names I didn't recognize. "Also, my wife, Hayley Snow, showed strength and calm under pressure, aiding two citizens who might otherwise have drowned. We will be awarding certificates of merit to each of these people at the next city commission meeting but wanted to express our gratitude today as well."

The crowd clapped and cheered, and I felt a rush of blood to my face. It was nice to be recognized but also weird as heck.

The Mango Murders

Especially given the fact that the entire case was still a disaster. A tall man behind me gave what felt like a purposeful shove, and I whipped around to give him a piece of my mind. Ulp. It was my ex, Chad Lutz. Weird upon weird. It was as if I'd conjured up Chad just by thinking about him earlier.

"Sorry," he said, "someone pushed me, and I lost my balance." Slowly his face changed from apologetic to uncomfortable as he recognized me, probably feeling as awkward as I was to meet up so closely. "I was on my way back from lunch, and I saw the crowd," he said. "They've got a rat's nest on their hands, don't they? Congratulations on your citation. Not surprised to see you here in the thick of the latest crime debacle, Miss Nosey Pants."

"That's Mrs. Nosey Pants to you," I snapped back, and after a momentary stare down, we both burst out laughing. I'd spent so much time recovering from and then resenting his bad boyfriend dumping behavior that I'd forgotten his sense of humor.

"I don't suppose you've heard anything about the boat incident from any of your shady clients?" I asked.

He reared back, looking outraged, but then started to laugh again when he realized I was tweaking him. "No one's told me anything, but then they don't. They share with Deena." His secretary. At least he understood his limits as a people person, and he'd been smart enough to hire my friend and pay her well.

Chad squinted. "I suppose you've already got the whole thing figured out and don't need me to tell you that our newly installed mayor was a major partner in the *Pilar Too*?"

Before I could press him for more details, I spotted Nathan approaching, looking stiff and grim. Had these two met? I couldn't think how, and I didn't want to be the one to introduce them. With an unpleasant jolt, I remembered they'd had difficult encounters when Chad's girlfriend was poisoned some years back, and I was one of the prime suspects. I couldn't bear the idea of getting wedged in between them, but I couldn't see a way to get out of the situation other than grabbing Nathan's hand to drag him away. That wouldn't work anyway. He was not the kind of man to dodge pain—it was in his police officer's DNA to charge right at it. But nor was he the kind of guy to hash through ancient emotional trauma, not privately and certainly not in public.

Nathan thrust his hand out and pumped Chad's, in a kind of macho police officer way that said without saying, "She's mine now, and I could take you with one hand behind your back." I was horrified.

"I'm Nathan Bransford, Hayley's husband. Sorry that you were dumb enough to let her go, but on the other hand, thanks for that, as it worked out well for me." He finally let go of Chad's hand, leaving Chad looking at it as if Nathan might have broken some digits. I gawped at my husband, who put his arm around me and pulled me tight, like they were hungry dogs, and I was a piece of meat Chad was trying to steal.

"Nice to meet you too," said Chad, with a wavery grin. He turned on his heel to retreat from us, for which I couldn't blame him one bit.

"What was that all about?" I asked my husband through gritted teeth.

"I don't like that guy, and I don't like him sniffing around like you're a dog in heat."

"A dog in heat?" My brain rolled through a dozen responses, from "are you kidding?" to "get a grip." But I thought of what my mother would have said—he's under a lot of stress in his job and with his parents in town and with us pulling dangerous stunts. This was his first major press conference in his role as Deputy Chief, and it wasn't exactly a raging success. Seeing Chad would have pushed his most tender buttons. I cupped his adorably dimpled chin in my hand and told him he had nothing to worry about. Then I added: "You know I'm grateful that he ended the relationship. It turned out to be more of a mercy killing than a loss—once I got used to the idea of living in paradise alone."

He laughed, but I saw him searching the crowd, for what? The perpetrator of the explosion who might have come to the press conference to learn how much the cops knew?

"Do you really have no idea who was behind the disaster?" I asked. "That's what it sounded like."

"No, nothing confirmed."

I leaned in close to him. "Could you give me a heads up on the ID of the victim? I swear I'll keep it to myself."

He heaved a heavy sigh. "We think it's Nan Copley."

"Good gravy," I said. "I swear she was not on the guest list." I had just finished looking at the amazing cake recipe she'd submitted to the *Key Zest* contest. "Did someone report her missing? Is that how you knew?"

He'd begun to look annoyed. "Look Hayley, I'll tell you more when I can. But yes, we had a report from her office manager."

Then Nathan's phone went off indicating a text had come in. He slid it out of his pocket. His expression changed from annoyed to exasperated.

"It's my mother. She wants you to meet her and your stepmother at Frenchie's for a late lunch. They've got a table and are about to order."

Chapter Sixteen

As for the corn, well, even off-season corn is pretty tasty mixed with oil and vinegar, and makes a good combo with the shell beans. It's a nice dish, worth interrupting the murders for.

—Adam Gopnik, "What's the Point of Food in Fiction?" *The New Yorker*, April 2007

I could think of nothing other than Nan Copley on the way to Frenchie's. How tragic for her to be trapped in the hold when the explosion occurred. Was the blast meant specifically for her? Or was that just bad luck? Why was she on the boat if she hadn't been invited to the party? Then I remembered again the gorgeous vanilla mango cake that she'd submitted to our contest, but we had not chosen. I could literally feel my heart sinking. As uncomfortable as it made me—very!—I needed to find out if there was a specific connection between this woman and my mother's business. Then slowly tease out the conflict about the published recipe. I parked my scooter and hurried toward the little restaurant, nearly wiping out a woman on my way.

It was Martha Hubbard, carrying a white bag that probably held pastry. She held it up. "Even a chef needs a day off from time to time. You were lost in thought . . ."

"I'm coming from the press conference. They've identified the victim, though they aren't sharing the name yet."

"Nan Copley," she said, with a quick nod.

Yikes, word—even unspoken word—traveled fast in this town. "Did you know her well?"

"You know everybody knows everybody." She paused. "How do I put this? She wasn't beloved, she was ruthless. Do you know Chef Richard from Lola's?"

I nodded. "We had an excellent meal there a couple of nights ago."

"He opened that place because she essentially forced his first restaurant out of the space he'd designed and rebuilt to his specifications. He was renting her space and learned this lesson the hard way: if you don't own it, don't put money into it that you don't mind losing."

"Yikes. He's probably worried about being fingered as a suspect, even if blowing up a boat he was a passenger on seems ridiculous." I remembered that he'd been distraught after getting a phone call while we were watching him cook. Could he have known the victim's identity that early? How would that happen? Maybe those feelings didn't have so much to do with the woman's death as they did the possibility that he might be implicated in the disaster.

I gave Martha a quick hug and hurried on to my lunch date.

Frenchie's was a small casual breakfast and lunch restaurant and bakery a few blocks from the Southernmost Point. The owners had moved from Paris to Key West in 2011, bringing

The Mango Murders

their baking expertise and a French flair to their place. My stepmother and mother-in-law were ensconced at a round table in the front window with a full view of the long counter filled with pastries. My mouth began to water the instant I stepped inside.

Sliding into the remaining chair, I said, "Pastry porn, perfect. I didn't even realize how hungry I am! That's not quite true—I was dreaming of a big sandwich but didn't have time to eat before the press conference." I looked from one to the other and grinned. "If only my mother was here, we'd have a perfect trifecta of the mother figures in my life."

Allison smiled. "Of course we asked her, but she's busy overseeing Gloria's next event. Apparently, tonight's party at the Key West Woman's Club is the biggest one yet. You people went all out for her celebration—I know she feels the love." She brushed a strand of hair off my forehead. "Hope you don't mind me saying you look a little peaked."

Just the mention of looking peaked made me realize how tired I was feeling. But I grinned again because I did not want to appear unenthusiastic about Miss Gloria's birthday arrangements as they were reaching their crescendo. "I'm beginning to think we might have over-planned just the tiniest little bit." I held my thumb and forefinger up with a sliver of light between them. "Though she's well worth it, don't get me wrong."

The waitress arrived to deliver Helen and Allison's lunch, and I ordered a tuna sandwich with olive oil dressing, salad, tomato, red onions, olives, anchovies, and hard-boiled egg on a croissant. Plus, a cappuccino and a side of potato salad. "I'll probably order dessert a little later." I paused, then held up a finger. "Why not put the order in now and save you a trip? I'd love a chocolate croissant with a double espresso for dessert."

"This girl can eat," said Allison to Helen with admiration. "You keep at it now, Hayley, and enjoy the ride, because once you turn 50, all those calories get applied directly to your waist and hips." She patted her own waistline, which was comfortably plump.

"Forget that. You look amazing." I forked up a well-browned potato from her plate and saluted. "Until then."

"I bet you've had a busy day," Allison said. "I had a massage, which was divine." But she sounded wistful, as if she'd like to be involved with something more fulfilling than pure self-indulgence.

"Miss Gloria's family is exhausting. We did the houseboat tour, which most people would love—not those women!" The waitress delivered my sandwich, and I took a big bite, chewed, and swallowed. "I do have some interesting news from my boss, Palamina, but not too much from the authorities."

"Where do we stand?" Helen asked, pushing her own plate away. The bruising around the cut on her forehead had reached the ugly yellowing stage, set off by the white tape covering the stitches.

I explained that I hadn't learned a lot from the press conference, other than the fact that the police had confirmed a death but appeared to be thrashing around for leads to explain the explosion without much success. "Nathan asked the public to come forward with tips. There are quite a few law enforcement agencies working on the incident," I said, my eyebrows peaking. I tried to keep annoyance from seeping into my voice. "Though he's not that eager for *our* input. I'm cutting him some slack because he had a lot of people harassing him." I skipped the part about our little interaction with Chad, because I didn't want to share every neurotic life twitch with Nathan's mother. "I did hear that the current mayor was an investor in the boat that went down."

"Interesting, though I can't imagine he'd want to blow up a boat on which he was a passenger. Seems very risky," said Helen.

"Unless it wasn't really meant to blow up," said Allison. "Maybe it went further than what was intended."

"I agree we're really nowhere," said Helen. She poked at her rejected salad, looking discouraged.

"Except..." Then I pulled the photocopy of Palamina's stalker-girlfriend from my backpack. "This woman, who sounds disturbed, might be lurking on the island, looking to damage Palamina's credibility. The sailing trip could have been the perfect opportunity." I explained how she'd apparently ruined my boss's marriage and seemed unable to hear the word *no* as final. "She comes down here every year on the anniversary of the date they started seeing each other, which is this week. Even though Palamina tells her not to bother."

Allison smiled. "Either she's a grand romantic, or—"

"A stalker," said Helen, frowning. "Was she an invited guest?"

"Absolutely not, she would have snuck on." I showed them the photos that my boss had shared. "At some point, I'm going to show this to Lorenzo to see if he recognizes her from Mallory Square. I don't *think* she could have been his client. Although that woman was upset about her relationship."

"Aren't we all at some point?" Helen mused.

"My mother and Sam haven't seen it yet either. They might recognize her if she'd been a stowaway."

"Was this ex-girlfriend at all nautical?" Allison asked. "Meaning, would she have the know-how to sabotage a boat? Was she that angry with Palamina?"

"No idea," I said, feeling deflated. "Here's another thread." I showed them the list of recipes that had been entered in the contest the week before our boating event. "My mother's cake was chosen over the other entries, even though we really did judge them blindly. Though I suppose it's possible that my cooking DNA recognized hers at some deeper level."

"Cooking DNA? Never heard of it. That would be motive for an attempted mass murder?" Helen asked, every muscle in her face a question mark.

It did sound ridiculous, put that way. Though I suspected my mother-in-law might be lacking cooking DNA altogether—I'd never experienced her cooking anything. Which wasn't a fair observation, because I'd yet to visit her home. However, she wasn't the kind of guest who asked what was for dinner and how she could help.

"I admit it sounds odd, but what else explains our choice? One of the submissions was a spectacular three-layer vanilla and coconut cake with a mango puree filling. It was the fanciest recipe and—it turns out that it came from the woman whom they possibly found dead in the hold of the *Pilar Too*. Though Nathan refused to confirm her identity at the press conference, he told me in confidence. Her name is Nan Copley. It's already the scuttlebutt in town, though how they found out is beyond me."

"Oh my gosh," said Allison, leaning forward with wide eyes. "You're saying the cake and the death are connected? Why was this person in the hold to begin with? Was she trying to target your mother?"

"How did they identify the dead woman? What else do you know about her?" Helen asked.

The Mango Murders

I explained that I had no idea about the forensic process. Then I added what Martha had told me about Chef Richard's experience. "Nan Copley was a chef/caterer who pretty much stole his space after he'd paid to have it renovated to his specifications."

"Stole it in what way?" asked Helen.

"He made the mistake of renovating her rental space with his own funds," I explained. "And then she took it back without reimbursing him a cent. By the way, he was also on the boat."

"So you're proposing that our victim blew up the boat because of grudges she held against your mother and another local chef. However, she did a lousy job and ended up blowing up herself as well." Helen wrinkled her nose. "I feel this is desperation speaking, reaching out its boney fingers at you."

My hackles bristled, but Allison stepped in to smooth the waters.

"I agree that it sounds like a stretch, but let's not dismiss any ideas too quickly. Were there photos taken at the party?" my stepmother asked. "Maybe you'd see something in one of them that could explain what happened. One of those women or even someone else acting in a suspicious manner that you didn't notice at the time because you were so busy?"

Helen looked at her with interest, as if this was the first time she really noticed Allison was there. Which was probably unfair of me because they must have been talking about something before I arrived, but still . . .

"We all had iPhone cameras and we were supposed to snap candids in between serving snacks and drinks," I said. "I don't remember taking a single one. Luckily, we'd also hired an official photographer. However, all that footage was lost at the bottom of the bay along with our phones and his camera. I still haven't had time to get my cell phone replaced."

Nathan's mother was studying my face. "Didn't you say something about a drone at that wedding scheduled for the same night as your event? I wonder if they accidentally got something useful to us?"

That felt right and true and ultimately could hold the key to the whole mystery.

"How do we find out?" asked my stepmother.

The waitress arrived with my dessert. I dug right in, stopping long enough to say: "Try googling the website Drone and Photo. Alex Press does a lot of real estate photography, but I think he works on local events on the side. But if he was hired to do a wedding, he probably won't share the footage with us. I know from helping cater big events for anxious brides that they can be super protective of their photos."

"Watch me work." Helen quickly tapped that information into her phone, came up with a number, and dialed. When a man answered, she explained in her most no-nonsense voice that she was the mother-in-law of the bride he photographed several days earlier. "Now she absolutely refuses to share the link for the drone video with me, even though my husband and I paid for your services by writing her a big fat check." Her voice shifted to a sweet wheedle. "If you could kindly send me the link to that footage, it will save a lot of family drama, including possibly an early divorce. That's if I could ever talk sense into my son."

I heard the rumblings of the man replying.

"Yes, I understand that she specifically asked that it be sent to her and her alone, but I only want to look it over. I swear on the head of my not-yet-born first grandchild that I won't put one frame up on Facebook or Insta. You wouldn't catch me dead on TikTok." They had more of a back and forth, with Helen growing more animated and adamant.

"Yes, thank you so very much," she said. "Text the link to me at this number. I will not share anything. The police will contact you if they need to." She instantly realized she'd made a faux pas. "The marriage and wedding police, I mean." She forced out a peal of laughter.

An alert came instantly to her phone, and I could picture the photographer deciding to do whatever was necessary—quickly—to finish with her.

"You are astonishing," I said, wondering to myself whether I should believe anything she said in the future. She fibbed so easily.

She ducked her head. "Making up stories to get people talking is one of my superpowers."

While I cleaned my lunch plate down to the slick white finish and polished off Allison's uneaten potatoes, the women spent a few minutes studying the footage from the link that Alex had sent. As we'd hoped, though the drone was focused on the wedding tents right in front of Bistro 245, Mallory Square was close enough that he also filmed the harbor. We watched as the *Pilar Too* came into view from around the point at Sunset Key. It felt so creepy to see the progress of the boat I'd been a passenger on, knowing that disaster was coming.

I peered at the tiny screen, squinting for the splash that a few witnesses had mentioned before the flames and smoked began to spiral from the boat. So far, the details were not as revealing as I'd hoped. At that point, the video footage swerved back to the wedding venue, where the bride and groom danced their way to the party tent with moves that appeared tightly choreographed.

"Can you send that to my email?" I asked Helen. "I can't see that it tells us anything new, but I can make the picture much larger on my computer screen when I get home."

With a few taps on her phone, she sent it off. She paused, rubbing her chin. "Should I send it to Nathan?"

"That could save us another scolding," I said, grinning. "You might want to gloss over how you got it but pinkie-swear him not to share."

She spent another minute tapping. "I'll see if Janet has anything else that might be useful."

Helen texted my mother to ask whether she had replaced her phone and been able to retrieve any of the event photographs from her cloud. While waiting for a response, she set the phone on the table and picked at the remainder of the chocolate croissant that I had insisted on ordering for the three of us to share but so far eaten almost entirely by myself. I sipped my double espresso, hoping for a big jolt of energy. We watched the dots on the message screen until a set of photographs appeared.

"I didn't take many because I was so busy getting the food out," my mom said. "But these came from early on when Sam was able to snap a few shots of our guests arriving. I've sent them to Hayley's address as well."

A second text came in. Helen read it and showed me the screen.

"Is Hayley with you? Please let her know she has an appointment with the physical therapist, Heather Harvey, tomorrow to work on her neck—3 p.m. on the fourth floor of the BBT building. Also, please tell her that she needs to go to the phone store!

I don't feel right, not being able to reach her L O L." After that she'd added several hysterically laughing emojis to show that she was not really a desperate mother, only concerned.

"I guess I'm everybody's gopher at this point," said Helen with a lopsided smile on her face. "She's here. I'll tell her," she dictated into her phone, then sent the message off.

"Let's take a look."

She scrolled quickly through the dozen photographs that my mother had attached. Most were groups of two or three people, dressed in Key West cocktail attire, generally sprightly tropical but not formal. I pointed out the ones that I knew. In the end, that was most of the guest list—either I knew them personally or had seen them on social media or in the newspapers. I recognized the dark-haired woman I'd helped rescue after we'd been dumped into the water. In the photo, she was carefully made up, wearing a sparkly top, flashing a dazzling smile. So very different from the way she'd looked soaking wet.

"That's Amanda. She co-owns Wicked Lick Ice Cream with her husband, John. I can't say what she might have seen, but I know she'd talk to me if I stopped by their shop. She was very grateful that I helped her when she thought she was drowning."

I tapped on another photo that had captured local artist and sculptor John Martini chatting with a well-known local painter, Peter Vey. Behind them stood a tall woman with a big smile and wheat-colored hair. The photo had been taken at a distance so the background was blurry, including her face, and she was angled away from them, toward the sea. But maybe . . .

"I don't recognize this woman." I pulled out the photos that Palamina had sent me of her former girlfriend, Eva aka Athena, so I could compare the two. "I'm thinking it might be her." I tapped on the paper.

My stepmother reached across the table to look at Helen's phone and the photocopy. "I don't know," she said, gesturing at Helen's phone, "the nose is different. Smaller. And this lady's eyes aren't droopy like that other photo of Eva."

I peered at the screen again, not seeing exactly what she was seeing. It was too hard to make out the details in the candid shot. "Maybe she had plastic surgery in the process of attempting to win back Palamina."

That sounded so silly and preposterous. I heaved a discouraged sigh, suddenly limp with exhaustion. "I confess to feeling stumped. Maybe there are some other people in the Key West food world I could interview. I wish I'd gotten more definite leads from the former mayor. If we could think of someone who knows her well, maybe they'd get more out of her than I did. Or we could go back to the harbor and try to talk with Captain Roche. Or his next boat-slip neighbor. Later, when I'm home, I'll try to brainstorm foodies with a grudge." I cackled, thinking that title might make a good reality TV series or at least an Instagram reel.

Helen stared at me. "You're all over the place with ideas. Some of them might lead us somewhere, others sound ludicrous." She straightened, as if winding up for a lecture. "You need to organize your thoughts, put people in order of who's most likely to have done something so extreme. And why. If you think the perpetrator was the captain we talked to at the harbor, for example, has this other fellow, Roche, stolen his business more than once? It's hard to imagine that losing one gig like your sunset cruise would create so much animosity. If you think it's related to the mayor, what unpopular moves did she champion? Also, if signs now point to the new mayor having an interest in the damaged boat, how does that play into a possible motive? Could he have been after an insurance payout? If so, it stinks of financial desperation." She wrinkled her nose again, as if smelling something rotten. "Food grudges? I can't see it."

She wasn't wrong about any of that, but I still felt like a balloon stabbed with a fork—and that must have shown. Allison put her hand on mine and grimaced in Helen's direction, her blue eyes flashing icy. "I wonder if you have any idea how harsh you sound? Hayley is whip smart and she's trying super hard to make sense of a very confusing case that was also personally traumatic. I can't see why you'd want to tear her down." She paused to glance at me and squeezed my hand. "Maybe that's not your intention, but that's the way you come across."

Helen pressed her lips together but didn't respond other than giving the briefest nod. I squeezed Allison's hand back to show her I was grateful that she'd stuck up for me. Because I did feel blindsided by my mother-in-law's words. I knew this about her: she got sharp and sometimes lashed out when feeling stressed. Nathan had picked up the same trait, and I didn't like it in either of them, even though I understood it and told myself I should try to overlook it. Or in Nathan's case, maybe mention how I was feeling, hoping he'd absorb that information for next time. Then let it go. I sure wasn't going to correct my mother-in-law.

"You're right, I'm sorry," Helen said, reaching out to pat my other hand. "This situation feels very personal, doesn't it? We've both been touched by it." Now her hand hovered over the bandage on her forehead. She acted so tough, but that motorcycle had to have frightened her.

"OK, if I can set my preconceptions aside"—she smiled at me—"let's talk food. You mentioned that your mother's recipe ran in your magazine, and you also report that your mother was catering this event. It still seems unlikely to me that she was a target—I mean really, a caterer?" she added in a softer voice, with a glance at Allison. "I'm willing to consider the possibility though. Maybe you should tell us more about what's happened in Janet's career since she arrived on the island. How did things go when she first came down to Key West and how have things unfolded since?"

I thought about what to say, what might turn out to be useful. I didn't want to blather aimlessly for fear Helen would lose her patience and scold me again. "In the beginning, I wasn't so thrilled with her decision. Who needs their mother nudging her way into their new life?"

"I can understand that," Allison said. "You were claiming new territory. A place and friends that belonged only to you, not your family. Plus, you were floundering a little and who needs their mother witnessing that?" She smiled and clasped my hand. "You've grown so much down here. We're very proud of you."

Helen was obviously impatient but trying to keep that in check. "But she came whether you were in favor or not. Then what?"

"She was struggling at first, she was lost. You may remember that she'd driven her first catering business into the ground because she spent too much for the prices she was charging. This is not a secret, and it wasn't all bad. She wanted to cook with only the best ingredients, but then those products cost more than she earned. But gradually she got her footing and figured

The Mango Murders

out how to make things taste amazing for a reasonable price. Word-of-mouth helped spread how excellent her cooking is. Sam has been a big asset because not only can he cook, he understands business."

"Where do things stand now?" Helen asked.

"She's a preferred vendor," I said. "There's a lot of competition in this town because many people host weddings and fundraising galas and other parties down here. I think her business really started to take off when she landed the Cuban American event at the Truman Little White House a couple years back. That was a surprise to a lot of people. She was new and not known for cooking Cuban dishes, but she's very personable and lovely and reasonable. Plus, she hired Cuban American workers to help with that weekend, so she didn't serve anything inauthentic, and at the same time, she supported their community. She has a very good way with people, including impossible brides. As I said, she has her super-secret weapon and that is Sam. He loves being her sous chef, and he keeps her grounded. Plus, he's adorable and charming and that helps when they are serving the food or dealing with anxious brides."

"I'm not hearing murder motives," Helen said, clicking her short nails on the table. "I'm hearing a success story, gradual enough that most observers and competitors would understand and accept it as well-deserved."

"You're probably right," I said. "It makes more sense to focus on understanding the *Pilar Too* captain's business. If that doesn't pan out, it's probably something political. Maybe it was even a big mistake, and someone shuffled that propane onto my mother's cart and took it downstairs in the dumbwaiter with no intention to sabotage anything." Both mother figures looked skeptical.

"You're right," I said, sighing heavily. "Much as I hate to think this, someone planned it." After I finished hoovering up the last chocolate crumb, Helen and Allison urged me to go home and get some rest before tonight's party.

"You look a little peaked, even after a hearty lunch. This week has been a lot and it's not over yet," said Allison. "Plus, you need to get a new phone."

"Do you mind if I borrow these photos?" Helen asked. I nodded. "How about we zip over to the waterfront and interview that captain about his next-door boat neighbor on our way home?" she asked Allison.

The harbor wasn't on their way home, but I could see Allison was excited to be in on some action.

"Be careful out there," I told them. "Someone on this island is feeling desperate. Desperate enough to sabotage a boatload of passengers, and possibly mow you down." I looked directly at my mother-in-law. "Let's all be smart and vigilant."

Allison pulled me into a quick hug. "We will, and you do the same."

Chapter Seventeen

"Besides, if the conference sponsors aren't happy," Sigrid said, plunging her knife into the sandwich so the yoke flowed like yellow lava over the ham onto the crunchy stalks of potato, "Dustin's out of a job."
—Lucy Burdette, *Death in Four Courses*

While I waited to pay the check that I'd insisted I needed to cover for professional reasons, a horde of questions about this case scrolled through my mind. For instance, why in the world would someone drop off the boat and swim to shore while the party was in full swing? That only made sense if the person was doing something dodgy to begin with. Such as unscrew the top to the propane tank that wasn't supposed to be there so it would blow up later. Who would do that? How could they guarantee it would go as they'd planned? It was both a vicious plan and not failsafe. Another possibility was Palamina's ex, but really that seemed silly, at least after discussing it with Allison and Helen.

As tired as I was, I didn't feel quite ready to go home. We needed answers. First, I'd swing by John Martini's studio. He was known for being plainspoken, and he was well connected in town. He might have heard rumors about a possible perpetrator. Maybe he could identify the woman in the photo who came in behind him and Peter. My mind wasn't completely ready to give up on the possibility that it could have been Eva.

From John's studio, it would be easy to dip into the Wicked Lick for a cup of ice cream. Not that I was the least bit hungry after my lunch feast, but I only needed to buy one small cup and taste judiciously. Either Amanda or her husband might have noticed some crucial detail before we were dumped into the harbor. I could also jumpstart research on a round-up review of ice cream shops on the island while I was visiting their shop.

Martini's studio was located on Emma Street in the Bahama Village section of Key West, formerly a movie theatre in a neighborhood named for its Black Bahamian residents. I tapped on the door of the cement building painted in bright blue with bright green trim. *Terminal Art Works* the sign on the wall proclaimed. Since the door was cracked open, and no one had answered my polite knock, I stepped inside.

The interior was a remarkable space, another world from what waited outside. Soaring two stories high, the wooden roof was supported by steel beams. Some of the walls were partially tiled in pale blue with brown designs, and the remainder were plain concrete, like the floor. The entire cavernous space inside was populated with larger-than-life steel figures, ranging from whimsical to grotesque and Picasso-like. Tiny bodies with big heads had birds perched on them. They were painted in red and yellow and scattered around the studio. Other body parts constructed of rusty steel waited for assembly.

The Mango Murders

The place was downright freaky. I had to wonder what was going on in the mind of the artist when he designed this work. Toward the far end of the studio, rustic tables held more steel pieces waiting to be welded together, plus large saws and other industrial equipment. The wall on this side was papered with old photographs, newspaper clippings, and a diploma declaring Martini to be an honorary Conch aka Key West native. In this town, that was not an honor that was easily won.

"Hello?" I called out timidly. No answer. I moved a little further into the studio looking for the artist. In the far back of the space, I found a drafting table with sketches and a rustic lamp, and behind that, a window that opened out to a messy courtyard. Everywhere I looked, the corners and sides of this workspace were crammed with interesting objects. I almost tripped over a piece of furniture that looked as though it was part of a very old couch, covered in vinyl, the seat torn open to expose straw stuffing. In front of that, I saw a pair of work boots and a finished painting. Behind that, a red scooter decorated with *Safer Cleaner Ships* and *One Human Family* stickers.

"Hello?" I called again. I nearly jumped out of my skin when I heard a voice right behind me.

"Can I help you?" It was John Martini, a small man with a scruffy beard, dressed in faded jeans and a wool beanie hat. He didn't look pleased.

"I'm so sorry to interrupt." I introduced myself and explained that I was looking into the explosion off Mallory Square and that I knew he had been one of our esteemed guests. "I'm so sorry about the way it turned out and hope you haven't suffered any untoward effects." He shook his head, lips pressed together as though he had nothing to add, so I barreled on. "I'm curious about why you accepted the invitation?"

"Really?" he asked, as if wondering what kind of an odd duck interrupted his work zone with a silly question. "I went to that event because Palamina Wells asked me to. She promised that your e-zine would be focusing more in the coming year on saving our island from greedy developers and crooked politicians, than reporting fluffy stories about omelets and flamingoes. She wanted my help in shaping that message." He laughed and gestured at the articles on the wall related to saving our paradise from getting overrun by cruise ships and even more building permits. "I suppose I am known for speaking bluntly to the press."

"I think you are," I said with a grin. "I was looking over some of the photos taken before the explosion and noticed that you came in with Peter Vey and a tall woman with blonde hair with pretty reddish highlights."

He frowned, leaning against a bright blue metal figure with a small red bird perched on his head. "Yes, Peter and I boarded together. Neither of us came with a date so I can't speak to the blonde woman." He shifted, beginning to look impatient. "Unless you have a photo?"

"I have one at home and can text it to you later," I said, remembering that I'd given my photocopies to Helen. "Meanwhile, you know a lot of people in this town. Have you heard anything about who caused the boat disaster?"

"Nobody's filled me in on that," he said. "Are you connected with the authorities working on this?"

"If you count being married to the deputy chief of the Police Department as a connection, I suppose I am." I snickered. "But

I'm more connected because A, I was on that boat and more people could have died or been seriously injured. And B, it ruined two important goals: the boost we hoped to attain for our magazine and extra publicity my mother dreamed of for her catering business. Everything was blown up and washed away in that scary half hour." I snapped my fingers. "All our hopes along with that captain's livelihood, flushed away. That's not even mentioning the poor woman who perished in the hold. I've heard people talk about this, saying it was a blessing only one person died. But I'm sure she has friends and relatives who will grieve deeply. What kind of blessing is that?"

He was squinting at me now as though I'd gone off the rails. I probably had. Maybe it hadn't been such a great idea to slurp down a cappuccino followed by a double espresso. I was flat out wired.

"One last question," I said. "Did you notice anyone dropping off the boat before the explosion?"

He rubbed the whiskers on his chin. "Hmm, I saw plenty of people drop off and dive off and get thrown off right after the explosion. But I don't remember anyone before that."

I felt disappointed and discouraged. Whatever I'd imagined he'd have seen or heard because he was an artist who noticed things in his environment, either he hadn't, or he wasn't sharing it with me. "Would you let me know if you hear of something related to the case?" I asked, handing him a business card. "Or if you remember who the woman in the photo is?"

I took Angela Street to Whitehead and across, and parked a block from the ice cream shop, crossing fingers that one of the owners would be working. As I approached, I saw Amanda behind the counter scooping what looked like chocolate ice cream for a child. Smiling and laughing as she added sprinkles and gummies, she looked nothing like the desperate woman I'd helped to rescue.

I waited until she'd rung up her customers and they'd left the shop. She flashed me an automatic "greet the customer" smile.

"I'd love a small cup of the cold-brewed Cuban coffee ice cream. But I also wanted to see how you're feeling," I said. "That water adventure was quite a shock."

Her hand flew to her lips and her face paled. "Oh my gosh, Hayley, I didn't recognize you. I meant to call you and thank you, but I still don't have a phone. I acted like such a dope in the water, but I can't swim, and I panicked."

I shrugged. "No worries at all. I was glad to be in the right place at the right time. As for the phone, that makes two of us. I swear I'm going to the T-Mobile store tomorrow and get myself straightened out. The *Pilar Too* business aside, it's been a crazy, crazy week."

"The ice cream is totally on me," she said, holding up the cup she'd just scooped, which did not look small. "It goes really well with dark chocolate sauce."

"Sold," I said. She spooned a big helping of glistening chocolate on top of the ice cream. "Aside from checking in with you, I stopped by because I'm helping to sort out what happened."

She handed the ice cream across the counter. "There are lots of rumors flying," she said, her eyes wide. "From flying saucers to someone trying to take out the whole Chamber of Commerce in one fell swoop."

"A case of extreme government hostility?" I asked, grinning just a little though it wasn't really funny. "Since not all of them were invited, it's hard to see that working." I pointed at my cup with the plastic spoon. "This is amazing."

She nodded her thanks. "We freeze it with liquid nitrogen, which works so quickly we don't have to store the ice cream long. That means everything tastes fresh."

I leaned one elbow on the glass counter. "I went to the press conference at City Hall earlier, and the authorities still seem perplexed. Since you and your husband were right there on the scene, I imagine the police have already talked to you. But sometimes a person remembers more as the shock of the immediate situation wears off." I stopped there to see what she might fill in.

"We were so thrilled to be invited to your party." Her voice was wistful. "You probably know we're pretty new to Key West and certainly new to the food scene, so the invitation was special." She brushed a few dark hairs off her forehead. "Honestly, I was starstruck by all the fancy food people and the Key West dignitaries. I'm trying to think what might have been unusual." She closed her eyes for a moment and pressed her fingers on her temples.

"This might seem silly, but I did overhear someone refusing to wear a name tag. She said it would ruin her silk blouse, which had cost half a paycheck."

"Interesting," I said. "I didn't see that happen, but it's not outlandish. One time I wore a suede jacket to a meet and greet and they insisted I put on a sticky name tag. I've never gotten the stain off the jacket. It was so pretty, too, exactly the right mossy green color for my eyes and hair."

"Yeah, I get it," she said, her carefully shaped dark brows furrowing, "but the funny thing is, she wasn't wearing a silk blouse. It was more like a wash and wear, definitely not an expensive item like you'd see in an Eileen Fisher catalog. Working in Miami, I used to pay a lot of attention to fashion, so I notice these kinds of things. I remember wondering if for some reason she didn't want to share her name, and the shirt was her excuse. Though that didn't make much sense because we were there to meet people and network, weren't we?"

"We were," I said. "What did she look like?"

She looked at me and held her palm above her head. "She was taller than either of us, with reddish tints in her hair. I asked her about her connection to Key West and she got very mysterious, saying something like "oh, it's in my blood. My heart's on this island." Maybe not that exactly but that was the gist."

"Strange," I said, as my mind darted to Athena, Palamina's ex. What if she meant Palamina was her heart? But how would she have gotten onto the boat without being spotted, and what were her intentions? Was she the person who blew up the boat? I really did not have time or energy to investigate any more slim threads that might answer these questions. I sighed and pushed my business card across the counter. "Thanks for the ice cream. I'm glad you've recovered. Please let me know if you think of anything else."

Chapter Eighteen

He spoke blasphemies other chefs recognized as hard-won truths. "Any chef who says he does it for love is a liar," Mr. White said. "At the end of the day it's all about money. Can you blame him, or any other chef, for wanting to live like his customers?"
—Dwight Garner, "A Bad Boy's Manifesto,"
The New York Times, April 8, 2015

Miss Gloria had chosen the Key West Woman's Club to host the last event of her extended birthday party season. She had announced that the final family dinner at Seven Fish tomorrow night would not count as part of her official celebration, because that would push things over the top. Besides, that last meal was family only, and they'd probably not be speaking to each other by then. I felt badly that I didn't have time to check in with her before tonight's party, but as it was, I'd barely have time to get ready.

Just out of a much-needed shower with one towel wrapped around my torso and another on my head, I could hear Miss

Gloria greeting her sons on the deck of her houseboat. "Whoo-hoo, party boys! How do you like my birthday girl outfit?"

I braced for comments about her wearing a sweatsuit to a fancy party, but the rumblings of her sons were just low enough that I couldn't make them out. I was sure I'd hear more at the party. They all clattered down the finger toward the parking lot. She'd talked them into leaving early so they could stroll a few blocks of Duval Street before the dinner guests arrived. The daughters-in-law had never been on our main drag and dismissed it as dirty and full of drunks and half-naked people without ever seeing it. "But it's part of my Key West, and I want you to experience everything," Miss Gloria had insisted.

I finished getting dried off, buffed up, and dressed in my favorite pale green linen sundress with a handkerchief hemline set off by a crocheted trim. It skimmed my figure without clinging to the lumps and bumps, acquired in the last few weeks of tasting too much and exercising too little. Besides that, it set off the auburn tint of my hair. After applying blush and mascara, I walked the dog and fed both animals.

"I promise next week I will pay you two guys more attention than you can stand." Ziggy looked expectant, and doggishly happy. He believed me. Evinrude sat on the counter, facing away from me, switching his tail. He did not. I kissed each of their heads and opened my computer to check the email and texts that had been unavailable without a phone.

I had too many emails to read, including several from Palamina about work issues that she must have realized I wouldn't have time to address. I skipped right over those.

The artist John Martini had texted me. *I've remembered one more detail. I believe the woman you asked about was*

The Mango Murders

wearing a necklace that looked like a silver spoon that had been shaped into a fish. It was rustic and beautiful, and I'd never seen anything quite like it. I wanted to memorize the details for a possible future project, but I realized she might think that I was looking at something else. If you find a photo of that fish necklace, please send it on.

Nothing helpful there. What could a fish spoon necklace have to do with anything? I knew of a man who had extreme expertise in finding metal objects under water. He'd recovered many wedding rings and other treasured items. If he could search the sea bottom where we'd splashed down after the fire, and if he could find that necklace, it might confirm, what? That the unknown woman was on our cruise and had lost her jewelry in the disaster? For the sake of John Martini's art, I'd send on the photo if I came across it, but it wouldn't be a priority. We had a lot of bigger problems here.

I closed the laptop and hurried out to my prescheduled Uber ride.

* * *

Wide white porches and tall columns against the red brick set the Woman's Club building apart from other structures on this same Duval Street block. Unless there was a party in the front yard, most passers-by didn't realize this home represented more than a century of Key West history, philanthropy, and community service. By the time I arrived, party guests were already gathering on the front porch's white wicker benches.

The inside of the home was equally beautiful, with wooden floors, old-fashioned wallpaper, more wicker seating, and balloon window treatments. Chandeliers, large mirrors, stained-glass windows, and displays of old-fashioned China and glassware reminded visitors of more elegant, formal days.

For once, my mother wasn't having to cook all the food. She had insisted on preparing some hors d'oeuvres in advance—non-fussy dishes such as mounds of Key West pink shrimp, her famous hot pepper jelly cheese wafers, and a fancy Italian cheese, olives, and charcuterie board, so that Martha Hubbard could focus on the main course. Even with her cooking responsibilities minimized, Mom had been at the club house most of the afternoon to make sure the decorations were set up to her liking. The house looked even more stunning than usual, with glorious tropical flowers spilling out of their vases everywhere, among photos of Miss Gloria with her family and friends at all stages of life. Tables had been set up in the living room, dressed in white lace with pale pink napkins, good silver polished to a soft sheen, and more flowers. Already the rooms felt alive with chattering guests, even though we'd had to make some hard decisions about the invitation list. Having lived on the island for over thirty years, my neighbor had befriended and was adored by a lot of people.

I found the guest of honor in the parlor, formerly aka the men's smoking lounge. She looked adorable, positively radiant. We'd spent a lot of time last week trying out hair mousse and then combing her short white pixie, so the little peaks stood up to her satisfaction. She pulled a fast one by showing me two different sweatsuits that she pretended to be choosing between, each of them baggy in the knees and elbows, though studded with her favorite rhinestones spelling out Key West. In the end, she wore navy silk balloon pants, a white lace top, and a

The Mango Murders

sparkling birthday crown with *Birthday Princess* written in sequins that I'd ordered for her on Etsy. It had roses and pink tulle scattered all over and glittery gold trim on the points of the crown. Wearing it, Miss Gloria glowed like all the good fairies I'd imagined in my childhood. I hurried over to squeeze her into a hug and kiss her.

"You little dickens," I whispered. "All this time I worried you were wearing a saggy, faded old sweatsuit to your own party."

"A gal has to have some secrets, even from you," she said, her eyes sparkling with laughter. "It was fun to tease you and watch you be all careful and considerate of my awful taste."

"You're not only a dickens, you're a little devil," I said laughing and pulling her into another hug.

Nathan arrived as Miss Gloria's son Frank was welcoming all the guests and thanking her local family for throwing the party. "Please enjoy the champagne and wonderful hors d'oeuvres," he told the crowd. "Not to worry, there will be plenty of time for short toasts and roasts during dessert."

I wove through the crowd to Nathan and gave him a peck on the lips and a big smile that I hoped didn't look forced. I could feel the tension lingering between us—we were still dancing around each other following the argument the night before. I hated fighting with him.

"That was one heck of an awkward press conference, especially the denouement." Speaking of Chad without mentioning his name. "I appreciate you telling me in advance that it was happening. I was glad to be there, and I thought you did a good job."

Nathan grunted, frowning. "Not many would agree but I appreciate your support."

"Anything new on the victim?" I asked.

"Still not official, but coconut telegraph tells us it was Nan Copley." Key West-speak for word of mouth.

Nathan's father, Skip, strode up and clapped him on the shoulder. "You look like you're still pouting about your golf loss the other day, buddy." He laughed loudly, took a big swig of his beer, and turned to me. "How's my favorite daughter-in-law tonight? Will there be anything on the menu that I can eat?"

Three things I might have said: One, Nathan despised back-clapping and golf both. He wouldn't care if he won or lost, unless someone insisted on rubbing it in. Two, I was Skip's only daughter-in-law, so calling me the favorite was a low bar indeed. And three, he ate like a toddler. If we'd planned Miss Gloria's party around him, we could have offered carrot sticks and PB & J on white and saved a lot of work.

"Of course," I said, offering a simpering smile and kissing him on the cheek. "We totally planned the feast with you in mind."

I left the two of them to argue over their golf scores and made the rounds, introducing Miss Gloria's out-of-town people to local friends, including her mahjong buddies, my coworkers, and her pals from the Friends of the Key West Library, with whom she sorted book donations, and the Friends of the Key West cemetery, with whom she gave tours. Then I refilled my champagne glass and ducked into the kitchen to check on Martha.

I took the lid off the nearest pot that simmered on the stove to revel in the pungent scents of sauteed onions, celery, and peppers. On the counter, big bowls of pink shrimp, scallops, and Florida spiny lobster waited their turns to be added. "It smells

The Mango Murders

incredible in here. How's it going? Do you need reinforcements?" I asked.

Martha grinned and tipped her chin at the two apron-clad ladies who were chopping vegetables at the center island. "Got all the help I can use. Any more bodies would only be in the way."

Then her face grew serious. "I meant to ask you this question, but I kept forgetting. Was Nan Copley on the cocktail party guest list the other night? This has been puzzling me because I can't picture how she fit in with the rest of the crowd that you invited."

"That's a very good question," I said. "I'm not sure that she would've been invited on behalf of *Key Zest*, but I'll check with Palamina. I'll also ask my mother. She could've issued an invitation just to be courteous, from one chef caterer to another."

I left the kitchen thinking, if she wasn't invited, what in the world was she doing on the boat? How did she end up dying in the hold? *If* that was what happened. Nathan had still been a little cagey about Nan Copley's identity. A badly burned crime scene made it difficult to identify victims. Besides, next of kin always came first. I'd try again later to squeeze him for more autopsy details on both the woman and the *Pilar Too*.

I returned to the party, circulating through the guests to make more connections, our friends Eric and Bill to Frank and Henrietta, Miss Gloria's mahjong buddies Phyllis Gagner and Mrs. Dubisson to Chief Brandenburg and former Mayor Teri. I'd called her best friend Mrs. Dubisson since I moved to the Houseboat Row neighborhood, but tonight, celebrating Gloria and liberally plied with champagne, she was insisting everyone drop the formalities and call her Annie.

"We heard you on the radio describing how you rode in a Navy jet," said Annie, giggling at the Chief. Were her knees actually buckling a little? "You are so brave. Weren't you the only guest who didn't upchuck?"

The chief had been invited to ride in a Blue Angels jet at the speed of sound this year, and he'd been interviewed about how much he loved the experience by most of the Key West media. He thanked her as a wave of red flushed his face and the rest of us laughed at his discomfort. I pulled him aside for a moment.

"Anything new on the *Pilar Too* case?" I asked. "Have they confirmed that the victim was Nan Copley?"

He cracked a big grin. "Always the detective. I have nothing new that I can say on that issue." He smiled again, knowing that I'd recognize that line as the standard police public relations issue. Which could mean exactly what he'd said, or possibly, a lot was happening they weren't prepared to share.

I turned to chat with Bill, who'd helped me solve a murder case at the Little White House a few years ago, and his psychologist husband, Eric. Eric rolled his eyes at Henrietta's departing form. "I don't get the feeling she appreciates her mother-in-law," he said.

"Bingo," I said, pointing at him. "Maybe only someone with your training and experience could explain why Frank chose such a pill for a wife."

"I'd have to charge for that opinion." Eric laughed. "Any news on the motives behind the boat disaster?"

"Nobody's telling me," I said. "Do you have any armchair hypotheses?"

"I'd look at love, lust, loathing, or loot," he said, grinning. "Something in that neighborhood, or so the experts would say."

The Mango Murders

Mayor Teri came up behind and grabbed my fingers. "Do you have a minute?" she whispered. "I was thinking about our conversation this morning." I followed her to the front porch where there were fewer partygoers and the bar-hoppers on Duval were too far away to listen in. "Have you visited the Mango Madness exhibit at the Studios of Key West? People really outdid themselves this time." Mango Madness was an annual event held at the Studio's main art gallery during the mango season to showcase the art of local Key West people.

"I chatted with folks there, and as you can imagine, the boat explosion is on everyone's mind. Several people mentioned that our new mayor has business dealings with the captain of the *Pilar Too*."

"Meaning he might have arranged to have it blown up for what, insurance payouts?"

"You didn't hear that from me," she said with a wink.

"Of course not. But I could tell Captain Roche loved that boat like it was his firstborn. It would have to have been an awfully big payout."

"Agree," she said. "It might be a puzzle piece, but we don't know where it fits. Or it could be a piece from a different box altogether."

I spotted my mother leaning against the door jamb leading to the kitchen, taking a well-deserved breather. I hurried over and leaned in close to her so other guests wouldn't overhear. I did not want to ruin the festive vibe with questions about the murder.

"The question has come up about who invited Nan Copley to the party on the boat. Was it you?" I asked.

"I would not have asked her," my mother said, frowning. "I don't think it's an exaggeration to say the woman despised me. That invitation would only have stirred up a hornets' nest. It wasn't only me. I think she felt terribly rivalrous about anyone who was succeeding when she was not." Mom put a hand on my forehead. "You're working too hard, sweetheart. You look pale. Maybe let it go for tonight and just have some fun?"

"I'll try." I grinned as she went back into the kitchen. Danielle had come into the dining room and waved hello at me. We exchanged quick hugs, and she gazed around the space, taking in the floral arrangements and table settings.

"The place looks amazing! Somehow, you've captured the exact essence of Gloria."

"Thanks. Mom did the lion's share. Listen," I said, "would you mind dashing off a quick text to Palamina to ask her if she invited Nan Copley to our party?"

"Now?" she asked, squinting in disbelief.

I nodded.

Danielle rolled her eyes but sent the text as I'd asked, adding, *Hayley wants to know.*

The name doesn't ring a bell, Palamina texted back, *but I will look at the guest list and advise.*

Three dots on the screen and then, *how is the party going?*

"Absolutely perfectly," I dictated to Danielle, figuring it would not do any good to shade the truth. Palamina's was one of the names hovering on the overflow fringe of invitees. I had assured Miss Gloria that she would not expect to be invited and would probably at this point feel better staying home. She wasn't exactly a social butterfly, except for work events where she had to sparkle.

"No word from Athena?" I asked Danielle to text.

The Mango Murders

No! came the quick response.

I could picture the look of horror on her face, but I felt I needed to be sure this woman wasn't involved in the disaster. I told Danielle what to type next. *If she was in town, any guesses about where she would be staying or hanging out? Just so I can keep my ears and eyes open.*

I'd asked her this earlier, but she hadn't replied. Palamina wrote back: *She didn't care about food so I can't speak to restaurants. She sometimes stayed at the Casa Marina. She liked the water view and found their bar quite civilized. Don't ask for Athena, that name is a total conceit. Her legal name is Eva.*

This was the same hotel where my parents and in-laws and Miss Gloria's family were staying. I would quiz them about whether they'd seen anyone who fit that description. Another text came in on my friend's phone.

But she isn't on the island. I swear I would feel the sour and angry vibes if she was anywhere near.

"Why are you obsessed with Palamina's girlfriend?" Danielle asked.

A good question. I'd been shocked by Palamina's entire backstory spilling out this past week, after years of learning nothing personal. It was impossible not to want every gory detail of Eva contacting her every year on the date she thought was their anniversary. I had Danielle sign off because maybe it was true my questions were nosy, bordering on harassment. Besides, I couldn't think of anything else to ask my boss, and my mother was ringing a silver bell to call the guests to dinner.

The guests buzzed around finding their places, and Martha's delicious dinner was served: seafood chilau, described as a cousin to shrimp Creole, mango and greens salad studded with blue cheese and spicy toasted pecans, and fresh baguettes from Old Town Bakery. Once the dinner had been eaten and the dishes cleared, large slabs of key lime pie and coconut cake were offered for dessert along with coffee and tea. Feeling my usual obligation to try everything, I nodded yes to one of each.

Miss Gloria had turned down the idea of a gigantic sheet cake pierced by eighty-five candles. "It will be embarrassing when I can't blow them all out. Plus, you know sheet cakes are never as good as a good old-fashioned homemade layer cake. Maybe one of the ladies at the Woman's Club will offer to bake." As with all her preferences for the party, we had agreed.

I swiped a bit of the frosting from my slab of coconut cake to try to figure out the ingredients. Cream cheese, I thought, and butter and powdered sugar. Did it include mascarpone? A dash of vanilla? With coconut flakes pressed into the icing, this reminded me of a recipe I'd seen recently, but I couldn't think where. I wondered if it could possibly be as delicious as my friend Eric's coconut cake, and then I thought maybe we should have asked him to bake. On the other hand, coconut cake for a hundred plus would have been a big ask.

Miss Gloria stood up to speak to her guests.

"Thank you all for coming so far to celebrate me. I am deeply grateful and honored. What I have learned in eighty-five years is that wrinkles and creaks mean a life well-lived, not an old lady circling the drain." The audience hooted with friendly laughter. "I've also learned that friends and family mean everything. Everything," she repeated, her voice a little wobbly. "After Frank died, I wondered how I could feel like continuing to live without him. We had so many grand times together, and I loved him so dearly. Not that I was thinking about doing myself in," she added quickly. "But I was deeply sad."

She swept her hand around to take in the gathered crowd. "You, my family through biology and by choice, shepherded me out of that darkness. It is very, very helpful that most of you are younger and sturdier than I am, and some of you even cook." The audience snickered. "In case anyone has had enough of me, I can tell you that my future plans include living into my next century." The room broke out into laughter and applause.

After the toasts and testimonials were finished, I stopped to chat with Miss Gloria's daughters-in-law for a moment. "You are so lucky to have her in your family," I said, meaning every word. Gloria materialized next to me with Helen, Allison, and my mother in tow.

"I wanted to be sure you'd met these people," she said to her daughters-in-law. "They are the most powerful women on this island right at the moment, and lucky Hayley is related to all of them." I wondered if there was an underlying and not-so-subtle message about how much I appreciated the mother figures in my life, compared with their dismissal and disdain.

"You have a mutual admiration society going on here," Henrietta replied, her lips thinning into a smile. Tonya grimaced behind her.

I hugged Miss Gloria. "That was an amazing speech. I'm lucky to have them—" I swept my arm to include my trio of mothers, "and super lucky to have you as my bonus relation." Her sons approached to whisk her off to another conversation.

While my mother chatted politely with the daughters-in-law, I asked Helen and Allison who they'd talked with earlier in the day at the harbor, and what they'd learned on their visit.

Helen said, "Of course Amos Roche wasn't there because his boat was trashed. It would be too sad to linger around an empty slip."

"But his next-door neighbor was," Allison said, sounding a bit like an eager puppy. "According to Helen, he was a lot more forthcoming this time."

Buddy LaRue. The youngish man with a flowered shirt and ponytail. "He remembered something important?" I asked.

"Maybe he remembered details after we spoke with him the other day. Or maybe we were just more persuasive this time. Your stepmother is quite the flirt." Helen's lips twitched into a smile.

"I'm not . . . I didn't . . ." burbled Allison.

My mother-in-law cut her off.

"Anyway, we didn't hear that much from LaRue. But his first mate, Louise, was full of helpful tips. She said Captain Amos was not watching carefully the comings and goings of staff setting up for the cruise party. Your mother must have hired a swarm of helpers. In other words, no one kept close tabs on what got loaded on that boat." She frowned as she studied my face.

I swallowed the big surge of worry this raised, hoping it wouldn't reflect badly on my mother and the way she ran her business. She'd been super busy that day and had asked the captain if she could drop off some supplies on carts on his dock, early the day of the party. Sam planned to roll them aboard once he arrived, if the captain didn't have time or didn't feel this was in his job description. I could see now this wasn't a perfect plan. Unfortunately, our guest and staff list felt that same way—a little out of control. We thought we had a good system for checking people in, but when the invitees descended on the gangplank, especially with the sunset cruise crowds pushing onto the docks bordering the harbor exactly at the same time that the boat was about to launch, maybe not so much.

"We had lots on our plates," I said cheerfully, not wanting to hash out my concerns right here.

"We should go mingle," Helen said with a sigh. "Nathan wanted to introduce me to some of his police friends."

As she turned to chat with other guests, I caught Allison's arm.

"Listen, while you're at the hotel tonight, keep an eye out for my boss Palamina's ex. She's tall and strawberry blonde, and thin and attractive. I think she was the one in that photo we were looking at earlier at Frenchie's. It's possible she's staying there, and possible she was somehow mixed up with the boat explosion. Let me know, OK?"

Allison hugged me. "Will do! Helen took the photos back to her room, but it's possible I'd recognize her."

As my relatives drifted away, leaving me again with Henrietta and Tonya, I saw Lorenzo standing alone. I couldn't think how to avoid introducing them, even though I doubted that they'd be open to his spiritual gift. I drew him closer to the women and explained how he set up his table and umbrella nightly at Mallory Square and read tarot cards for visitors.

"Not always visitors," Lorenzo said, brushing a few crumbs off his purple tie. "I have repeat local customers as well."

"Like me," I said, turning my gaze to the in-laws. "I find it extremely helpful to talk with him. It's like there's a universal energy stream that he can tap into and understand the way most people cannot."

"Really?" Henrietta asked. "I have to be honest, that's a little woo-woo for my taste."

"Ditto," said Tonya. "Most of the fortune tellers I've come across are more interested in fleecing their customers with fabricated truisms than helping."

Lorenzo folded his hands together and looked steadily at the women. "I know it sounds strange, but I've always been able to understand things in a different way than many people can. If a person is open to my gift, I'm happy to share it. My job is to help those who come to my table seeking clarity about their lives. Believe me I took a lot of bullying for my gift when I was a kid."

I couldn't help wondering if these women might have been the bullying kind in their younger years. Didn't matter because Lorenzo was a dear friend and Miss Gloria's guest, and I would not allow them to rudely dismiss him. "I always wondered how you got started with tarot card reading," I said.

"Believe it or not, my mother bought my first deck of cards when I was eight. She was a Pisces and therefore, had incredible intuition. She sensed that these cards would be important to me. Later I started to listen to a radio show with Harriet and Leonard Freeland about tarot and I knew I'd found kindred spirits."

"I'll give you an example of what he notices that the rest of us might not," I said to the women, as I could see their expressions glazing over with disbelief. I described a little about the customer he'd been talking with when the boat explosion occurred. Suddenly I thought of the photo of John Martini and the other artist, posed with the tall woman behind them whom no one seemed to recognize, though I was beginning to wonder if it was Eva. I'd still not had the opportunity to ask if Lorenzo knew her. Although it didn't make sense that she could have been his customer—the timeline didn't work. Unless she'd not actually sailed with us. Or unless she was the person who dropped over the side of the boat. But he'd been quite sure that his client was not wet. Maybe she'd come aboard the boat, then disembarked and hurried to Mallory Square to talk with Lorenzo? I shook myself out of those thoughts and back to the moment.

"My point is, Lorenzo could see the pain she was feeling about her marriage reflected in the cards she chose. People talk to him about their deepest worries—he helps them see and understand things that may have been hovering under the surface. Unfortunately, he didn't get to help this woman digest the reading because our boat blew up."

"Fascinating," said Henrietta. "He's a marriage counselor too." She turned to her co-daughter-in-law. "I believe we should affect a final mingle and then prevail on the men to take us home."

My friend bowed, touching his clasped hands to his forehead, murmuring, "Such a pleasure to meet you."

I would apologize to him for their rudeness next time I saw him alone.

Martha Hubbard emerged from the door leading to the kitchen, looking tired but very content. I hurried over to give her a big hug. "Your dinner was fantastic," I told her. "I wouldn't have changed a thing."

"Thanks. One person turned out to be allergic to shellfish, but we swapped in a chicken breast so no harm, no foul. That comes with the territory." She leaned over to whisper. "There's going to be a wake at the Schooner Wharf for the foodie crowd to tell stories about Nan Copley." She glanced at her watch. "Starting in half an hour. Want to come along?"

"Definitely," I said. "Can I ride with you? I came in an Uber."

After thanking a stream of party guests taking their leave, I decided that I had to tell Nathan about the upcoming wake at the bar. There was no reasonable explanation for why I would leave the party with Martha, rather than going home with him. I found him chatting with Sam. I kissed Sam on the cheek. "Great job tonight with the hors d'oeuvres and everything else you did. Miss Gloria couldn't be happier."

Then I pulled Nathan aside and explained about Martha's invitation.

"I'd like to go, and I know you'll worry that I'll get into trouble. But I'd like to go without you, because I might hear something that people would not tell me if a fearsome police guy was lurking nearby."

He rubbed his fingers underneath his chin, rasping a little patch of whiskers he had missed while shaving for the party. "I think you're right on this one. Why don't you go ahead with Martha and mingle with the other guests. I'll come separately and hang out away from your crowd. That way if there's any trouble, I'm there to help. I can listen from a different angle and then drive you home when you're done being nosy."

Laughing, I gave him a quick elbow to the stomach, though I couldn't argue with his plan. I made the rounds with the remaining guests, including Miss Gloria, who was still holding court in the parlor. The sparkly pink birthday crown was a little crooked, and she had a few dabs of chocolate ice cream on her lace blouse, but otherwise she looked happy and cogent.

The Mango Murders

"Do you have a ride home?" I asked.

"More offers than I know what to do with." She dissolved into giggles and held her glass out for a refill from a man carrying champagne. I could warn her to be careful, and not drink too much or stay out too late, but she was eighty-five for Pete's sake. For once, I minded my own business.

"I'll see you tomorrow, birthday girl, I love you!" I blew her a kiss and left through the kitchen and out the back door to join Martha on her scooter.

Chapter Nineteen

There was a palpable level of hostility radiating between them. They could have boiled water with the heat of their animosity.

—Rachel Linden, *Recipe for a Charmed Life*

The Schooner Wharf Bar was located on the dock that ran alongside the old harbor. Rustic and open to the sea air, it often featured live music and always, a lively crowd of both tourists and locals. Martha parked on the access road that ran behind the bar alongside the Marker hotel. We walked past the bigger-than-life-sized John Martini sculptures of colorful steel reindeer and rabbits, reminding me of my earlier visit to his studio.

Martha interrupted my thoughts. "I don't know quite what kind of crowd to expect," she said in a low voice as we approached the bar. "I wouldn't say Nan was a particularly popular person in town, but she's lived on the island a while and the food industry sticks with their own. Plus, I think someone is buying drinks, so that's always a draw."

The Mango Murders

Across the room, I spotted Chef Richard. I remembered what Martha had told me about the trouble between him and Nan Copley. If true, I could imagine that he felt bitter. But now he was probably worried that he might be considered vindictive, and therefore, a suspect in her death. He probably hadn't meant for his comments to be passed around town. He had to show up or look guilty.

Martha saw me looking in his direction. "He wasn't the only one who had trouble with Nan. She fired servers with impunity and was notoriously hard on the kitchen staff. You had to have a strong personality to stand up to her. She drove people to drink with her nitpicking. She wanted everything perfect." She looked hard at me. "I mean, *literally* drove people to drink. A couple guys I know showed up for their shifts with a fifth of alcohol and drank it down to empty by the time the kitchen was closed. Every night."

I shook my head with amazement. "She had a lot of enemies, from the sound of it. Hopefully we'll hear from people who were fond of her too. Or it will be just too sad."

"Her restaurants *did* run like clockwork," Martha added. "That was due to her demanding only the best, from purveyors, front of the house, back of the house, everyone. The food was mostly excellent."

Raven Cooper and her band were belting out Janis Joplin's *A Little Piece of My Heart* as we entered the bar, which made it hard to chat anymore. I followed Martha as she wended her way through the crowd to the end of the bar where the foodie people were gathered. She was greeted enthusiastically and introduced me to a few of the people nearest.

"Of course, you remember Analise," she said, as an attractive dark-haired woman threw her arms around me. Analise ran a very popular food tour in town celebrating Cuban and Caribbean influences on Key West food and history, and she'd been instrumental in helping me solve a murder in which Martha herself had been implicated.

"You've had a baby girl since the last time I saw you," I said. "Congratulations! Being a mother suits you, you're glowing."

"Tired too, keeping up with her," she said, the broad grin belying the circles under her eyes. "But I wouldn't trade it for anything." The very same thing my good friend Connie said about her two toddlers.

I squeezed her shoulders and turned away because Martha was introducing me to someone else. "Hayley was on the boat where Nan Copley was supposedly killed. Her husband's with the police department."

"Have they identified who killed her and why?" a woman asked. Suddenly I recognized her as Chef Edel Waugh, who'd also come too close to a murder several years ago that almost tanked her new restaurant. She'd been one of our guests on the ill-fated cruise. I explained the little bit that I knew and was authorized to share.

"I suppose it's hard when the victim is not universally adored." Edel frowned. "It makes for too darn many suspects."

"For sure," I said. "But we think it had to be someone connected with our cruise. What isn't clear is whether the perpetrator meant to actually blow up the boat or kill Nan Copley. I think the cops are taking a wide-angle view." It took all the control I had not to look over toward the alley behind the bar where I knew Nathan was lurking.

"Follow the money," Edel said as she drifted away. "Didn't Deep Throat teach us that in *All the President's Men*?"

"What would you like to drink?" Martha called to me, as she moved toward the bartender and managed to snag his attention.

"Maybe a nonalcoholic beer or ginger ale," I said. "I had a couple of glasses of champagne at Miss Gloria's party, and I don't want to get pulled over on the way home." Although I'd be riding with Nathan rather than driving myself, enough of a party was enough.

"They do make a delicious nonalcoholic spritz with notes of bitter orange and rhubarb."

"Sounds perfect."

She returned with two frosty glasses, just as the singer announced that shortly, a few people wanted to say some words about their departed friend and colleague. Others were welcome to speak as well.

I looked around as I sipped on the drink, wondering who else might have insight into the disastrous boat trip. I was surprised to see both Captain Amos Roche and Captain Buddy LaRue in attendance. They were in heated conversation. I squirmed through the crowd so I could get close enough to listen in.

Roche leaned into LaRue's space. "I've heard that you are spreading rumors about my boating abilities. I had nothing to do with that incident. It was on my client who did a poor job of vetting guests and left the door wide open to disaster."

I did not like to hear this at all. The propane tank that apparently caused the explosion did not even belong to my mother and Sam.

LaRue said, "Isn't the captain of a ship responsible for both cargo and passengers? That's what I remember from studying for my license." He had a sly cat smile on his lips that obviously made Roche madder.

A large man wearing a flowered shirt stepped in between them. "This is a remembrance of someone lost, not the time and place to fight. If you want to fight, take it outside."

The two captains turned away from each other, both muttering. I was a little sorry to watch them break apart, as I suspected I might have heard something useful if the conversation had continued. Although it could just as well have deteriorated into a fist fight, benefiting no one.

I edged a little closer to the captain of the *Pilar Too*. "I hope you're feeling better." I patted my forehead, noting that he was wearing only a large Band-Aid, rather than the full gauze wrap he'd worn in the hospital.

He focused on me and seemed to finally recognize where he'd last seen me. "Fine," he said, "if you don't count having lost my only way to earn a living."

I nodded to show my sympathy, then gestured at Buddy LaRue. "I know you guys don't see eye to eye on everything,"—Roche snorted—"but did your neighbor notice anything off the day of the cruise? Do you have a theory about what happened? We've been over and over the guest list and can't imagine that anyone we invited came with the idea of blowing up your gorgeous boat."

"Not my circus, not my monkeys," he said, pivoting toward the bar again. He paused to say over his shoulder: "Your mother was responsible for the guest list and the servers. None of that was on me."

The Mango Murders

But he had crew, didn't he? I didn't dare ask that out loud. I'd tell Nathan about this conversation and let him follow up because I thought I'd squeezed all I could out of him. Which in the end, wasn't much. I hated the idea of feeling suspicious of my own mother, but had she missed something important in her event planning?

Among the small crowd who'd been watching the argument, even in a sundress rather than her sailing uniform of short white shorts and striped shirt, I recognized the first mate from Buddy's boat, Louise Wardell. She was watching her captain sling his arm around a young woman nearby and plant a big smooch on her cheek. He was obviously drunk. Louise was sturdy and muscular, rather than willowy like the other woman. I thought she might be jealous.

"I'm Hayley Snow. Thanks for speaking with my mother-in-law yesterday," I said, moving a little closer to her. "It must be scary to think someone local randomly blew up a party boat."

She squinted, blinking back tears. "Randomly? I doubt it. Amos Roche is a pill with no moral compass. He's done his best to torpedo my boss's business. It's the way he deals with the world, and he obviously crossed someone's line."

"Tell me more about Buddy's business. Have you worked for him a while?"

Her face brightened. "He's a wonderful captain and I've learned so much about sailing and the sea. It's not his fault that business is down, there's so much competition in this town." Her gaze darted over to Captain Roche. "I think he's had woman trouble lately, too."

I widened my eyes, inviting her to tell me more.

"Buddy's very private about it, but I've heard him bickering with a woman over the phone. I know from lousy relationships," she said, in a voice that sounded sad. "My boyfriend was supposed to come down this week, and I had amazing things planned. I'd hoped this would juice things up and maybe we could start talking about us living together. I would move back to Orlando where he lives or welcome him here. But at the last minute, he decided not to come at all." One tear slipped out of her eye and ran down her cheek.

The description of the client Lorenzo had been talking to when our cruise blew up flashed to mind. OMG, had this woman been Lorenzo's client? This would help explain why the police were so interested in her. If there'd been serious trouble between the two captains, she would have been a witness to it. I decided I had to ask.

"The *Carpe Diem* did not go out the night the *Pilar Too* blew up, right?"

She nodded, a look of suspicion flitting over her face.

"Were you by any wild chance talking to a tarot card reader on Mallory Square that evening? I ask because he felt so bad about the reading getting interrupted. I have his card in case you wanted to follow up." I began to rustle in my small bag looking for the little stash of business cards I kept there. Now her expression looked panicked.

"That wasn't me." She spun around, exited the bar to the dock, and melted into the crowd.

Across the room, a pretty woman with bouncy curls and big blue eyes was bending Nathan's ear. He watched her intensely, and I felt my own spike of uncomfortable jealousy. Surely, I wasn't jealous of the very loyal, very dedicated man I was married to, who was only doing his job. He was not here to pick up girls, he was here to listen to the speakers and observe the attendant mourners. Sometimes a murderer showed up at a wake, or even worse, appeared at a funeral. I'd seen this with a few of Nathan's other cases. There were lots of possible reasons for taking that risk, including an urge to gain information about the progress of the case, avoid suspicion by appearing as one of the bereaved, and assess the reactions of the other attendees to see what they were guessing.

Raven Cooper returned to the mic. "At this time, if we could have your attention, Betty Darst, a second cousin of the deceased, will say a few words."

The blonde woman who'd been talking to Nathan approached the stage. No wonder he'd been so interested in what she had to say.

"Thank you. I appreciate all of you coming out to honor my cousin Nan. Regretfully, we hadn't been in good touch lately, since my move to California ten years ago. But my mother and hers were very close, more like sisters than cousins. They loved cooking together, and Cousin Nan was the child who paid the most attention in the kitchen and carried their recipes forward. We all adored her coconut layer cake. She had invented some kind of decadent frosting with marshmallows, and I believe she won a contest for that." She flashed a winning smile around the room, as I grimaced inside. "She was a competitive woman, in the kitchen and out. I remember as a kid that even in a neighbor's pool, she always won every race."

Behind me Edel muttered: "She lied like a sieve about those recipes. That layer cake came from the Woman's Club cookbook even though she claimed it as her own creation.

How did she have the gall not to think someone would find her out?"

I could see Chef Richard nodding in agreement off to the side. He leaned over to whisper something to Martha. As chefs, all three of them would know how important it was to give attribution to the cooks you leaned on when developing a recipe. But would that be a motive for murder? In such a spectacular way? Nan Copley had been angry about my mother's recipe being chosen over hers, but hers wasn't a stolen coconut cake. Once again, nothing about this case made sense. I moved closer to the three of them.

"I hear what you're saying. Nan may have fudged on copyright," I said, hoping to fish for more details.

I watched the frowns deepen on their faces.

"OK, so maybe it was more than fudging. But would one stolen coconut cake lead to murder? Any thoughts on who she might have tangled with on this?"

"Would anyone else like to share a few words about Cousin Nan?" asked Betty, on the stage. There was an awkward silence. Finally, Martha raised her hand and moved toward the podium.

She adjusted the microphone and smiled grimly. "Nan Copley made beautiful food that also tasted delicious. I remember an amazing meal she made for a group of us. We sat at picnic tables overlooking the water. It was magical." Martha described in detail a baked grouper stuffed with Key West pinks, alongside a rice dish studded with charred corn and shishito peppers and kissed with cilantro, lime, and spicy chili oil. My stomach began to rumble, even though I was a million miles from hungry.

The Mango Murders

"Her food was to die for," Martha added, and then raised her glass. "To Nan. We ate better on this island when she was a part of it."

Betty Darst returned to the microphone to thank Martha and announce that she would be buying a round of drinks for the crowd in honor of Nan. In the burst of cheering and clapping that followed, Martha threaded her way back to me.

"That was a very nice memory," I said, watching her face carefully. "You made me crave that rice dish especially. You must have known her pretty well if you were invited to a fancy dinner party."

"Not really," she said with a breezy wave as if it was nothing. "There was a big crowd. It would have been too painful if there was no one speaking for her tonight." Her face looked sad though. "It's true though, that was a special evening."

Across the room, Nathan was signaling to me, tapping his watch. Tick, tock, I could imagine him saying. I hugged Martha. "I need to get home. Please, please call me if you hear anything more about the cruise or Nan's death?" She gave me a thumbs up and turned to chat with another group of local chefs.

I wormed through the throng crowding the bar and joined Nathan in the back alley. We walked quickly to his parking space on William Street, three blocks away. The air felt too warm, settling heavy in my chest, though that weight could also have been leftover gloominess from Nan Copley's party. Once we were in Nathan's vehicle, I said: "That could have been the strangest wake ever. I hope mine will be a little more heartfelt."

He glanced over at me quickly. "Hayley, you are beloved. We'd be sobbing too loud to hear the speakers."

I swatted his arm and fastened my seatbelt. "What did you learn from Betty Darst?"

"She said Nan called her earlier this week to catch up, which was not commonplace. They weren't in regular contact, so it took her by surprise."

"This happened before the cruise incident?" Wait, duh, obviously. Since she died on the boat, it had to be earlier. "Dumb question. Did she want anything in particular?"

"I didn't get that impression. More like she wanted to connect, to touch base. They talked about what they'd eaten lately, and she told Betty that business had been a little slow. A couple days later, when Betty heard that her cousin had perished, she started to wonder if Nan had had a premonition about the disaster and that scared her. Maybe she'd sensed that someone had it in for her. But they didn't discuss this specifically. It was a hunch she felt later."

"If Nan had a premonition about a disaster, why in the world would she sneak onto the boat?"

Nathan shifted to face forward and started up the engine. "No idea."

"How did Betty get here in time to headline this memorial service when you haven't officially notified her?"

"That's a damn good question," he said, with a frown. "This town leaks secrets like a rotten roof leaks rain. How about you, did you hear anything unusual?"

"I almost had to break up a fist fight between the two captains. Roche seems to think it was my mother's fault that the propane tank was mysteriously loaded aboard. I hope that's not what the authorities are deciding as well."

The Mango Murders

I glanced over at him again, figuring that he would not tell me something like that until it was definitely confirmed, even if he believed it was true. He said nothing, so I continued. "Roche claims no one was watching very carefully for either the particulars of the guest list or the loading of supplies. Which between you and me, could be true. We were doing the best we could, but looking back, we needed more help. But listen, Roche had a crew working on that boat too, it could just have as well been one of them."

"Could have," Nathan said, giving nothing away in his expression.

"Have you looked into that? Are you going to look into that? I know it's not something criminal, but she could be charged with reckless endangerment or something like that, which would totally ruin her business if not her life."

Suddenly the pressure that had been building up in my brain felt like it had spread to my sinuses, and I couldn't help bursting into noisy sobs.

"What in the world is wrong? Do you need me to pull over?" my husband asked, slowing the SUV and pulling over to the Eaton Street curb so he could take my hand.

I rustled around in my backpack for a tissue, blew my nose and wiped my eyes.

"I'm OK, you can drive. I'll be fine really, everything suddenly felt so sad. Miss Gloria being so old. She can't last forever and what in the world will I do without her when she's gone? And then there's a wake without any close relatives and hardly anyone willing to speak. I mean how sad is that? Now my mother's in the spotlight for being careless even though she works like a dog and does her job beautifully. She's not a careless person."

"You're working too hard, too," Nathan said as he pulled into our parking lot. He took both my hands and squeezed. "We're all going to leave this world at some point. It's a given. The best we can do is appreciate each moment with the people we love. Yes, you'll be sick with grief when you lose Miss Gloria, but you're not wasting any time with her. You're enjoying her and loving the heck out of her and those memories will matter." He leaned over to kiss me.

"Thanks," I said. "That was beautiful, and oh so mushy. Not very Nathan-like at all."

I scrambled out of the car before he could protest.

Chapter Twenty

It's part cookbook, part hosting guide, part gratuitous gawking at Stewart's life meant to inspire envious awe or awful envy.
—Jaya Saxena, "Martha Stewart's 'Entertaining' Let Me Party Like It Was 1982." *Eater*

The next morning, I woke feeling a little hung over and slightly queasy, with an underlying sense of loss that always came after a long-planned event was completed. Postpartum party depression, my mother and I always joked. On the one hand, I was happy—the party was a success in all ways—great food, fun cocktails, a glorious setting, good company—everything Miss Gloria had dreamed of.

But still, as I'd said to Nathan to explain my sadness and sudden outburst last night, the question remained: What would come next? Would Miss Gloria be around to celebrate her next big milestone? Would our friends and family still be around in a year, or two years, or five? I felt embarrassed to have gotten so emotional in front of my poor self-contained husband, but the week felt like it had spiraled out of control.

Maybe it would help if I tried to understand it piece by piece. After pouring myself a cup of coffee and a bowl of cereal, I took those back to bed with the animals curled up on either side. I jotted down my thoughts on a yellow pad. There were three components to feeling overwhelmed: Miss Gloria's party, the wake at Schooner Wharf, the disaster on the cruise and my fears about my mother's role in it.

One. I'd learned over the past few years not to pay too much attention to my inevitable post event gloominess, because it always lifted. Then I could enjoy anticipating and planning for the next high point. I'd heard that writers and artists experienced something very similar once they finished a big project. The ones who lasted over the long run allowed themselves to mourn the completed project—briefly, and then bask in the success and get excited about new ones bubbling on the horizon.

Two. Besides that, the Schooner Wharf wake had been utterly depressing. I couldn't remember a funeral or gathering that radiated less genuine sadness for the deceased person. Plus, a murderer was still on the loose, baffling the police and frightening citizens. It felt very personal, because I'd been on the scene at the explosion and the incident had destroyed both my mother's and *Key Zest's* hopes for a big boost in business. At least in the short run.

Three. I was beginning to worry seriously whether the chaos surrounding our event had set the stage for the murder. If we'd been better organized for the cruise, could we have prevented the entire disaster? I felt sick even thinking that and wanted to do everything I could to help. Reflexively, I reached for my phone but came up empty-handed.

Yikes! Again! Top of today's to-do list: Get a new phone.

The Mango Murders

I rolled out of bed, returned to the kitchen, and opened my laptop. While it loaded, I refilled my coffee mug and warmed up one of the mango scones left over from hosting Miss Gloria's in-laws. Once it was toasted, I slathered the scone with left over cream cheese frosting. While I ate and drank my coffee, I jotted down as many questions as came to mind. Who set the explosion up? Why? Was Nan Copley killed by mistake? (Honestly, the comments I'd heard about her at her wake made her seem more like villain than victim. She might have pushed someone too far.) Who was the mystery woman in the photo with John Martini and Peter Vey? Who had aimed a motorcycle at either me or my mother-in-law? Why did Palamina choose the *Pilar Too* as the venue for our event? Was the appearance of my mother's cake recipe in *Key Zest* the beginning of this ugly landslide? Who was Lorenzo's mystery customer, someone related to the cruise disaster or a randomly upset woman? Could it possibly have been Louise Wardell? Who dropped off the side of the boat, if that actually happened?

I remembered that I hadn't had time to look at the drone footage from the wedding party occurring the same night as our big party. I searched for the link and clicked. The photographer focused mostly on the wedding party but also panned out over the water. Again, I watched as our catamaran emerged from behind the islands and cruised into the harbor. As the camera swung back toward the wedding, I did see a splash from our boat.

Now we had three different observers—the drone footage, Becky the boat captain, and Tobin the acrobat—who confirmed that someone had dropped off the side before the explosion.

Suddenly I noticed a text I'd missed in my queue. The message was from the woman who'd helped us after the motorcycle ran Helen down.

"Hayley, I'm glad you thought to give me your business card, and I hope your mother-in-law is OK! As a nurse—even on vacation, I'm always seeing life through my training. I was not thrilled watching her march off with her head bleeding instead of calling an ambulance. LOL. My daughter took an iPhone video of everyone getting off that big cruise ship. We noticed when we looked at it later that she had captured a bit of that crazy motorcycle driver. Maybe this will be useful to you in tracking this person down and having the police follow up?"

I sent her a quick note of thanks, and assured her that Helen seemed fine, feisty as ever. She was right though—I shouldn't have permitted Helen to talk me into a ride to the hospital on my scooter. Then I watched the video, twice, first at the regular speed and then in slow motion. It was by no means a high-quality production, rather jerky and out of focus. The motorcycle had emerged from the direction of the alley that led toward Duval Street. Then it had zigzagged through the crowd and aimed directly at my mother-in-law. This was no accident, no random target. Helen was precisely in the bullseye. I stopped the video at the point where I thought I'd have the best view of the face behind the helmet's shield. I could only say that it looked like a woman rather than a man, from the shape and size of the face, and the long hair that feathered out from the bottom of the helmet. On the other hand, plenty of men wore their hair long on this island, so it wasn't fair to judge on that detail alone.

I quickly drafted a note to Nathan, attached the file and sent it off, feeling pleased with myself for realizing that wasn't my job. Maybe their super IT people could blow it up so the driver could be identified. I watched one more time, this time focusing on our faces, seeing the expressions morph from surprised to horrified and frightened. I had to admit that Nathan was right. Something we had stirred up in our questioning had brought out the wrath of this bike rider.

I scraped the last bit of frosting from my plate, thinking that it reminded me of the coconut cake we'd had at Miss Gloria's party last night. Often at the Woman's Club events, the members liked to use recipes from one or the other of the old cookbooks. I pulled out the copies of both the 1949 and 1988 editions, given to me by the former president the first time I visited. Indeed, there was a coconut cake in the 1949 edition, one that I now remembered seeing in a column written by the historian at the Key West library. It had been submitted by Etta Patterson, who'd gotten a lot of mileage from the recipe by serving it to several actual US presidents. The cake part seemed exactly like the one that Nan Copley had entered in the *Key Zest* contest. That didn't bother me too much, because many layer cakes were constructed of similar ingredients. This icing, however, was different. Etta had used marshmallows and a whole grated coconut. The first was an ingredient I would not have endorsed with enthusiasm, and the freshly grated coconut would not be something today's cooks could easily manage. Maybe Nan had been unfairly accused of stealing recipes.

Then it occurred to me that perhaps we should be looking for someone who wasn't at the party on the cruise, rather than someone who was. Because why in the world would you blow up a boat on which you were a passenger?

As I looked at my list, two things jumped out at me as questions I could tackle without putting myself in danger, and thus in Nathan's bad graces. If all went well, I could do them both at once.

I started by texting Palamina to ask her if she would meet me for coffee at Five Brothers. I told her that I wanted to listen to what the other patrons might be saying about Nan Copley. This would be the perfect opportunity, since following the wake last night, her name would be all over town. It would be fresh on everyone's mind. Still, it would look less suspicious if there were two of us sipping coffee and chatting rather than me eavesdropping alone. I asked her to bring the guest list that I thought I'd left on my desk that included regrets. Then we could brainstorm about what I'd been learning about the boat disaster. What I didn't say was that I wanted to find out once and for all why she chose the *Pilar Too* for our vessel.

Five Brothers was a coffee shop and grocery store located at the corner of Southern and Grinnell Streets. It was old-fashioned and family run with no place to sit inside. Lots of locals, including a rotating cast of police officers and apparently Nan Copley herself, spent morning hours chatting and wiling away time on the benches outside the main door. After Palamina texted, agreeing to meet me in half an hour, I decided to walk the mile to the shop. I could take Ziggy for a decent outing and get a little bit of exercise to work off some of what I had been eating.

I texted Palamina back. *If you get there before I do, please order me a café con leche, and a guava pastry.* My stomach was rumbling as I looked at the menu, so I added . . . *Maybe a Cuban sandwich too, it's probably time we refreshed my round up of Cuban sandwiches. I'll eat that for lunch later. Much later.*

She would be horrified with my order, but those of us who weren't stick figures like her had to eat regularly. Maybe by assuring her it was for a late lunch, she'd be less judgy. Ziggy saw me getting ready to go out and trotted into the bedroom with his leash in his mouth. "Yes, Mr. Ziggy, you are going this time. You've put up with a lot this week." I ruffled the short fur between his ears and hooked him up to the leash.

By the time we arrived at the shop, huffing and sweaty, Palamina was already sitting on one of the benches with two coffees and a brown bag that smelled fragrant and unbelievably delicious.

"Perfect timing," she said, shifting over so there was room for me on the bench, "everything is still hot. How did Gloria's party go? From your texts last night, it sounded like it might've been a little hard for you to focus."

That made me hoot with laughter. I dropped my voice low. "It's hard to think of anything other than what happened with our sunset cruise and why. Nathan has not said this, not directly anyway, but I'm concerned that my mother will be accused of being careless. Which is totally not fair because on that busy dock, anybody could slip something onto a cart at any time. I'd be more inclined to think one of Roche's crew was involved." I heaved a big sigh. "We haven't had a chance to interview any of them because the boat's gone so no one's hanging around the dock. I have to trust that Nathan will do the best he can to figure this out and protect us."

I kept my eye on the other folks lounging beside the benches, and two police officers in blue uniform standing nearby, whom I didn't recognize. Schafer and Newcomb, the tags on their shirts read. New guys on the force, I supposed. Several people with sunburns who sounded like tourists were yakking about their Key West bucket lists, very pleased with themselves for having found a local spot off the beaten track. At the end of the bench, a weathered looking man wearing jeans with big holes at the knees was holding forth about the unfairness of hiking up rents on Garrison Bight. This was where our houseboats were docked, but I was quite certain he didn't live there. I wasn't friends with everyone who docked their boat in our marina, but I knew them by sight. Sometimes, I recognized their voices by the sounds drifting over the water from their boats. His was unfamiliar.

"Next thing you know," the man said, "they'll be raising rents on the docks along the harbor. As it is, it's hard to make a living. How long can we justify telling our customers that we have to raise our fees again in order to survive?"

Several others of the locals interrupted with a chorus of agreement about raising rents. Buddy LaRue wasn't here, nor was anyone talking about the death on our cruise, or Nan Copley herself. Not yet.

I focused back on my boss, keeping one ear open for a shift in topic or tone of the conversation. "Did you bring the list?"

She nodded and handed it over. "Anything jump out at you?" I asked.

"Not at first glance, but then you know the local characters better than I do."

"I'll study it when I get home." I folded it in quarters and tucked it into my back pocket to look at later.

"Can I ask you a question?" I didn't wait for her to answer. "Why did you choose the *Pilar Too* for the event? Maybe it's not related to the incident, but the question keeps coming up."

Palamina's expression was pained. "Really? I can't think how this has anything to do with the boat blowing up."

"But it could," I said, determined to stick with the subject until she spilled. "Please, this might be the end of my mother's career. Maybe ours too."

She puffed out a big sigh and focused on the flaming red royal poinciana tree across the street. "I'd say that decision came from the gut. When we first talked about the idea of a big party, remember how none of the options we discussed sounded quite right?"

I remembered, because Danielle and I had brainstormed every possible venue on the island. Palamina didn't like any of them.

"Right after that, I went over to the docks and looked at the boats that might be available. The *Pilar Too*, in spite of its silly name, was downright gorgeous, you have to admit that," said Palamina.

"I admit that it made a wonderful statement. Until it didn't, and all that flotsam and jetsam and our guests were bobbing in the water." We exchanged rueful smiles. "It was horrifying and terrifying," I said. "I don't think the horror of it has completely sunk in." I squinted at her and took a bite of my flaky pastry, followed by a sip of café con leche. "You chose the boat vendor by its appearance. Anything else go into that decision?"

She shifted on the bench, glanced down, and brushed away what looked like an imaginary speck on her capri pants. "My husband adored Hemingway. He always wanted to travel to Cuba to see the original Pilar, which is supposedly kept on the Hemingway property outside Havana. We were planning to go together, but as you know the marriage didn't last long enough to go on vacation." She frowned deeply, lines furrowing on the edges of her lips. "But that has nothing to do with anything. I don't know, as I said, this boat was beautiful, and it called out to me."

"So you talked with Captain Roche at that point?"

She nodded. "I described what we had in mind, and he said he could handle it. He'd hosted many bigger events. He sounded OK—what do I know from cruising? But he seemed enthusiastic about the party and assured me his crew could handle a crowd like that. He took me on a tour, and we mapped out where the different stations could be, and I kept thinking how much Damian would have loved the boat."

Her face looked sad, desperately sad. Like puzzle pieces shifting into place, her choice of that boat for our event came clear. I didn't think it had anything to do with why the *Pilar Too* blew up, who dropped off the boat, or who had it in for Nan Copley. Underneath her prickly exterior, my boss was a lovesick puppy, and she chose the craft that her estranged husband would have adored.

As we were chatting, I heard several phones buzzing. The guy a few seats away from us grabbed his out of his pocket to look. "Oh my God! They found Buddy LaRue's body."

"You're kidding," said the man next to him. "Where? Did he have a heart attack?"

"In the mangroves across from the airport."

"Murder? Suicide? Accident?" The man who had asked those questions laughed even though it wasn't the slightest bit funny.

I felt sick at the thought of another death and hoped it wasn't connected to our sunset cruise. Had there been enough bad blood between Captain Roche and this man to lead to murder? They had definitely had an ugly interaction last night.

The Mango Murders

In tandem, the police officers both looked at their phones, then their radios crackled with instructions, and they rushed off to the cruisers parked on Southard Street.

"This changes everything," I muttered to Palamina. "I was beginning to think LaRue was behind the explosion. But if he's been murdered or killed himself, that can't be so. I've got to get home and call Nathan, and I've got to get a new phone right away."

Chapter Twenty-One

She could taste the sense of anticipation, sharp and bittersweet.

—Harini Nagendra, *A Nest of Vipers*

Ziggy and I fast walked home, with the Cuban mix sandwich leaking juice onto the brown bag in which I carried it, calling to both of us. "It will be an early lunch," I told the dog. "But I think we deserve that. Honestly, it's been a crazy, crazy couple of weeks."

Ziggy wagged his tail in agreement.

Despite feeling panicky about the latest news, I realized there was nothing that I could do. This wasn't my problem. But still, it felt like I needed to know the facts. If I couldn't reach Nathan, or he was not at liberty to tell me anything, Miss Gloria would probably have heard some of the details on her police scanner.

I checked my calendar once I got back to my laptop, reminding myself that I had a physical therapy appointment out near Publix shopping center. This would give me enough time to go to the T-Mobile store to purchase the new phone I desperately needed. Next, I checked my email.

Amanda, the ice cream shop owner, had written to report that she remembered a woman asking the people around her whether they smelled gas. "People were noncommittal," she added. "Nobody said they could smell it, and no one seemed the least bit worried. That included me—we were all having the best time! Then I'm pretty sure the woman said, 'I'm going downstairs to see if someone left a stove burner on.' I might be wrong, but I think it was the same woman who refused the name tag."

She'd left her phone number, so I dialed her back on the landline and was shunted to voicemail. "It's Hayley. I wonder about the timing," I said. "Did the explosion happen right after that? A while later? Anyway, I'm off to do some errands but let's talk soon."

Allison had also emailed saying she'd been asking around whether Eva aka Athena was staying at the Casa Marina. "Of course, the front desk wouldn't tell me anything. But I suggest that you come right over if you have time."

I did, just barely. She wouldn't tease if she didn't have something that might matter. It could be super important, considering this new information about Buddy LaRue's death.

I fed both animals and gobbled down half the Cuban mix sandwich, tucking the rest into the refrigerator. I couldn't stop thinking about Palamina mourning her marriage, desperately sad about losing her husband. I would feel exactly the same way if I'd made a foolish error that resulted in Nathan calling it quits. I left a message on Nathan's email, reminding him that

I would be out most of the afternoon, going to my new physical therapist, and hopefully to get a brand-new phone as well. I also reported what Amanda remembered about the guest who smelled gas on the boat.

"I love you," I added, thinking again about Palamina and Damian. "See you for dinner at Seven Fish at 7 p.m. Let me know if you're able to pick us up or if I should hitch a ride with Mom and Sam."

When I emerged outside, I was surprised not to see Miss Gloria or her cats on the deck, though it was getting hot so maybe she'd retired into the air conditioning. I tapped on her screen door.

"Who's there?" Her voice came out as a low croaking noise I'd only heard the one time she had the flu.

"It's Hayley. Can I come in for a minute?" Another croak of assent.

Miss Gloria was lying on the couch looking like a sack of white rice with a hole in the corner. She had an ice pack draped over her forehead.

"It's been years since this happened to me, but I almost feel like I have a hangover," she said in a whisper.

I tried not to laugh. "How late were you out?"

"2 a.m. We ended up at Sloppy Joe's. I wanted to go to Garden of Eden's clothing optional bar next, but the others voted me down. That's when Annie Dubisson called us an Uber. Thank goodness for good friends! Can you imagine if I'd pranced down Duval Street in my birthday suit? People have been known to do that after they've had way too much fun, and the bounds of decent behavior are breached. I'd never live that one down."

I snickered. "No, you probably wouldn't."

She pressed her hand to her eyes, her skin translucent over the veins and tiny bones. When she blinked her eyes open, tears had gathered in the corners. "It was an unbelievably special night, and I owe so much to you. You and your family worked so hard to pull that off."

"You are worth every minute that it took."

Her police scanner crackled reminding me what I'd come over for. "Have you been listening to the latest news?"

She sat up suddenly and dropped the discarded ice pack on the end table. "I knew I needed to tell you something. They found that captain's body early this morning. Someone had clunked him on the head and then put him out to sea in his own dinghy. The motor was running. No telling whether he ever would've been found if an early morning kayaker hadn't spotted what he thought was an empty boat and called the Coast Guard."

"Were there signs of a struggle? Did they say anything about suspects? Do they think the kayaker was involved?"

She clapped the ice pack back onto her head. "Not so many questions all at once. You know they aren't gonna put all that out on the police scanner. They are quite aware that I and the rest of the world are listening in."

"I'll leave you to recover." I blew her a kiss. "I'm off to the physical therapist and to get a phone. Finally. Will you be OK to go to dinner tonight?"

"I wouldn't miss it," she said. "I'm afraid my sons and their wives won't leave without this final exclamation point. They're exhausting don't you think?"

"They mean well," I said. Although I wasn't convinced that that was true.

Chapter Twenty-Two

A recipe has no soul . . . You as the cook must bring the soul to the recipe.

—Thomas Keller

I hopped on my scooter and drove across town to Flagler's big hotel bordering the Atlantic Ocean. Allison was waiting outside the grand entrance with a valet dressed in khaki pants and a blue polo shirt.

"This is Alex," she said, once I'd joined them. "He's been so helpful to us this week."

He blushed and bobbed his head—he and my stepmother had definitely hit it off. I imagined she'd greeted him warmly every time she saw him, and probably tipped well to boot.

"He's not sure he remembers much about the woman you're looking for, but he definitely remembers her car."

"Her car?" I asked the kid.

"Yes," he said his tone serious. "It's a turquoise Thunderbird, vintage, convertible, with stick shift and original leather seats. It's a stunner. When she asked me to park it in a special place, I was happy to do that. She said she was only staying a couple days on this visit, so I'm a little surprised that she hasn't come back for the car." He rubbed his temple, looking perplexed. "I swear she said a proposal was in the works, so she might be spending lots of time here in the near future planning a big wedding."

"Oh," I said. "She was hoping to get married here? Lovely." If she'd planned to propose to Palamina, that would have landed as well as a key lime pie dropped from the viewing deck of the lighthouse. "Those are very clever observations," I added with an admiring smile. "Would you mind showing us the car?"

We walked between the vehicles, many of them high end, luxury cars, until we reached the furthest corner. The blue convertible was off by itself, near a maintenance shed.

The valet blushed again. "She said she didn't want to take the chance of any dings or dents, which sometimes happens in a public parking lot. But she also didn't want to park under a tree where a coconut or a heavy palm frond might fall on it. So I chose this spot."

"Very thoughtful," I said, thinking she must have offered him a *very* large tip for the special treatment. We both thanked Alex effusively, as he trotted off to a help a customer who had pulled up under the hotel's portico.

"Would you mind taking a photo of the license plate and texting it to me and to Nathan?" I asked my stepmother. "I'm on my way to get the new phone right now. Use your judgment on what you tell him about why it might be important."

She busied herself taking pictures from several angles.

"Wouldn't the front desk confirm that this was Eva's car?" I asked her.

"Their lips are sealed. Which I suppose is a good policy if you are going to have high profile guests staying at your hotel. I'll keep poking around."

"Where's the rest of the family?" I asked.

"Believe it or not, Rory seems to have been bitten by the golf bug. He's out playing again with your father and Nathan's."

I gave her a quick hug and hurried to my scooter to drive up Flagler to the newer and busier section of town. I still had time before my physical therapy appointment to stop into the T-Mobile store. Hopefully, all fingers and toes crossed, I could pick up a new phone, get my data transferred, and get back to the old normal. For all the touting of experts about how reducing screen time was good for mental health, it felt like mine had only deteriorated since losing my phone.

Inside the store, I confirmed with the young woman on duty that I could indeed replace the old phone on my current plan, and that with my username and password and Apple ID, she could help transfer my apps and photos and everything else to the new phone. I chose the next iteration of my old phone, purported to have an even better camera, then chose a case, and paid.

"I was on the sunset cruise that blew up and sank the other night," I told her. "I am dying for a new phone. I've been lost in a communication desert without it."

"It's going to take me a good half an hour to get this set up," the clerk warned me. "I have several jobs ahead of you. Seems like half the people on the island lost their phones on that boat."

I felt a spike of annoyance, as the store was empty. Not a single other customer. But this wasn't her fault and even if it was, pitching a fit would not improve my chances of getting the job done quickly.

The Mango Murders

The clock on the wall told me I had five minutes to get to my appointment. "This could work out just fine," I said in a reassuring voice more for myself than the clerk. "I have a medical appointment and then I will pop back over."

Heather Harvey, Miss Gloria's physical therapist, had an office in the BBT building, one of the few tall buildings in the New Town section of Key West. It appeared old and tired though, ready to be knocked down and replaced by something more modern. I went inside the lobby, pressed the button to call the elevator, and waited several minutes for it to arrive. On my way up to the fourth floor, the machine clanked and jerked, and I hoped I wouldn't get stuck. I still had a bit of PTSD from being trapped in the elevator of the Steamplant apartments some years ago with our *Key Zest* landlord and friend, realtor Cory Held. I couldn't get out of this creaky box and into the hallway quickly enough.

Heather's office was at the end of a dingy hall. Hers was a small but welcoming space with a PT bed, a tiny desk for her computer, and a cupboard that I imagined was full of physical therapy equipment. She greeted me at the door, a cheerful blonde woman with a welcoming smile.

"Come right in and have a seat." She waved at the stool beside her desk. "Your neighbor told me how you'd been on that doomed Mallory Square cruise. She said on the phone that you have some symptoms related to the explosion?"

"Yes," I told her. "I wouldn't normally rely on my elderly neighbor to make my medical appointments, but I've not been able to replace my phone." I took a breath. "I must have wrenched my neck when I hit the water. I hoped it was going to go away by itself, but it hasn't." I tipped my head gingerly to the right and pointed out exactly where it hurt.

"I've treated a few other people who were on that boat," Heather said, her eyes wide and comforting. "It sounded very scary."

She invited me to take a seat on the therapy bed and led me through a few gentle stretches so she could evaluate the injury. As she worked her fingers across my neck and upper spine, I studied the photos and diplomas on her wall. There was a sweet photo that looked like it had been taken at her wedding with her new husband and a golden retriever.

"You essentially have whiplash, which I know I can help," Heather explained, once she'd finished her examination. "Although your injury sustained while hitting the water would have occurred at a higher velocity than many automobile accidents. I say that to explain why you'd need to get an X-ray before I could treat you."

I felt a rush of disappointment, surprised to notice how close I was to tears. Again. The delay made good medical sense, and she was wise to insist on it. Crying wouldn't get me anywhere—it was just annoying. I'd felt like a ball of mush ever since the boat incident. I pushed back the threatening deluge and let out the big breath of air I realized I was holding. "Absolutely nothing is going quite right today. In fact, it's been a lousy week. To be honest, I was hoping for a quick fix."

She offered a sympathetic smile and gave me her business card. "No quick miracles in this business. Have your doctor send the X-ray results to this email and then we'll get started. Have they determined the cause of the accident?"

"They determined that the explosion was fueled by a canister of propane that had been loaded into the lower level, though I haven't heard what sparked it. I'm not sure we can ever know

The Mango Murders

that. It appears that someone loosened the cap. Maybe the woman who was the only casualty. I can't imagine she meant to die, but maybe she wasn't able to get out in time or it happened sooner than she expected. Or maybe she had nothing to do with the gas but went to the bathroom at exactly the wrong time."

While she typed some notes into her computer, I stopped myself from babbling more details by gazing at the golden retriever in the wedding picture. I wondered whether Nathan and company had thought to ask other guests whether they smelled gas. Surely, they wouldn't have overlooked such an important question. At least I'd reminded him that Amanda had overheard this very conversation.

Next to the wedding photo was a colorful print that reminded me a little bit of the Spanish artist, Jean Miro.

"That was a gift from John Martini," she said smiling when she saw me studying the art.

"He was on our sunset cruise as well. All of us were pretty shaken up."

The smile fell from her lips. "I don't think he'd mind me saying that I had his shoulder fixed up almost as good as new, and then he wrenched it when the boat blew up. All the work we did together, undone in a moment in that explosion. But we'll get him sorted out."

She was so positive and competent that I believed her. "He's a remarkable artist," I said. "I've always wanted one of his sculptures—a small one, since they weigh a ton and we live on a houseboat." We both laughed.

"Actually," she continued, "he was here right before you. He was planning to take a ride out to White Crowned Pigeon Park to look at some materials for a new piece. You know that big green barn-like building almost to the end of the road?"

"I haven't been back there," I said. The road to that park ran along an airport runway, separated from the airport property by a big chain link fence. Nathan liked to take Ziggy there when he jogged. Less traffic, less noise, fewer crazy dogs and people.

"I think he said the city was offering some chunks of rusty metal to whoever would be willing to cart them off. He was going to look them over to see if anything might be useful in his next project. Between you and me, I think he's hoping to persuade the authorities to give him that old plane. The city and the airport authorities have been wrangling for years over what to do with it. Imagine the artwork he could build around that."

"What old plane?" I asked.

"You should go see it," she said, "before they tow it away for good. A Cubana de Aviación flight was hijacked in 2003 on its way from a small island to Havana. Oddly enough, it was diverted to Key West, where it's remained ever since. I think at some point it was used as a training facility for firefighters and police, but now it's abandoned to the elements. The city and the airport authorities have been wrangling for years over what to do with the aluminum carcass. Hence, John Martini's interest."

"Interesting," I said, my thoughts pinging over to how he hoped to get artistic inspiration from the necklace of the woman on the boat. Was she the same person who refused the name tag? Could this possibly have been Louise Wardell? Acting in Buddy's interest? Although she was alive and well—making me think that perhaps she'd been the person to turn the nozzle on the gas canister and then drop off the *Pilar Too* before it blew up.

The Mango Murders

"He's exactly the person I wanted to talk with again, but of course I still don't have a phone."

"Want me to text him?" she asked.

This wasn't a bad idea. I had a feeling that if I could show him the clearer photo of the woman who'd photobombed him, he'd be able to help with her identification.

"Sure. I'll run by the T-Mobile store first, grab my new phone, and be over at the park in twenty minutes?" Then maybe I could persuade him to look at the event photos again.

I took the stairs on the way out of the building rather than repeat the trip on that rickety elevator. With dull gray walls—last painted years in the past, I suspected—and rusty metal stairs, the stairwell could have stood in as a spooky filming location for any horror movie.

Once safely outside, I returned to the store to pick up my new phone. The clerk cringed when she saw me coming.

"Unfortunately, we're having some trouble with our Internet and that means your download is going very slowly. Best guess, it will be another hour."

I huffed my annoyance, but I wasn't going to waste the next hour watching the clerk like a boiling pot. Popping into Publix for supplies was a bad idea because the groceries would wilt in the afternoon heat. At least running out to the park to chat with John Martini again would kill a little time. It might even garner some useful information.

Chapter Twenty-Three

When you contrast her recklessness with your frugality, your disapproval radiates from your words like heat from a waffle iron.

—Kwame Anthony Apaiah, "The Ethicist", *New York Times*, April 10, 2024

There are not too many wild places left on the island of Key West, except for the marshy areas that are too wet to build on. Wildness is more easily found on the water, in the mangrove islands, or out in the far reaches of the Dry Tortugas National Park. Here on land, development has slowly encroached on the open spaces. Empty lots have been crammed with buildings and entire neighborhoods have been erected on pure dredged fill, so that more residents and visitors could be shoehorned in. I could understand the urge: everyone who visited this place wanted to own a piece of paradise.

I had never been to White Crowned Pigeon Park, never heard of it really, but Heather described it as an untrammeled area that ran parallel to the Key West airport. I drove down Flagler and turned onto Government Road, winding through a small neighborhood and into open areas leading to the park. A chain-link fence topped with barbed wire ran along the right side of the road, separating the public areas from the airport. Within a few minutes, I reached the old plane that Heather had mentioned. An aluminum ladder leaned up against the body, and a set of wooden steps led to the door. CUBANA was painted on the side in fading gray, the color of the stairwell I'd raced down. I could picture the terror of the passengers who'd been unlucky enough to fly on the hijacked plane. Now, it was a hulking carcass, a shadow of long-ago days. Unless Mr. Martini had a lot of money and pull, it was hard to see how he could get his hands on this skeleton of a plane. I kept driving, reaching the end of the road, identified by a small sign as the City of Key West paintball fields. Next to the bright green shed that Heather had described, I spotted a storage area containing oversized rusty chains, heaps of scrap metal, and abandoned machines—the pieces the city must be hoping someone would haul away. The heap was covered by a corrugated roof and fenced in with chain link—no sign of John Martini.

I turned around and drove back the way I came, noticing two homeless women who'd set up camp next to a weathered picnic table, with a shopping cart full of belongings and two black and white spotted dogs. They sat in low hanging beach chairs in the shade and watched me approach.

"Good afternoon," I called. "Did you happen to see a bearded man about so tall"—I held my hand six inches above my head—"drive by on a scooter?"

They looked at each other and shook their heads. "Too hot to be out," said the older woman. "Not much traffic today."

I waved my thanks, and drove on, finally spotting a sign that identified the Fran Ford White Crowned Pigeon Preserve. In the trees behind the sign, someone had erected a very rusty mailbox with the red flag up, as if it was waiting for the postman. The sun was beating down hot and hard, and I wished I'd brought my water bottle. I saw nothing alive. No birds, no animals, not even an iguana. Overhead, I heard the thwap, thwap noise of a helicopter. I squinted up. It looked like tourists headed toward the Dry Tortugas. Or possibly, military. Everything about this place spooked me.

In the bushes behind the mailbox, I thought I saw the glint of red metal. As the sound of the chopper blades receded, I heard a noise, maybe a muffled voice.

"Help!"

A muffled voice that sounded absolutely real. I parked my scooter and took a few steps closer. A red scooter had been pushed into the thick brush, and now lay on its side. It did not look as though the person had parked and gone for a hike or a picnic, and meanwhile their bike had fallen over. It looked like something awful had happened. I paused to listen and heard it again.

"Help!"

Once I got close enough to read the stickers on the scooter—*Safer Cleaner Ships* and *One Human Family*, I knew it had to belong to John Martini. He was one of the good guys in our Key West world and I'd seen that very scooter in his studio. I considered turning around and riding to the nearest home for help. But if his life was in danger, could he wait even the five minutes my ride would take? Plus, another five or ten while I explained everything to the homeowner and begged them to call the cops?

I took a deep breath and pushed my way into the undergrowth. I found him in a thick stand of shrubs and ferns. His hands and feet had been tied, and he'd been muzzled with a bandana like the red one he'd been wearing at his studio. His eyes got wide when he saw me.

I crouched down beside him and began to work the knot. "Sorry, this might hurt a little. It's been pulled very tight."

He nodded his head and squawked a noise that sounded like "thanks."

"I don't have a phone, so once we get you untied, I'll take you out on my scooter." My fingers felt sweaty and clumsy, and I began to hum with encouragement. "Almost there. I'll get you out. Don't worry. Who in the world did this to you?"

As the bandana finally loosened, I felt a sharp jab of pain in my back, and my hands were yanked behind me so I fell to my knees. A gravelly female voice spoke. I craned around to see who it was, catching only a glimpse of a ponytail in a ball cap, a medical mask, and angry eyes.

"If you say one word or scream or fight, I will shoot him and then you. We're taking a walk one at a time, you first." She gave me another jab in the back. "Stand up."

I believed her, so once I was pulled to my feet, I trotted ahead. But a million thoughts were running through my mind. Who was this? Why bother with either John Martini or me? Would I ever see the people I loved again? Was I the biggest dope in the world? Yes, but was there a way out? I'd seen not a single person who might call for help, except for the ladies by the picnic table and their camp was far enough away that they likely couldn't see or hear us. I could scream but I might get shot.

She pushed me along until we reached a wooden path lined with metal railings that led deeper into the brush of the salt marsh. The air was thick with humidity, and I could smell myself sweating with fear.

"My car is parked on the other side of this walk. When we get there, you'll be riding in the trunk. If we pass anyone, not a word, understood?"

"Understood," I squeaked, listening to the clap, clap of our shoes on the wood planks and feeling more discouraged and frightened with each step. But in the distance, from the direction of her car, I heard more footsteps, and a sharp woof. She slung her free arm around my waist, like lovers out for a stroll, keeping the gun pressed into my back as warning.

She had told me not to speak, but this could be my only chance to signal I needed help from whomever it was. I pasted a great big wide grin on my face. The kind of smile that Miss Gloria cautioned me never to use because it showed I was obviously too tired or disinterested to be authentic. "Even a stranger would know you're a phony," she'd said.

But as I grinned foolishly, Helen and Allison came around the next bend, along with Ziggy, who was dragging them at a quick clip. The dog stopped stock still when he saw us, every muscle in his sleek black body clenched, uttering a low warning growl. I felt a powerful urge to throw myself into my stepmother's arms, but the woman jabbed me with the gun's barrel again. I tried to signal with eyes only that my relations should do nothing to upset her.

"Good morning," I squeaked. "It's a lovely afternoon for a stroll, wouldn't you say?"

"Lovely," my stepmother squeaked back, her expression frightened. Helen's face was completely blank.

"Not one more word," the woman hissed.

The Mango Murders

She hustled me past the mothers. Then I heard fierce snarling and out of my side-eye, saw a blur of black fur. Ziggy threw himself at the woman and sank his sharp teeth into her calf. She went down with a shriek, grabbing at her leg, now running with blood. Helen lunged forward, shoved both of us hard, and then scrambled for the gun that had been knocked loose as we stumbled. She clocked the woman on the temple and stood over the slumped figure.

"Take my belt," she instructed my stepmother. "Tie her hands and call 911."

She yanked the mask off the woman's face.

"What the hell, Hayley?" she asked. "Isn't this Nan Copley, the one whose picture was in the *Citizen* this morning? I thought she was dead."

Chapter Twenty-Four

Speaking from experience, chicken soup can heal both a sore throat and a broken heart.
　—Molly Adams, "My 85-Year-Old Grandmother Ate 8 of These Every Day," *Simply Recipes*, September 24, 2024

I heard police cars screeching up Government Road with sirens blaring. Two officers pounded down the path and took charge of Helen's prisoner, while a third retrieved John Martini from the bushes. He hurried up the walk toward us, trailed by the disheveled sculptor rubbing the red marks on his wrists. I recognized Officer Ryan, who had ferried me home after the boat explosion a week ago.

"Could you give us a thumbnail sketch of what exactly is going on here?" he asked.

I untangled myself from Allison's hug and explained how I had come looking to talk with John Martini about clues to finding the criminal responsible for the explosion. "I thought it might have been either Buddy LaRue's head crew member, Louise, or my boss's girlfriend Eva who caused the incident. I was pretty sure John could confirm this."

The Mango Murders

Officer Ryan held up his hand. "Let's slow down here." He turned to Martini. "Let's start with you."

His voice came out in a series of raspy croaks, and Allison handed him the bottle of water she'd been clutching. "I'd heard about the metal chains they were hoping to give away"—he waved toward the paintball field—" so I took a ride up to look them over. There wasn't much I thought I could use. But on the way out, I spotted that rusty mailbox."

"That thing is so cool. And spooky," I added. "It's almost like the residents it belonged to have disappeared completely. Vanished."

"Yes." He nodded vigorously. "That was going to be the theme of the new piece if I could somehow wrestle the mailbox to my studio. Something about how the old guard, including the wise ones who understand our island's history, has rusted away to nothing in our town."

Officer Ryan looked impatient. "So you were looking at the mailbox, and—?"

"That woman emerged from the bushes, threatened me, and tied me up." He looked a little sheepish. "After Hayley visited my studio, I started thinking about doing some investigation of my own. I went back over to the *Carpe Diem* to talk with Buddy and his crew. He wasn't there of course, because he'd been murdered. Louise, his chief mate, was devastated. He'd told her he was in trouble and might have to disappear for a while. She thought he was being dramatic, as was apparently his wont. So I took a ride to the mangroves where his boat had been found. Seeing nothing unusual, I headed out here. While I was studying the mailbox, Nan Copley surprised me. She was worried that I was nosing around into Buddy's business. She wasn't going to allow me to blow the whistle." He glanced at me. "She was following you originally, all the way to my studio."

I clapped a hand over my eyes. "I'm so sorry to pull you into a dangerous situation."

"Meanwhile," Officer Ryan asked me, "how did you end up here?"

"I went to physical therapy for an evaluation of my whiplash, and Heather happened to mention that John was going to be here looking at some raw materials. I wanted to talk to him again about the necklace."

"The necklace?" asked Officer Ryan.

"It's a long story and maybe Nathan should tell it, but I suspect it's what they'll use to identify the real victim. It was a fish made out of a spoon, hung on a black string, which probably burned away in the fire. Anyway, Heather said she'd text him to tell him to expect me because I still don't have a phone. Sure enough, I found him, but he was hogtied and left in the brush."

"Why in the world did she leave him tied up in the bushes?" Helen asked.

"If you don't mind, ma'am," said Officer Ryan firmly. "It will work better if I ask the questions."

Did he know he was scolding Nathan's mother? It would've been funny except nothing felt too funny now.

"He was tied up in the bushes while she waited for you," Officer Ryan said. I gulped. "You found him and then what?"

"As I tried to untie some of the knots, she came up behind me and threatened me with her gun. But I still didn't know it was Nan because of the mask. She said we were walking to her car where I was going for a ride in the trunk." I shivered, not wanting to imagine what the endpoint of that ride would have been.

"Anyway, as we went along this path, my mother-in-law and stepmother appeared out of nowhere, thank God in heaven, and then my mother-in-law Helen let go of the leash and Ziggy attacked Nan. After that, she managed to snatch up the gun and my stepmother called you."

"How did you happen to come along at just the right time?" I asked my relatives. "Oops." I glanced at Officer Ryan. "Sorry, you're asking the questions."

"Go ahead," he said, sounding defeated.

"It's a complicated story, but we stopped at Houseboat Row to talk over the case, but found you weren't there. Miss Gloria got worried when she didn't hear back from you after your therapy appointment, and it was clear that your phone was still not working. She called Heather Harvey, the therapist, who told her that you were planning to take a ride out here to talk with Mr. Martini. Since we were already out and about, Gloria asked us"—she pointed to Allison and herself—"to swing by the park and see if your scooter was here. She had a very bad feeling. She suggested we come in through the neighborhood so we wouldn't alert the bad guys and scare them into hurting you. We agreed and came in the back way, pretending we were dog walking."

"I loved the binoculars," I said. "Brilliant touch."

"That was Allison's idea," said Helen with a smirk. "She thought we could pass for birdwatchers. Joggers, not so much."

"I think this is enough for now," said Officer Ryan. "We will be following up shortly. Do you need medical attention?" he asked Martini and me.

"Not at the moment," I said. "Maybe I'll feel some new aches and pains once the adrenalin recedes. Right now I really want to go home."

Officer Ryan took all our information, with assurances that we'd need to tell our stories again.

* * *

My mother was waiting at the houseboat, having been alerted by Allison about the latest excitement. She ran down the finger and pulled me into a giant hug as soon as I got off my scooter.

"Come inside," she said. "It's beastly hot out here and you ladies need something cool to drink."

Back in my own kitchen, I rewarded Ziggy for his bravery with bites of the leftover shredded chicken I'd tucked into the freezer after a dinner last week. He wiggled with appreciation.

"You were brilliant," I told the dog. "You absolutely saved the day."

"He definitely did," Allison agreed. "Though I'm certain Helen would have come up with something. I was scared to death when I saw you with that hideous grin on your face."

My mother poured us frosty glasses of sweet tea garnished with big slices of lemon and key limes. She set a glass in front of me, along with a snickerdoodle she'd found stashed in the freezer.

Confusing myself completely, because tea and cookies did not ordinarily cause meltdowns, I burst into tears. Mom pulled me into another big hug, rubbing my back in comforting circles. "It's been a terribly stressful week hasn't it, between the accident and the fear that it wasn't an accident and then Helen's motorcycle incident and then all the stress with Miss Gloria's family and you trying to make everything perfect for her, and then, to top it all off, this woman trying to abduct you at gunpoint. It's no wonder you feel like the world is too much."

Once my sobs abated, she held me away from her, examining my face, then brushing my damp cheek with two fingers. Exactly the place where I'd noticed some new freckling this morning.

"I know. I need to be careful to use more sunscreen."

A big smile spread over her face. "Hayley Catherine Snow Bransford, your hormones have been showing all week. Is it possible that you're pregnant?"

I felt the clunking feeling of my stomach falling, followed by a hysterical bubble of laughter, and then cold fear. This could explain why I felt constantly ravenous and also exhausted. "Oh my gosh. We weren't trying for this, and we hadn't even discussed it. I've been drinking coffee and alcohol all along. I've probably ruined the poor baby." I pressed my fingers to my face and wailed: "We're not ready! I don't know how it happened!"

The three mothers exchanged a glance and began to laugh. "You don't have to say another word, because we're pretty sure we know how it happened." That was my mother, who would know I'd later regret spilling any intimate details to my mother-in-law.

While I absorbed the shock of the news for a few minutes, the mothers chattered about possible due dates and where in the world we'd put a baby and all its accompanying stuff in our little houseboat.

I motioned for a time out. "These questions are all very important, but it occurs to me that I need to figure out how break the news to Nathan when the time's right. Let's not say anything at dinner, because I should tell him first, don't you think? Maybe get a pregnancy test to be sure?"

"Probably right," Helen said. "Knowing my son, I predict he's going to be stunned. When he gets over that, which could take a couple of weeks, maybe even months, hopefully not years, he's going to be thrilled." Her phone rang and Nathan's name scrolled across the screen. She handed it to me. "I'm sure this is for you. I don't want to speak to him because I'm afraid I'll spill the beans."

Chapter Twenty-Five

> *It is not often that someone comes along who is a true friend and a good cook.*
> —Jenny Rosenstrach, *Dinner, A Love Story* newsletter, March 23, 2024

Seven Fish has been one of my favorite restaurants in Key West since I wrote my first review when I was auditioning for the job at *Key Zest*, what felt like eons ago. They had moved from a small storefront on Olivia Street to a big new building on Truman, and I'd visited both places many times. The ambience was different in the new venue, but the food stayed exactly the same—fresh and simple and delicious. We'd asked to be seated in the smaller side room, as we'd have fifteen at the table, and the restaurant could get noisy when it was busy.

Allison, Rory, and my father were already seated at the far end of the table with Miss Gloria's sons and daughters-in-law. I blew her a kiss for sacrificing herself to chatting with those unpleasant women. She would know that I needed to be close to my people for tonight, not trying to make nice while dealing with their negativity. I took a seat across from Helen, keeping my mother on one side, and saving Nathan the place on the other.

"We ordered some appetizers for the table, hope that's OK," Allison said.

"Appetizers are always OK," I said, my mouth watering at the prospect of sautéed grouper sushi rolls, grilled shrimp, and wild mushroom quesadilla. But should I choose the fresh yellowtail snapper in their signature Thai curry sauce or the sweet and crunchy banana chicken? Those caramelized walnuts killed me every time... Or even their showstopping meatloaf? I always felt a little guilty ordering that dish in a restaurant known for fish, but still it—

"Earth to Hayley," said my mother. "The waitress is wondering what you would like to drink?"

"Could the bartender make a mocktail? Something festive with a couple of maraschino cherries and a little umbrella? We did a lot of celebrating last night so I'll start slow." No need to explain that I was pregnant—pregnant!—and shouldn't be drinking alcohol. Nathan deserved to absorb the news privately before I let that particular cat out of my bag in front of this motley crowd.

"Of course," said the waitress laughing.

I chatted with the others for a few minutes until Nathan rushed in and swept me into a hug.

"Good god, Hayley," he said. "I can't believe what I'm hearing from Officer Ryan."

"It wasn't her fault," Helen and Miss Gloria said at the same time.

"It was purely coincidental," Miss Gloria added, "though definitely mistakes were made, since she had neither an Apple

The Mango Murders

watch nor a phone so I couldn't track her. I could have sent the police in earlier if I'd known exactly where she was."

Nathan pressed his palms to his eyes, then pulled a phone from his pocket. "I stopped by the T-Mobile store and picked this up—the clerk sends her apologies for the delay. I'll be happy to get you an Apple watch if you'll only stay home with it."

I kissed him and then hugged my phone to my chest.

"But here's the thing," said Miss Gloria, leaning forward to look him in the eye, "you know she isn't going to stay home. She has to go out to eat for her job, and she has to follow all those hunches that you police types don't even notice. Maybe a better idea is to buy her the air tags they use to track luggage and have her stash one in her bra. The bad guys aren't likely to search her underwear, but they might steal or trash a smart watch."

"Stop!" I said. "Enough talking about me as if I'm not here. I'd much rather hear about Nan Copley."

Nathan nodded. "We'll continue this discussion later, but meanwhile, I'll tell you what I can. We've brought in Louise Wardell, Buddy LaRue's second in command. She's filled in a lot of blanks and will be interviewed again tomorrow morning."

"I could have sworn she was the killer," I said. "She's the one I hoped John Martini could identify when I went out to the salt ponds to chat with him. She's definitely strong enough to have been able to manage the captain's murder and then push him out to sea."

"Nope, it was Nan Copley. All she's saying so far is that you"—he nodded at my mother—"stole her career."

"I'm so sorry she felt that way," said my kind-hearted mother softly. "I had no idea she was paying attention to what I was doing."

"Never mind the fact that you stole her grandmother's upside-down mango cake recipe and won the *Key Zest* contest with it," Nathan added. I could tell he didn't believe that for a minute.

"Ridiculous!" Sam said. "That was a perfectly traditional upside-down cake. You can find recipes like it in tons of cookbooks from Betty Crocker to the *Joy of Cooking* to Dorie Greenspan and David Lebovitz. We just played around so it fit the mango theme. When Hayley needed last-minute recipe entries two weeks ago, we thought this cake would be perfect. It was good for the mango season, but it might also shine a spotlight on our big outing. We didn't steal that recipe from anyone's grandmother, end of story. In fact, from what Hayley's discovered, Nan Copley herself pretty much lifted her cake recipe from the Woman's Club cookbook."

"That may be," said Nathan looking directly at my mother. "But it's not what she saw and felt."

"Oh my gosh. If it wasn't Nan Copley who perished in the hold," I said, suddenly putting pieces together, "it had to be Eva Flanagan. She's the only person we know to be missing." I turned to look at Allison and Helen. "That's why her turquoise car is still parked in the lot at the Casa Marina."

Allison's hand flew to her lips. "Oh, that poor woman."

"Why was she on the trip in the first place?" my mother asked. "She certainly wasn't on our guest list."

"We'll find out all those answers," Nathan said, turning to me. "We, meaning the *Key West Police Department*. Here's my question: Please explain what the heck you were doing at White Pigeon Park? I can't believe you wandered into that wilderness by yourself."

The Mango Murders

I smiled what I hoped was a beatific smile. "That's not exactly a question. To be clear, it's officially called the Fran Ford White-Crowned Pigeon Preserve. And I wasn't exactly in the wilderness—it's well trafficked. An airport runway runs right along that road. Plus, there were some homeless women who would have told the cops where to find me. Most important of all, the mothers and your dog showed up when I really needed them. Ziggy was the true hero of the hour."

Nathan opened his mouth to disagree.

Suddenly, as I looked at my husband's dear face, I could imagine his dimples and his green eyes on the face of a child, and it felt like my interior world had shifted like some giant tectonic plate. I couldn't keep it in.

"I have some news," the words came blurting out even though I'd had no intention of doing it this way, and I knew I should have confirmed it first.

I reached for Nathan's hand. "We're having a baby. I think. I'm almost certain."

He looked utterly stunned, and around him came a chorus of "What?" "You're kidding!" and "Congratulations!"

Finally, Nathan stammered, "You're pregnant? How did this happen?"

All the women at the table burst out laughing.

"Really, Nathan?" his mother asked.

He clapped his hands over his eyes and waved her away. After the hubbub had calmed, Nathan placed his hands on my shoulders, kissed my cheek, and said, "No wonder I've been more worried about you than usual. Although you've gotten into the usual terrible situations. Maybe deep down I knew this was about more than you."

My father and Allison came over to hug me. Both had eyes shiny with tears.

Allison said, "Hayley, I'm so excited for you, and for us. I can't wait to get my hands on that baby."

My father squeezed me tight. "I can't believe my baby is having a baby. You'll be a wonderful mother, just like your mother was."

As the appetizers were delivered and orders for more drinks taken, the questions continued to fly. "Do you know how far along you are?" "When did you discover this?" "Is it a boy or a girl?" "How do you feel so far?"

Miss Gloria's daughter-in-law Henrietta tapped her water glass to get our attention.

"We are delighted with your news, and we have some news, too."

This did not bode well. Leave it to sourpuss her to kill anyone's buzz.

"Gloria will be moving north to Michigan at the end of June. That gives her more than a month to get her things organized and say her goodbyes. I know this is difficult, and she rejected our plan once before, but her sons and daughters-in-law all agree that this time it's for the best. That barely floating little tub of a houseboat is no place for an octogenarian plus. Did you know they are predicting an above-average hurricane season this summer? More storms and bigger. Life down here is only going to grow more precarious. Michigan is the best place in the country for old people to feel safe right now. If you all love her as much as you say you do, you will support this decision even if it feels hard."

Not this again. I hated to see that my friend had been right with her prediction about her family—they were going to interfere with her perfectly fine life, the life that she'd spent almost forty years building and completely adored. She had to be devastated. But instead of dissolving into helpless tears, Miss Gloria slapped her hand on the table, her face brightening as she looked around at her family and friends.

"I know I sort of agreed to that, but I didn't sign anything in blood. Now I've got a new plan!" she exclaimed. "I'm not going anywhere until Hayley's baby leaves for college." She turned to look at me and Nathan. "Remember how we talked a while back about how at some point you guys would be ready to move away from Houseboat Row and maybe buy a sweet house with a yard and a mother-in-law suite behind it? With fruit trees like mangos and avocadoes and figs, and room for a swing set, and built-in babysitting. We didn't talk about the exact timing, but it appears it's now." She shifted her gaze between me and Nathan. "No offense, but apparently, you two are short on the facts of life. Maybe your mothers didn't review that information with you?" She widened her eyes, first at Helen, and then my mother.

The entire table burst out laughing again, and I could feel my face getting as hot red as Nathan's.

"Done!" said my husband, who never did love the houseboat life as much as Gloria and I did. "Let's toast to built-in babysitting and a big yard for the kid! And to Hayley, who's going to be the best mother of all, present company excepted."

"Cheers to staying on this island until I harvest my last mango in paradise!" Miss Gloria crowed.

There were cheers all around, except for poor Annie Dubisson, who looked like she'd just lost her best friend in the world.

"Nathan," I said, grabbing his hand and squeezing, "I know you've had to absorb a lot in the last fifteen minutes, but do you suppose we could find a two-bedroom mother-in-law cottage? If we're going to have one octogenarian living in our backyard, wouldn't two be even better?"

"Hurray! I'll drink to that," said Miss Gloria, clinking her friend's glass.

"I've got realtor Cory Held on the line," said my mother, holding up her phone. "She's got a ton of listings that could be perfect. Would it be convenient to look at prospects tomorrow?"

Chapter Twenty-Six

One thing I learned, and continue to learn every day, is that the food we enjoy most connects to our deepest memories of when we felt happy, comfortable, nurtured.
—Ina Garten, *Be Ready When the Luck Happens*

Nathan had rushed home from work to escort me and my mother on a quick tour of the listings that Cory Held had generated. My head was spinning, and we had two more days of appointments to go. Only once we'd narrowed the field down to a few homes we adored, would we take the octogenarians with us for a second visit. All of us agreed that Nathan and I had to decide first.

Once we were finished for the day, Nathan insisted on walking us the short distance from the parking lot to our home before returning to the police station, even taking my hand to help me aboard, as though I was a giant and fragile egg. Which I supposed was not far from the truth. My dear friend Connie came running up the finger and threw her arms around me.

"You're pregnant! I'm so, so happy for you! Our kids will be the best buddies. Except—" her face fell—"Miss Gloria says you're moving away from Houseboat Row."

"Not far," I said. "My first choice will be the Meadows." The neighborhood full of single family homes with historic touches and private gardens that was located just over the Palm Avenue bridge. "It's such a short walk. We'll visit every single day. We'll take everyone to the library for kids' programs and go to parent-teacher night—we'll do everything together!"

She hugged me again and hurried back to the sounds of squabbling that wafted from her little blue floating home. What was I getting myself in to?

Miss Gloria popped out of her own cabin and skipped down the finger to us. "Any good prospects?" she asked eagerly.

"It was a lot to take in," I said, glancing at my husband whose face was a map of grim frown lines.

"Tell us what else you learned about the murder," I suggested, to protect him from a house-by-house recitation of high points and flaws. Living through it once had been painful enough for him. I could fill in my friend in excruciating detail once he went back to work.

Nathan looked relieved to be off the house hunting details and back on his familiar law enforcement turf. "As I mentioned yesterday, both Buddy LaRue and Nan Copley were involved in the disaster. Motives: LaRue was insanely jealous of Captain Roche. He was certain his boat would be chosen for the *Key Zest* party. He thought Roche's Hemingway look-alike boat was nothing but a gimmick, and he couldn't understand why he kept losing business to them. This definitely wasn't the first time he thought Roche had stolen his business. Meanwhile, Copley was furious that Janet and Sam were chosen to cater the big event. This all started earlier with the Cuban American festival at the Little White House a few years back. She thought she would be a shoo-in for that event because she'd been cooking on this island for a lot longer than Janet."

He leaned forward to make eye contact with my mother. "Ever since you landed—or stole—that job, depending on who you're asking, her heart has been a festering wound. She felt like that plum should have been hers. She followed each of your successes with disbelief and grew angrier and angrier. To make things worse, everyone's business was hit hard in the aftermath of the hurricane and the pandemic, including hers, so she experienced your booming business as plain and purposeful robbery."

"So what did they have in mind? Did they actually mean to blow up the ship?" I pressed my hand to my forehead. "Was this a suicide mission? If so, it was a catastrophically ridiculous plan."

"Not at all," Nathan said. "Their intention was to ruin the party. Buddy left the propane tank in one of Janet's carts, which he knew would be taken to the lower level in the dumbwaiter. Nan was supposed to slip into the storage area, unscrew the top, turn on the gas burner of this little stove so the pilot light would be on, and then get out of the way. She claims they didn't intend to set it on fire or blow it up, only cause a scene with the leaking gas to show that Janet and Sam and your captain were careless. Then maybe the cruise would have to be aborted, and your reputations ruined."

I blew out a breath in disgust. "I don't think she's telling you the whole story," I said. "I can't believe she let everyone think she was dead when she wasn't! That's plain mean. Also, what about poor Buddy LaRue, sent off dead in his own dinghy? How does she explain that one?"

"As you might have suspected, Nan Copley has been lying through her teeth. On the side of the good guys, I told you that

LaRue's first mate, Louise, came forward to talk about what she noticed and what he told her. She's the woman who was talking to Lorenzo when your boat blew up. She was horrified of course. She said that both LaRue and Copley were throbbing with jealousy," he said. "She'd heard them arguing over the past couple of months, and she reported that they'd been meeting up every morning at Five Brothers for coffee. According to Nan Copley, who was quite willing to throw her pal under the bus now that he's deceased and can't speak up for himself, Buddy LaRue had grown fiercely jealous of Amos Roche, who also was attracting the attention of investors, like our new mayor. LaRue felt it wasn't a fair competition."

"Sitting right next to the fancier boat with all those customers trooping in must have killed him," my mother said with a sigh.

Nathan nodded, looking steadily at her. "Meanwhile, Chef Nan Copley had grown furious with your success."

"Her success has come because she writes the best proposals and cooks the best food and hires the best people to help and pays them well." I could feel an outraged heat creeping up my chest and spreading across my face.

"We know that," Nathan said in a soothing voice. "But Nan didn't believe it. Apparently, she'd also submitted multiple proposals to cater events, but hers weren't getting accepted. One day she and LaRue ran into each other while getting morning coffee at Five Brothers. They started chatting about their resentments and their anger gathered steam over a period of months. The breaking point was when your recipe was chosen as the winner in the *Key Zest* contest."

"I always wondered what people talk about when they sit outside Five Brothers on that bench," said Miss Gloria. "Have you noticed? It's like a vacuum that must be filled. There's always someone there. They seem to stay for hours. That place serves strong coffee, too. They must be marinated in caffeine by the time they finally go home."

"The recipe she submitted was fraud, plain and simple!" I felt outraged on my mother's behalf, which caused the onset of a blast of heartburn, and then a coughing fit. My mother raced into the kitchen to get me a glass of water.

"You need to try to stay calm," she said, returning with the glass and patting my back.

"For nine months?"

They all burst out laughing.

"Technically six," Nathan said with a grin, his adorable dimples flashing. He took my hand. "You know this could have happened the night I came home late, and you were dressed in Saran Wrap."

I swatted his arm away.

"Stop! Stop! We're not going there," Miss Gloria yelped, covering her eyes. "You two need to keep those details to yourselves. How about tell us the rest of the murder story? That's something we can all appreciate. You've left us hanging on the bench with a cup of strong coffee."

Nathan grinned again. "According to Nan, she and Buddy LaRue began to wonder if there was something they could do about this. They cooked up the scheme of trying to sabotage your Mango Madness sailing event. As I said, Buddy LaRue placed the propane on Janet's supply cart. After Nan slipped into the hold during the party to unscrew the propane tank, she would then drop into the water and Buddy would pick her up. She claims they only intended for there to be a scare, not an explosion, and certainly not a murder."

"Who's going to buy that story?" Miss Gloria asked. "Now I remember reading an article about her in the *Keys Weekly*. They asked her to comment on the last Olympic games because she'd been a very good swimmer in college. According to her, she was especially successful because of her flip turns and the long distance she could hold her breath under water. All that personal detail came up because she was discussing winning techniques for breaststroke and butterfly. At the time, I thought she should have quit talking about herself and paid more attention to the real athletes."

"Fascinating," my mother said. "Obviously she wasn't the victim, she was the one who escaped." She looked at Nathan. "Are you going to tell us the rest of the story now?"

"Right," Nathan said. "As you said, obviously Nan wasn't the victim. The victim was Eva Flanagan aka Athena, aka your boss Palamina's ex-girlfriend. Eva and Nan were almost the same size, and both had anchor tattoos on their ankles, which was the one part of Eva's body that wasn't badly damaged in the fire. We called her cousin Betty Darst to ask about identifying marks, and confirmed that Nan had that tattoo."

I couldn't help interrupting. "Eva/Athena must have snuck onto the boat to get close to Palamina and try win her back. I think she went down into the hold because she smelled gas. That's what Amanda told me."

Nathan nodded. "Unfortunately for her, that's when the boat blew up. Palamina has confirmed that Eva always wore that fish necklace. She'd found it at a street fair in Cuba, and it turned out to be our best shot at identifying her personal effects.

"Nan's confessing a lot because she's in a panic to get the charges dismissed," said Nathan, "which is not likely to happen in any case. She told us that once LaRue went after you and my mother with his motorcycle, it became clear that he was unraveling. One of our police officers who's stationed at Five Brothers every morning was approached by LaRue yesterday—he wanted to tell him something unofficially. He never got to have that conversation, but the officer came to me after Buddy was found, wondering if this had anything to do with this case. Unfortunately, it was too late to save Buddy from his pal."

"How are you feeling?" Gloria asked me. "After all this big news, plus that chase at White Pigeon Park or whatever the heck it's called?"

"Pretty good," I said, resting my hand on the gentle round of my stomach, which I had assumed was due to overeating. That was still true, but also, someone was miraculously growing in there. "In fact, it's kind of a relief to realize the state I'm in, because it explains a lot of things. Such as the fact that my emotions have been seesawing all over the place."

Miss Gloria's eyebrows peaked, and she gave a knowing nod in my husband's direction. "We've noticed that, sweetheart."

I slapped her knee. "No need to rub it in. Besides that, I seem to be constantly starving. By the time this baby comes out, I'll be big as a proverbial house. Bigger than any structure we've seen so far today on our house tour."

"Not to worry." My mother laughed. "I think I gained fifty pounds with you. Your father did not like that one bit. He informed me more than once that I was growing one baby, not a football team."

"No way! He didn't!" I exclaimed. "That's so rude. I'd kill him myself right now if he hadn't left town this morning. I'd murder Nathan before he finished the sentence." I wrinkled my nose in his direction. "You have been warned."

Mom grinned and patted his knee. "It will all be fine. Soon after the birth, I was back to myself." She gestured to her shape, which was curvy and fit her height perfectly, and pretty much matched my own.

"Speaking of the birth," I said, "I'm terrified." I gripped Nathan's hand. "You'll be there every moment, won't you? Even if it takes days and days of brutal labor, and in the end, they have to slice me open like a ripe cantaloupe? And then we land some woo-woo substitute doctor without a real medical degree who insists that new parents eat the placenta?"

The longer I talked, the woozier Nathan looked.

"OMG Hayley, you're scaring him to death. We'll all be there every instant—whatever you want, isn't that right Nathan?" my mother coaxed. He nodded.

"I'll tell you what I'm really worried about . . . I'm worried about how things will change. Do I have to give up my job? My friends? My freedom?" I stared at Nathan, who was beginning to look as terrified as I was feeling. "Will our marriage turn into nothing but a parade of diaper changes and arguments about who has to get up in the night?"

"Things will change, sweetheart," said my mom. "But think of all the women across the years who had work they loved and children too. Yes, life will be busy and there will be change, but mostly for the better. Never for an instant would I have given you up to get my old life back. You'll have as much help from your family and friends as you can stand."

Nathan had been listening carefully. Honestly, I was not eager to hear his take on this. *No wife of mine is going to work out of the home!* If he said something like that, I'd have to kill him. Then neither of us would get to raise the baby. I took a deep breath, sending cool air down my chest, and into the abdomen where this new being resided.

"You look like you have something to say," I told him. "Go ahead, I can take it."

"The only change I'm going to insist on is buying you an Apple watch," Nathan said. "And a new car. I've never been crazy about that scooter, and now with two of you to worry about, I won't take no for an answer."

"Sold!" said Miss Gloria. "It's thoughtful of you to be thinking of me at a time like this. I could certainly use a new ride." We all burst out laughing, bursting the bubble of terror that I'd felt rising up my throat.

"That's all set then. What can I make you for supper?" my mother asked.

"Supper sounds amazing. In fact, I'm kind of starving now. You know what I've been craving? Tuna noodle casserole. The exact recipe that your mother used to make."

My mother snorted with laughter again. "Hayley, sweetheart, she used a can of mushroom soup, a can of tuna, and some boiled egg noodles. Whipped it all up with a fork and added a little mayo if it looked dry."

"That's my recipe too!" Miss Gloria exclaimed. My mother and I howled until the tears came.

"Is that really what you want?" my mother asked me, once Nathan had returned to work. "I have a much nicer version with a béchamel sauce, grated cheese, sauteed onions and celery. Buttered and toasted panko with parmesan cheese on top. Sometimes one of my brides wants a homestyle dish to serve after the wedding reception, and that recipe is a huge hit. Caterer's tip: it helps soak up the alcohol the party people have imbibed."

I could feel my mouth watering. But not for the fancy catering version mom produced for after-wedding parties, for my grandmother's special. "The can of soup please," I said, a wide grin spreading over my face. "Your mother's recipe. That's what your grandbaby's asking for."

Chapter Twenty-Seven

Occasionally, when deep breathing isn't enough, the lava boils over and I say something I regret. The best way I know to repair the damage is with food.
—Jaime Lewis, "I Have to Apologize a Lot. These Cookies Help Me Ask for Forgiveness." *Washington Post*, April 29, 2024

After my mom had hurried off to shop for the casserole and Miss Gloria had left to take a nap, I reclined in the shade on my deck, listening to the clanking and whooshing of Houseboat Row. Would we really move away from this place? I'd miss it terribly. Evinrude hopped onto my belly and began to knead as though he was a pastry chef working on a slab of biscuit dough.

"There's going to be a new kid in town buddy," I said, rubbing his ears. "But you'll always be my number one son." I rested my head against the back of the chair, and faded into a nap.

An hour later, my mother returned with a brown bag and the casserole in a Pyrex dish. "Everything should be ready in about an hour. I'll set the table and make a salad. Did Nathan say he's coming home for supper?"

"I think so," I said. "Though he may be late. Do you need a hand?"

"Not this time."

As my eyelids fluttered shut again, a vision of Eva/Athena's last day on earth on our boat pushed into my mind. She had looked so happy in the one photo, as though she was on a mission that she was certain she could accomplish. I supposed it was a good thing that she had died thinking she was about to be reunited with her lover. Should I call Palamina to tell her this latest news? Perhaps that was a job best left to Nathan. But what I could do was dial her ex-husband and let him know that I believed she would be open to a call from him. She would be feeling so vulnerable and even sad—about everything.

I opened the tab on my computer screen that led to their wedding announcement, then googled Damian's phone number. Palamina would kill me if she found out that I was meddling in her business, but it wasn't only her business. Someone had blown up that catamaran and killed a woman and caused a lot of traumatic distress. Though on the other hand, her husband was definitely her business.

I took a deep breath and dialed Damian's number. His voicemail kicked in. He had a lovely deep voice that matched his handsome physical self. I lost my nerve and hung up before leaving a message. I decided to practice first by dictating a message into my new phone.

"This is Hayley Snow in Key West. I work for Palamina Wells at *Key Zest* and wanted you to know that I think she'd love to talk with you." I couldn't leave it at that—he'd never call her because that message was lame. I'd have to plan this out better. Should I say something about marriage being hard? Even a slog? How one day you think you have a disagreement settled and the next day you're litigating the same problem? That sounded like TMI. I tried again.

"We married people get into ruts, and it's hard to get out of them. Plus, we bring so much garbage and baggage into a relationship, it's a miracle that anyone lasts. How do those people who are married fifty years make it to the finish line? Maybe in a way, it's easier to get married super young before you have any of this history." I thought that over for a second, and then added—so it would feel as though I'd shared something too, "Although that's ridiculous because we all have history, always. For me, it was my parents' divorce."

I clicked the microphone off, thinking, thinking. Did that sound absurd and rambling? I tried again. "I wanted to be sure you knew that Palamina loves you very much. I think she'd be very willing and very grateful to try your marriage again, or at least have that conversation. She's too proud to tell you, but she considers Eva to have been a terrible mistake. Maybe she was panicked about whether she could make a go of love in the long term? I don't know, because she doesn't talk much about her family of origin. I do know she's swamped with regret about what happened between you, and I'm certain she'd welcome the chance to talk."

I clicked off, thinking again that Palamina would kill me in an instant if she knew I was telling him all of this. She'd kill me, and then he'd kill her for airing their dirty laundry to strangers. But as I was learning, people needed to talk about this kind of stuff, or it would fester inside. So, it seemed worth taking the chance.

"You see," I said to Evinrude, stroking him from the base of his ears to the tip of his tail. "There are ways to be helpful without putting oneself in danger."

I clicked the message on and listened to it the whole way through.

As it wound up, Miss Gloria tapped me on the shoulder, and I startled so hard I almost dropped the phone.

"What the heck are you doing?" she asked.

"Practicing," I said. "I wanted to call Palamina's estranged husband and tell him some of what's gone on this week. But I'm dictating my thoughts first, so I get the words right. I'm trying to say marriage is hard, and we all come to it with baggage, and it's hard to admit we've made mistakes, and so on. I'm really hoping he gives her another chance and they get back together. What do you think?"

She perched on the edge of the lounge chair next to mine, cocked her head in one direction, then the other. "Hmmm," she said finally. "That's a lot to tell someone you've never met. Wonder how it would go if you suggested those things to Palamina and let her decide whether to reach out and what to say. Marriage *is* hard," she added. "There are always ups and downs."

She was right, as usual. Then the underlying meaning of her words hit me, and I had to laugh. "You think I should be saying some of this to my Nathan and butt out with my boss."

She was practically twinkling with glee. She leaned over to kiss my cheek. "You said it, sister, you said it." She kissed me a second time. "I'm going inside to help your mother. You rest for now, OK?"

I nodded, leaning back again, my hand on my belly. Again, I felt the shock of realizing a new being was growing inside. My eyes flew open.

"Listen baby, I'm going to find those recipe cards passed down from my grandmother so I can show them to you when

The Mango Murders

you get big enough. Ix-nay on you gumming the edges, in other words. Reading those, you'll get a real feeling for what she was like—not much of a cook but a gem of a person. I'm sad you won't get the chance to meet her. But you'll have three amazing grandmothers, my mom and your dad's mother, plus Allison, my stepmom. They couldn't be more different, but you'll love them all. Plus, Miss Gloria, she's like a super grandmother or great grandmother. A fairy godmother, really. That was her just now—she keeps me in line, and honestly, I do the same for her. Annie Dubisson will be living in our back yard, too, an honorary great grandmother. Those ladies will babysit you when I'm busy. Don't worry, they both know how to take care of babies and they're strong enough not to drop you."

Yikes, what if this baby only wanted me and freaked out every single time I left the room?

"Listen," I told the baby, figuring he or she better know the truth from the beginning. "I'll miss you when I'm off working, but heck, you don't want me around all the time either. Ask your father; he'll tell you I get stir-crazy if I'm not busy." I sucked in a big breath of air. "Honestly, we'll figure this out together because I have no clue."

My mother's voice wafted out from our cabin. "Calling Hayley Catherine Snow Bransford. Supper's on and it's time to eat for two!"

THE END

Recipes

Mango Daiquiri

This is the featured cocktail that is served on the *Pilar Too* at the beginning of *The Mango Murders*. It's easy to put together. The simple syrup is made by simmering equal parts water with sugar until the sugar is dissolved. Everything else is self-explanatory, though you will need to drag the blender out of the cupboard. No one at the party was able to really enjoy the drink, but hopefully your event won't be nearly so dramatic!

Ingredients

One large ripe mango
3 ounces white rum
2 tablespoons simple syrup
1/4 cup fresh lime juice
One heaping cup of ice cubes

Place the ingredients into the blender, ending with the ice. Whirl them until the mixture is smooth and golden. Taste to make sure the balance of sweet to sour is to your liking.

Serve in pretty glasses. This should make three generous drinks.

Upside Down Mango Cake

May to June is mango season for real in Key West, so I obviously had to develop mango recipes for this book. Hayley's stepfather and mother make this cake for one of Miss Gloria's birthday week celebrations. You'll see while reading that the cake also makes a lot of trouble for the characters—but can a cake be responsible for murder?

Ingredients

1–2 mangoes
8–9 Maraschino cherries
12 Tbsp butter, divided
1/2 cup brown sugar
2 Tbsp honey
1 and 1/2 cups unbleached flour
1 and 1/2 tsp. baking powder
1/2 cup sugar
1 tsp. vanilla
2 large eggs
1/2 cup milk

Preheat the oven to 350. Butter a 9-inch cake pan, bottom and sides. (I used some of the butter above, figuring there's plenty in the recipe already.) Cut a piece of parchment paper to the size of the pan, put it in the bottom and butter that too. Peel and cut the mangoes into slices or cubes.

The Mango Murders

Melt 4 oz of butter in a small pan. Add the honey and brown sugar and heat, stirring until smooth. Pour the mixture into the prepared pan and then place the fruit into the pan, in whatever design you choose. Dot with maraschino cherries.

Meanwhile, combine dry ingredients except for the sugar in one bowl and measure milk into a glass measuring cup. In another bowl, beat the butter and sugar and vanilla with a mixer until they are light in color. Add the eggs one at a time, beating after each. On low speed, add the dry ingredients in three parts, alternating with the milk until everything is mixed nicely.

Pour the batter over the fruit and bake for about 40 minutes until lightly browned or until a knife comes out clean. Let the cake rest on a rack for an hour. Then place your serving plate over the top and gently invert the cake onto the platter. Serve warm or at room temperature.

Mango Scones with Cream Cheese Frosting

Hayley's neighbor Miss Gloria is celebrating her eighty-fifth birthday in this book. Lots of visitors have arrived on the island, including her two thorny daughters-in-law. Miss Gloria gets the idea of inviting them for a tour of residences on Houseboat Row, with scones and coffee on Hayley and Nathan's deck at the end. Hayley makes these mango scones, and my, they are delicious! You could make them without the icing, but as my husband would say . . . why?

Ingredients

2 1/2 cups all-purpose flour
1/2 teaspoon salt
2 teaspoons baking powder
1/2 teaspoon baking soda
1 teaspoon almond flavoring
1/3 cup brown sugar
One stick (a.k.a. 8 tablespoons) frozen unsalted butter
One egg
1/2 cup sour cream
2 1/2 tablespoons whole milk
One cup ripe mango, peeled and cut into small chunks

The Mango Murders

For the frosting:
4 ounces cream cheese, at room temperature
4 tablespoons unsalted butter, at room temperature
1/2 cup confectioners' sugar, sifted

Preheat the oven to 400°.

Combine the dry ingredients with a fork. Take care to mix the brown sugar in thoroughly.

Placing a grater over the bowl of dry ingredients, grate the frozen butter into the bowl using the largest holes. With a fork, mix the butter in well with the flour mixture.

In another bowl or large measuring cup, whisk together the egg, sour cream, almond flavoring, and milk. Stir the combined wet ingredients into the dry and mix until just moist. Fold in the mango.

Dump the batter onto a piece of parchment paper lightly dusted with flour and shape it into a circle. The batter will be wet and crumbly, but don't overwork it.

Cut the circle of dough into eight wedges and separate them slightly so there is space between each scone. (I cut mine into six wedges, which were very generous!)

Bake until beginning to brown, about 18 minutes. Serve as you like with more butter, whipped cream, the cream cheese frosting, or just as they are. These freeze well and can be defrosted and warmed up for a treat on another day. As a side note, I asked my hub if he wanted his frosted and he first said no. He changed his mind when he heard I was having frosting. After tasting it he said, "I don't know why you even asked me about the icing, it's amazing!"

These freeze well and can be defrosted and warmed up for a treat on another day.

Janet Snow's Tuna Noodle Casserole

At one point in the book, Hayley's craving her grandmother's tuna noodle casserole. She begs her mom, Janet, to make it for her. Janet says: "Hayley, sweetheart, she used a can of mushroom soup, a can of tuna, and some egg noodles. Is that what you want? I have a nicer version with a béchamel sauce, grated cheese, sauteed onions, and celery." Hayley can feel her mouth watering. But not for the fancy catering version, for her grandmother's special.

"The can of soup please," I said, a wide grin spreading over my face.

The recipe below is Janet's fancier version. It's not hard and it's delicious enough for company.

Ingredients

3 tbsp butter
3 tbsp flour
1 red onion, peeled and minced
3–4 stalks celery, chopped
1 tsp sharp French mustard
2 tbsp chopped chives
2 cups milk
1 can tuna in water
8 oz egg noodles
1 cup shredded cheddar
1 cup frozen peas

Lucy Burdette

Breadcrumbs
Grated parmesan

Heat the oven to 350.

Cook the noodles as directed on the package, drain, rinse with cool water and set aside.

Drain the can of tuna. Melt the butter in a saucepan and sauté the minced red onion and chopped celery until soft. Stir in the flour until combined. Add the mustard and mix that well. Slowly add the milk, stirring until you have a thick white sauce. Stir in the cheese until smooth.

Add the tuna, the peas, and the reserved noodles and stir gently. Fold the mixture into a buttered casserole dish, top with breadcrumbs and grated parmesan cheese.

Bake until golden and bubbly, 25–30 minutes. Serve hot with a nice green salad.

Hayley's Grandmother's Tuna Noodle Casserole, borrowed from the Brady House Specials

This recipe, which I attributed to Hayley's grandmother in this book, is borrowed right from *The Brady House Specials*, my husband's family cookbook. My mother-in-law loved to eat and was a good home cook, but she didn't make anything too fancy. There were seven kids in his family, so you can imagine that her main goal was getting something fast and filling on the table. We always get a laugh out of the note on the recipe that this simple casserole was Lewis's (#6 of 7 in the lineup) favorite!

Ingredients

6 oz can of tuna fish
Can of mushroom soup
1 can milk
Cooked noodles

Cook noodles until tender. Add tuna and mix with other ingredients. Put in casserole. Sprinkle with buttered crumbs and bake 30 minutes.

That's it!

Acknowledgements

While I was writing this book, we took a wonderful ride on the *Argo Navis* under the guidance of Captain Emyl Hattingh, sponsored by Key West Art and Historical Society. We sailed from the Key West Bight and past Sunset Key and Wisteria Island, enjoying a different view of Mallory Square and the rest of the harbor than we usually do while on land. This trip inspired the opening pages of the book, though the disaster that occurs on these pages is purely fictional.

Thanks to my family, Susan Cerulean, Jeff Chanton, and John Brady, who first suggested the White Crowned Pigeon Park as a good setting for one of my scenes, and to Jeanne Pasternak, who confirmed this. Sue and John are my very best supporters, in both writing and life.

A few new characters appear in this installment of the Key West series, based on actual Key West people: Heather Harvey, John Martini, Chef Richard, Amanda Velazquez, Betty Darst. None of them asked for this, nor are they responsible for how their fictional characters behaved. Thanks to Pat and Lew Mastrobuono who went to great lengths to find and purchase the fish necklace that I regretted passing up. Thanks to Susy for the air tags. Big thanks to my golfing pal Mary Pat for the

Acknowledgements

hormones. Thank you to former Mayor Teri Johnson, who worked so hard to navigate the problems facing our island. Opinions in this book are only mine!

While I was writing this installment, my attention was drawn to an article written by Dr. Corey Malcolm, the historian at the Key West library, on the subject of Etta Patterson's coconut cake. How could I not work this into the plot? Thanks to Dr. Malcolm and also to the Friends of the Key West Library who posted this story on Facebook, and the Key West Woman's Club who included it in their original cookbook. Thanks always to my favorite police consultant, Steve Torrence, and to Ron aka Lorenzo for his perspective and wisdom.

Jessie Crockett is a dream at brainstorming plot points—thank you! My writers group pals, Angelo Pompano and Chris Falcone, read everything and are the perfect combination of support and challenge, along with being dear friends. My Jungle Red Writers, amazing authors and human beings, inspire and support me every day!

Thanks to my smart and dogged agent, Paige Wheeler, and her team at Creative Media Agency. I also thank the amazing team at Crooked Lane Books, including Matt Martz, Dulce Botello, Rebecca Nelson, Thai Perez, Mikaela Bender, Megan Matti, and more behind the scenes. I adore my cover artists, Griesbach and Martucci, and my independent editor, Sandy Harding, who sees the roughest of drafts and makes suggestions that allow the book to grow into something so much better.

To the librarians and booksellers who buy these books and put them in the hands of readers, and to my readers—thank you, thank you, thank you!